# CHASING *Brynn*

A Tempting Novel
Book Two

# CHASING *Brynn*

A Tempting Novel
Book Two

ANGELA CORBETT

Cover design by Wicked By Design



Published in the United States of America by Midnight Sands Publishing, Utah

# *Dedication*

For my best friend, editor, and my person:
Dr. Ashley Argyle.

At first I thought I couldn't continue without you…
Now I know I have to continue for you.

In loving memory
Ashley Argyle, Ph.D.
November 29, 1979 - November 18, 2014

Owner of Inktip Editing

<u>English Literature Professor</u>
Salt Lake Community College
Denver University
Colorado Women's College
Metropolitan State University of Denver
City University, London
University of Alaska, Fairbanks

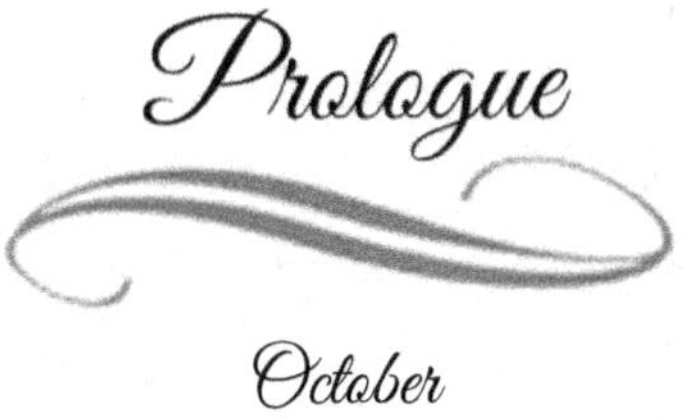

# Prologue

*October*

"So, do you like him?" A pretty brunette in a white long-sleeved sweater, jeans, and teal scarf cupped her warm mug of coffee as she asked the question to her equally beautiful blond friend.

"Yeah, a lot," the blond answered. She had cheekbones that I'd commit serious crimes for.

The two girls sitting at the table next to mine, in my direct line of sight, had been discussing their dating lives for a while. Thanks to the close quarters of the tiny coffee shop, our tables were inches apart and their entire conversation was being broadcast to everyone around them. I had discovered the blond was named Michelle, and the brunette, Lisa. I tried to tune them out, concentrating on my own guy issues.

It had come to this. I was staking out local stores.

For a man.

I sighed, staring into my non-fat Chai latte, the pretty foam heart design starting to fade as I moved the cup. What was wrong with me? I didn't do this. I wasn't one of those crazy girls who fell for a guy and started obsessing. I moved from guy to guy, looking for the one who had the best skills.

Then, I'd had an encounter with him.

Some people saunter into your life with pleasantries and little fanfare. Others come in with totalitarian authority, taking up all of the air in the room until you want to beg them for oxygen. He was the latter. Passion had swirled between us like a firestorm. He'd held my gaze like he owned me. And then he'd walked away without another word. I had no clue who he was; I didn't even know his name.

I'd been wondering about him for days, hoping I'd run into him somewhere again. It had almost become an obsession—one I'd been rather annoyed with. I don't obsess about guys. Ever. I'd learned my lesson about giving my heart to someone years ago, and didn't need to take a refresher course. In my opinion, relationships are wasted energy. Guys are good for one thing: sex. And lots of it. I was used to getting exactly what I wanted from them. This guy was different, though. He hadn't chased me, and it irked me to no end. I was determined to have another chance meeting with the mystery man, and get him out of my system for good so I could focus my attention on other things.

The girls' conversation stirred me out of my self-analysis. "There's just one problem," Michelle said. "He has size issues."

A line formed between Lisa's brows. "How small are we talking here?"

Michelle wrinkled her nose as she stirred her latte. "Baby carrots. Even that might be generous."

"Ouch," Lisa said, making a sympathetic face. "Are you sure he's not a grower?"

Michelle frowned, resigned. "Baby carrots *is* the grown size."

"Ohhhh," Lisa said, stretching the word out. "Might be best to end things now."

Michelle took a deep breath. "That's what I was thinking." She took a bite of her cookie and leaned back in her chair, her shoulders slumping in resignation. "What about you? How are things going with Jeff?"

Lisa gave a hefty sigh. "He's nice…it's just…he's not really interested in anything physical. It's kind of giving me a complex."

My eyes widened at that, and Michelle looked just as stunned as I felt. "What do you mean? You're gorgeous!"

Lisa pushed some food around on her plate with her fork. "I feel like he only wants me for my mind."

Mind, huh? That one was new. But I understood what it was like to only be wanted for certain reasons, and not the ones you wanted to be desired for. There was a time when I'd been in a similar position, and I'd hated it. It had changed my whole life.

"Seriously?" Michelle asked, dumbfounded. "Your mind? Not your ass? Because you have a stellar ass!"

Lisa nodded slowly in disappointed acceptance. "I mean, I'm glad he thinks I'm smart, but he basically told me I'm the only girl he's ever met who could compete with him intellectually, and he wants to focus our time together on that."

I almost laughed out loud. I didn't know the dude they were referring to, but he obviously had a serious ego and could use some relationship tutoring and probably a good kick to the kiwis. Michelle voiced it for me, "What a dick wagon! Tell that mind masturbator he can get his brain off with someone else! You deserve someone who wants you for everything you are, and makes you feel like the most important person in the world!"

I looked down, trying to hide my smile. I liked Michelle. I liked her a lot.

Lisa's face brightened at Michelle's compliments, and the validation that she was better than mind-masturbator-Jeff had made her feel. It seemed like all of the reinforcement she needed. "You're right. I do deserve better."

"Give me your phone," Michelle said, grabbing it from across the table. "We'll text him a middle finger emoji right now."

Lisa and Michelle both laughed as they sent the text. "At least my problem is easy to solve," Lisa said, picking up her coffee. "I can dump the asshat. But you really like your guy, and can't do anything about the carrot problem."

Michelle frowned, nodding at the same time. "There's chemistry, but I don't think it will last when the sex is bad. I'll probably break it off soon."

I groaned inwardly, wishing I could lean over and become part of their conversation. Yeah, big dicks were great. I was a huge fan of them myself—HUGE. I had even made them the topic of my Master's thesis until Syd suggested I go with something more academic, and I'd changed the title to *Sex in the Modern World.* I thought that *In Search of Schlong* was a much more entertaining subject line, however, and I felt confident that particular thesis would have garnered a lot more reads.

The point was: if the guy was a good guy, and the chemistry was present, there were plenty of ways for dudes to compensate for their shortcomings…whatever those may be. A guy who understood passion, desire, foreplay, and wasn't afraid of experimenting; those men were special. All men needed to be that enlightened. Likewise, women needed to know what to look for in a partner, and how to communicate their needs and desires. Men needed to know how to anticipate those needs and desires as much as possible to turn up the passion. Why weren't women and men being taught this information? I wanted to drag my chair right over to Michelle and Lisa's table and tell them exactly what their sex education classes hadn't. But barging in on a conversation I wasn't supposed to hear in the first place probably wouldn't be appreciated, nor would my opinion on baby carrots.

As I sat there listening to the girls dissect their relationship problems and talk about other guys they were interested in, an idea popped into my head. I grabbed a piece of paper and pen from my bag, and started jotting down my thoughts. Before long, I had three pages full, and that was just off the top of my head.

I smiled as I took another sip of my latte, and pulled my laptop out of my bag. If there was one thing I was an expert in, it was sex. And if I could help make it better for the population of Easton State University, Winchester, Colorado, and the general public, I would. I opened my laptop, and my sex advice blog, Mistress A, was born.

# One

January

## Tips and Tits: The Word from Mistress A

### Shiver Me Balls! Let's Talk About Dick Mittens

*Yes. They're an actual thing. And I'm not talking about the* Urban Dictionary *definition. Tiny pieces of yarn, lovingly crocheted—probably by someone's grandma, to keep a dude's balls toasty warm. I had several reactions when I saw this. Fascination. Confusion. A slight tinge of horror when I thought of grandma. I was curious though…was this a real problem for the male population? Were frosty balls an actual situation requiring special accessories? After a poll of several dick owners, I can tell you that yes, nut sacks do, in fact, get chilly…especially when the nut owners go commando. However, I feel this situation can be easily remedied* without *the use of a twenty dollar ball snuggler, and the loss of grandma's innocence. So here's the deal, dudes: when my boobs are cold, I don't order nipple gloves. I put on a shirt. I'd advise you to do the same with pants.*

My phone buzzed on the table next to my laptop. Sydney's name scrolled across the screen. She'd been my roommate for years, and my best friend even longer. She was my constant, my soul mate, and knew me better than any other person on the planet. I tapped on the screen to open the text.

*How was your date last night?*

Syd had always been interested in my dating life, but seemed even more so since she'd met the love of her life, Jackson West—master mechanic with blue eyes the color of Bora Bora, and panty-dropping everything else. He was a catch. She knew it, and totally deserved to be as sickeningly happy as she was. She also knew I had no interest in relationships, so I wasn't sure why she kept asking me about my lack of them lately. Maybe she wanted me to be as grossly adorable as she and Jax were. I wasn't interested.

I typed out a quick response.

*Research was uneventful. I'm still pissed you bailed on my Big Dick road trip.*

I'd found an article that listed men's average dick sizes by state. I wanted to check them out for accuracy—research, of course. But Syd had already found everything she was looking for, and wasn't interested in accompanying me on my quest. She was not a very good

Sam to my Frodo in that sense.

*That trip would have been a waste of time. You should be thanking me. And for getting you to change the title of your Master's thesis.*

I narrowed my eyes, annoyed that I'd listened to reason and agreed to change it.

*You got me to change the name. Penis size is still a very BIG chapter!*

*Haha. I'll be there in five. And I'm bringing friends.*

My fingers froze on the phone. Friends? What friends? My stomach twisted and I couldn't tell if I was about to be sick, or excited. Because Syd had one specific friend I was very interested in conducting some research with. *Very, very* interested. I had met him officially when Syd introduced us in this coffee shop, in November. That's when I'd finally found out his name: Cade Brett. That was also the day I realized the mystery man I had been looking for since October was actually Cade. I'd had dreams about my mystery man/Cade. Full-on fantasies even. And I didn't like it. I was the aggressor when it came to relationships. I decided when they started, and I decided when they stopped. I'd given up too much control in the past. Now I was the woman I wanted to be, and I certainly wasn't going to let a man get in my head and make me see cupcakes, relationship rainbows, and freaking love sparkles.

When Syd had introduced us, I had also found out that Syd is Cade's law school study buddy. The news had been shocking to say the least, and not at all what I'd expected given my history with him. He was on track to be a buttoned-up lawyer who surely wanted a white picket fence, cat, dog, and a kid or five. Those things were not on my life plan roster. I don't do relationships.

But I'd been thinking about Cade for months. Something had sparked between us from the first time we saw each other in October, and I'd decided he needed to be on my list of research subjects. He'd mentioned how much he loved The Grind, a local Winchester coffee and dessert shop. The name made it sound dirtier than it was, and when I'd first moved here, I might have visited the establishment thinking an entirely different type of grinding was going on. I'd been disappointed—but only until I tasted their coffee.

I spent a lot of time in coffee shops doing schoolwork and writing content for my blog, but ever since the mention, I'd found myself coming up with reasons to spend even more time at The Grind. I kept telling myself it was only because I wanted to screw Cade and move on. At least, that's what I hoped the reason was. I didn't want complicated, and in my experience, problems and relationships went hand-in-hand.

The door opened and a bluster of cold, January air pushed into the warm building. "Brynn!" I heard the high-pitched squeal of Paige, Courtney's sweet four-year-old little girl, and turned just in time for her to run into me with all of her force. If hugs could be measured, she had hit me with a knockout. I loved this kid. Courtney was Jax's sister, and Syd and Jax were a couple, so Syd was practically Paige's aunt. Syd and Courtney waved as they walked up to the counter to order while I sat with Paige.

"How's my favorite girl?" I asked, pulling her onto my lap.

She gave me a toothy grin. "Good."

"What did you do today?" I asked.

"Colored!" she exclaimed, breathless. She had more excitement for coloring than I'd had about anything…ever.

"What did you color?"

"Unicorns!" She reached in her violet bag and pulled out her coloring book, methodically opening pages and showing me her masterpieces. She was actually pretty darn good, and I wasn't sure I'd be able to color in the lines as well as she did.

We finished going through the coloring book and then she gasped, her eyes bright with excitement as she grabbed her backpack again. She reached her little hands inside, tongue out the side of her mouth as she searched, and then her cheeks pushed up into happy bubbles as she pulled out a She-Ra action figure, holding it up for my inspection. "Look what I got!"

I glanced up at Courtney, and then Syd, who had finished ordering and were settling into the chairs next to me. "I assume you gave her this?" I asked Syd. Syd loved She-Ra. She'd even named her dark blue '69 Camaro after the female princess.

"Actually, Jax did," Syd said, smiling at Paige. "But I totally supported the decision."

The corners of my mouth lifted. "I'm surprised Jax didn't get her a Camaro, too."

Paige rifled through her little purple backpack and

pulled out a small, dark blue Camaro. "It looks just like Syd's!" she beamed. She rolled it around on the table, then shifted her determined gaze to me. "Mom says I can't drive Syd's yet, but when I'm big, I'm going to have one *just* like it."

I laughed, and looked at Syd and Courtney. "She's going to be a handful."

"She already is," Courtney said, tousling the little girl's pretty blond curls. "Do you want to go play in the treehouse, Paige?"

The Grind was in a college town, but there were lots of students who were young and needed a place to take their kids. The Grind had built a special section for kids in the corner of the room, complete with a treehouse that lodged its own jungle gym. It was the busiest coffee shop in town, and that play area was one of the reasons. Never underestimate the appeal of something that entertains children long enough for a parent to have some quiet time.

"Yes!" Paige said, jumping off my lap. She put her toys back in her bag, handed it to Courtney, and ran over to the treehouse.

"She's my favorite," I said to Courtney.

Courtney's face lit up with pride and love as she put the backpack on Paige's empty chair. "Mine too."

"We're glad you're here," Syd said, placing a hand on Courtney's arm.

Courtney watched Paige for a few moments in silence, then turned back to Syd and I. "Me too. I came here because I needed to get away, and I missed Jax. Paige missed him too. I didn't think I'd stay, but I'm glad I did."

She unwrapped the marbled white and dark chocolate brownie she'd bought, and took a bite. "I feel safe here, and I'm lucky to have such kind, loyal friends."

I didn't know a lot about Courtney's past, but I knew Paige's dad wasn't in her life—or Courtney's. That had to be hard, especially being a single mom so young. A family tragedy had left both Courtney and Jax financially independent, so at least she didn't have to worry about money, but I couldn't imagine trying to raise a child without a partner. I'd lose my mind just trying to care for a plant without help. I wasn't sure about Courtney's relationship with her parents, but she was close with her brother, Jax, and it probably eased her mind to have a good male role model present for Paige.

The server came over with Syd and Courtney's drinks. I was jealous they had fresh coffee, and contemplated getting another, but did a quick calorie calculation in my head and decided that if I did, it would have to be black, no sugar, no milk. If I wanted to drink something that bland, I could drink straight water instead, so I pulled my bottle filled with lemon flavored water out of my bag.

"I'm excited for your house warming party next week," Syd said to Courtney.

"Me too!" Courtney said. "Everything is finally unpacked. I can't believe I found a place so fast. Single home rentals are usually crazy hard to find in this area, but I was lucky that I started looking around the same time the last semester ended at Easton. It gave me more options, and the house is really perfect. Two bedrooms, two bathrooms, and a fenced yard for Paige. She'll love it even more when the snow melts. Jax's apartment is nice, but it's small, and Jax and Syd need their privacy—"

"Don't be silly," Syd said, cutting her off. "You could have stayed there as long as you wanted."

Courtney nodded, wrapping her hands around her coffee cup to warm them up. "I know, but Paige and I needed a place of our own to settle into. Stability is important for kids." She lifted her coffee to take a sip.

"So is Paige not wandering in and finding Uncle Jax and Aunt Syd naked in reverse cowgirl," I pointed out.

Courtney choked on her coffee and couldn't stop laughing. Syd blushed and smacked my arm. "Seriously, Brynn?! She's his sister!"

I gave her a look. "Do you honestly believe Court doesn't know you're having sex?"

"No!" Syd stuttered, her face scrunching up as she tried not to look in Courtney's direction. "But we don't have to talk about it! It's uncomfortable."

Courtney had gotten her coughing under control. "I'm not uncomfortable."

"I am," Syd grumbled.

I rolled my eyes. "That's ridiculous. Sex is awesome. Everyone should talk about it all the time."

"Says the girl on her way to becoming a sex therapist."

I shrugged, unapologetic, and changed the subject. "Do you need help with anything for the party?" I asked Courtney.

"I don't think so. The house is clean and the food is being delivered."

Food delivery was smart, and exactly what I would have

done in her place. Ordering from somewhere simplified things. There would be no worries about trying to make something everyone would like, or accommodate all of the attendees' various diet and food requests. "Did you invite a lot of people?" I asked. Courtney hadn't been in town long, so I wasn't sure how many people she knew.

She shook her head. "Not a lot. Some people from Mom to Mom."

Syd and I volunteered at CARE, a local nonprofit that supported people with family members in area hospitals. Courtney wanted something to do with her time, and had started talking to Charlie, the executive director of CARE. Charlie mentioned Mom to Mom, and said it was a local nonprofit that provided assistance to single mothers. Courtney had started working there part-time. It was perfect for her situation because there were so many other moms in the programs who she could relate to and help. There were also a lot of kids, and Paige was able to play with them and take preschool classes there while Courtney worked. It was turning out to be a great situation for them both, and I hoped they were each meeting new friends.

"I'm glad that's worked out so well for you," I said to Courtney.

"Me too. I was worried about finding something that Paige could be part of. My co-workers are great to include her. It's definitely a perk, and I like being able to use my own experiences to help others."

I wasn't sure exactly what those experiences were. Courtney didn't talk about it much, but I was happy she was doing well, and liked her job. "What do you do there?" I asked her.

She took another bite of her brownie before answering, "A lot of things. I'm mostly support staff for the full-time employees, so every day is different. Sometimes I sit in on support group meetings, other times I'm making phone calls, working on fundraisers, inputting data, and running errands. A lot of my days are spent with the moms, talking to them, giving advice, playing with the kids." She glanced over at Paige, doing a quick check as she watched her daughter go down a yellow plastic slide. "My favorite part is the interaction, though. I like being able to listen to other moms tell their stories, and share mine if they're interested."

"It's probably a lot like making friends with someone," Syd observed, taking a drink of her coffee. "You get to know them, and slowly share more as you build trust."

"Exactly," Courtney said. "The different personalities are fun." She leaned in like she was about to reveal some kind of secret. "Lately, a lot of our discussions have drifted to Mistress A."

My heart started to race and I took a cleansing breath, trying to calm it down. Mistress A had gone viral soon after I'd started posting. I'd kept my identity a secret, and was constantly worried about outing myself.

Syd snorted. "Well, if the moms are trying to prevent more pregnancies, Mistress A is probably not the best subject to focus on."

I gave a derisive laugh. "Because a blog can get you pregnant?"

"It provides a plethora of information," Syd argued.

"Exactly! Information is never bad," I countered. "If more people had information, there would be fewer teen pregnancies, STDs, and people unhappy with their sex lives."

"I agree with Brynn," Courtney said. "We've used some of her posts as topics during discussion groups at Mom to Mom. It's actually pretty liberating to talk about sex so openly and not have to feel bad, or shove desires under a rug."

I raised my water bottle to her in salute. "I'm glad I'm not the only one who thinks she's awesome. I fully support anyone who's trying to get more sexy knowledge to the people."

Syd rolled her eyes. "*Everyone* thinks she's awesome."

I eyed Syd from the side, wondering who exactly "everyone" was.

"I hear people talking about her all of the time," Syd said.

To be fair, I'd heard rumblings about Mistress A as well. People loved sex, and loved being voyeurs. The thought that there was a real person out there with intimate knowledge about the subjects Mistress A was posting was extremely appealing to the masses. I'd done my best to protect my identity, though in today's digital age of data mining, everything from your website searches to your tampon brand preferences are tracked. I'd been careful though…I hoped.

"What are they saying about her?" Courtney asked. "Because at work, she's considered a goddess."

"How do people even know it's a girl for sure?" I asked,

trying to throw my two cents in and confuse the scent a bit. I was happy to provide more rumors about my alter ego, especially if they were false.

"I don't think she would have called herself Mistress if she were a guy," Syd said.

"You've seen *Catfish*, right?" I asked. "Some people are batshit crazy."

Syd shook her head. "My gut says girl. Even her site looks like a girl chose the design. She knows too much about a woman's body to be a dude. She's even explained period pain, something I'm certain no man on the planet would ever be able to articulate. Yep. I'm going with girl."

Syd had good instincts…hopefully better than most people. She was right about the site as well. I'd had it designed in shades of red, black, white, and silver. The Mistress A logo was a set of dark red lips, with Mistress A splashed across them in metallic silver. The background on the sides and top of the page was black with an elaborate filigree design over the black in a lighter shade of onyx. It was elegant without being too girly, so it would appeal to both sexes. I'd wanted it to look classy with a contemporary feel, and was happy with the results.

"People just want to know who she is," Syd said. "No one's been able to crack her real identity."

"How is that possible in the world today?" Courtney asked, taking another sip of coffee. I resented her metabolism. I felt like I'd gained at least a pound just watching her eat. "You can find out almost anything at the click of a button."

Syd shrugged. "She must know what she's doing,

because no one's figured it out yet."

I smirked. Or she knew someone who knew what they were doing and who owed her a serious favor after he had some bad Asian food and pooped his pants one day on the way to class and she saved his ass—in more ways than one. He didn't want that story getting out, and I wasn't above blackmail to get what I wanted.

"Some of the girls at Mom to Mom think she's a psych professor at Easton," Courtney said.

I frowned. "That seems unlikely."

"Why?" Syd asked, taking another sip of her caramel coffee, totally messing up the cute little heart they'd made in the foam. She didn't care. She didn't appreciate foam art.

"Because I know all of the psychology department professors. Their reactions to my thesis included a lot of choking and red faces—and that was *after* I changed the name from *In Search of Schlong.* I honestly question whether any of them have even had intercourse."

Courtney and Syd both laughed. "Well, if it's not them? Who then?" Syd asked.

I took another drink of water, trying to come up with a plausible theory. "It could be anyone," I said, lifting a shoulder. "Maybe it's a doctor, or a therapist. Maybe it's not even someone in town."

"Mistress A has made references to the Winchester area," Syd pointed out. "Most people think she's local."

I held back the sigh I wanted to heave. She was right. I'd slipped up in a couple of my first few posts, but I hadn't thought anyone had really caught on; I was still annoyed with myself for letting it happen. I'd changed the posts since, but the damage was already done. I'd been trying to draw attention away from Winchester and Colorado ever since. "Still, the internet is a big place. It could be a teenage kid, or a ninety-year-old woman on the other side of the world for all we know."

Syd shuddered. "That would be weird. Both of them."

I nodded in agreement.

"And the grandma thing makes me think of her dick mitten post."

Courtney and I both shuddered, and then laughed.

"Whoever it is has way too much knowledge to be a kid." Syd's logical mind was getting the best of her. There was a mystery to solve and she was like a dog with a bone when it came to things that needed answers. It was the law student in her, and it concerned me.

"Maybe," I said. "Kids know a lot these days, though."

Syd's expression was dubious. "I'm pretty sure they still don't know how to tie bondage knots."

My brows shot up. "Umm, how do *you* know anything about that?"

Color immediately pinked on Syd's cheeks. "I read the blog post," she mumbled.

I grinned. "Uh huh." I would have pushed and teased her more if we were alone, but she'd already gotten mad at the reverse cowgirl comment. I wasn't going to keep going and make it monumentally awkward. Courtney's lips were turned up in amusement, and she didn't seem fazed.

"Seriously," Syd said, trying to get away from the subject of her personal sexual preferences. "The blog's been up for over two months now. Do you think we'll ever find out who Mistress A is?"

I ran a finger back and forth over the top of my coffee sleeve. "I doubt it. The person has no reason to reveal their identity."

Syd's brows bunched together, a determined look blanketing her features. "Maybe someone needs to give them one."

## *Tips and Tits: The Word from Mistress A*

### My Penis is the Wrong Size...Now What?

*Look, I'm not going to be the one who lies and tells you size isn't important. It is. And girth is just as important as length, maybe even more so to some people. But being well-endowed in that area can also make dudes* **way** *lazy. Regardless of your size, you've got to know how to use it. A dude with a tiny weenie who understands passion, foreplay, and making a woman feel desired will be FAR more memorable than some guy with a ten-incher who swings it around with all the precision of a baby elephant playing with his trunk. Bonus points if you know how to keep things fresh, exciting, and talk dirty…and if you have a working knowledge of adult toys. If you're intimately acquainted with the "over eighteen" section of your local sex toy store, or even the online version, you will hit a girl's* *list of favorite lovers, guaranteed. Big or small, keeping things exciting matters. Asking a woman if you're going to get sex tonight is completely different from looking at her like you want to rip her clothes off, and then doing just that. And this advice extends to women as well. Just because guys are easy to please, doesn't mean you can do a little tug and blow, and then lay there motionless while he does his thing. There are countless ways to make sex more interesting and enjoyable for everyone…dudes included. Find a partner you can lose your inhibitions with and try new things. If you do, you'll never be dissatisfied.*

I shut my books and closed my laptop with a sigh. I left the library, pulling my heavy wool coat tighter around me as I made my way to my car. I'd been trying to work for hours. One of my projects for a psych class was on gender roles and how they affected relationships. I'd been doing research all day. My mind had spent most of the time wandering, however. I had several more blog post ideas I'd jotted down during what should have been my study time, and a solid knot in my stomach from my coffee shop girl date with Syd and Courtney earlier in the week.

Syd's threat about giving Mistress A a reason to step forward had been haunting me for days. Her life revolved around learning to recognize fact from fiction, and figuring out holes in people's stories. She was going to make one hell of an attorney. If anyone could find their man, or in this case, woman, it would be Syd. Frankly, I was surprised she hadn't listed me as her number one suspect. Maybe she had, and she simply hadn't informed me of it yet. She often kept things close to the chest until she had proof.

I wasn't looking forward to seeing her at CARE in fifteen minutes. I usually loved my time volunteering and my time with Syd, but being under her discretionary examination was not something I cared to participate in at the moment. Which kind of pissed me off because I'd never felt the need to keep anything from Syd before. She was my best friend. I never censored myself…why was I doing it with her over Mistress A? It's not like I thought she'd tell anyone. She was getting a degree in keeping confidences, and she'd *always* kept mine. She was also the least judgmental person I knew. It was silly to think she'd do anything I didn't want her to with the information. She wouldn't even tell Jax if I asked her not to. The knot in my stomach untwisted a bit, but it didn't go away. That bothered me. I wanted to tell her, but decided I'd keep it to myself until I could analyze why I didn't want anyone—even the most important person in my world—to know about my secret. In the meantime, I needed to practice my poker face for any time Syd was in the room and Mistress A became a topic of conversation.

I pulled into the parking lot of CARE and went inside the red brick building. CARE was located in a former house that had been converted to rooms for families who needed a place to stay while their loved ones were in the hospital. They had recently started a renovation project to add on to the house and make more space for residents.

There was a need for places like CARE. I'd gotten involved because Syd's mom had cancer when Syd was young. Syd and her dad had spent a lot of time in facilities like CARE. Syd said it helped give her some stability, and made the treatments and health crisis with her mom easier to bear. Thankfully, her mom had beaten the cancer and been in remission for years. But not all stories have a happy ending, and it's important to have a support network. Charlie had worked as the CARE executive director for years, and I loved the guy like my own dad. He was working in his office and I stopped, leaning against the doorway and wiggling my fingers in a little wave. "Hey, Charlie. How's your day?"

He looked up from the stack of papers on his desk; his computer monitor reflected in his eyeglasses. "Pretty good. It would be better if I didn't have to get this grant paperwork done. How about you?"

I tipped my head in acknowledgment. "It would be better if I didn't have so much research to do."

"Being responsible is rough."

I nodded my head in empathy. "Adulting is hard."

Charlie laughed and gestured to his right. "Syd's in the kitchen."

"Thanks!"

I stopped in the hallway to put my black coat, red gloves, matching scarf, and bag in a locker, then wandered into the kitchen. Syd was helping a group of kids make cookies. Peanut butter cookies with chocolate kisses on top were her favorite to bake. The kids loved pressing the chocolate into the cookies when they were fresh from the oven.

"Hi, guys!" I greeted them as I sat at the counter across

from Syd.

A chorus of "Brynn" rang out in various voices and decibel levels. Kids created an intense level of noise, especially when I'd spent my whole day in a library.

"Hey!" Maci said, putting her little hands on her hips. She was one of my favorite kids, and she'd been at CARE with her parents for several months. Her brother had been in a car accident and was now in physical therapy, recovering from spinal injuries. "I'm not a guy!"

I gasped, feigning surprise. "You're not?"

"No!" she huffed. "I don't even *like* boys!"

One of the boys, Todd, took offense to that. "We don't like girls either," he said, his face screwed up with absolute distaste. I wondered how long they'd both continue to share their respective opinions. I'd started having crushes in elementary school.

"Hey," I said, stepping between the two of them to split them up, "that's not very nice. It doesn't matter if you're a boy, or a girl, or an alien. You can all be friends."

"Aliens?" Maci said, her voice going up in awe.

"An alien?" Todd echoed, eyes as big as saucers. "You know some aliens?" I wasn't sure if the thought of my alien connection scared them, or made them think I was cool, but either way, they were all much more interested in my answer than they were in cookies. And it took a lot to take a kid's mind off cookies…especially when they were one of Syd's secret recipes.

I wasn't going to admit it to a bunch of little kids, but I was fairly certain aliens were the only explanation for some of the guys I'd dated over the years. "You never know what's out there," I answered with a shrug, and felt a little *X-Files*-y when I did it. Imagination wasn't a bad thing, and hopefully it wouldn't cause nightmares and get me in trouble with their parents.

Syd pulled the cookies out of the oven at that exact moment, saving me from having to explain my theories on aliens, or their existence to the kids—for now at least. I was sure it would be a future topic of conversation; one they'd probably ask their family members about, and discuss with their friends. Kids remember everything.

"Grab the chocolate and start unwrapping it," Syd said to the group of kids.

All six of them grabbed handfuls of the sweet, melty treat, and started prepping them to go on cookies. Syd let the cookies finish baking on the sheet for a little longer, then slid them off one by one onto the cooling rack. The kids were all armed with their first piece of chocolate, and ready for the moment Syd would call them into action. "Okay, press the chocolate into the middle!"

They each scrambled, and I laughed watching their personalities come through. Two of the boys put the chocolate on immediately. Todd decided one piece of chocolate wasn't enough, and he needed three. Another little girl spent some time finding just the right cookie because it had to be a special cookie to get her piece of chocolate. I understood that. Chocolate was delectable, and chocolate on peanut butter cookies was even better. It was basically a little peanut butter cup in cookie form. Maci took the longest of all of the kids. Once she'd selected her cookie, she stared at it, getting the position just right. If I didn't know she was only four, I'd say she was calculating angles in her head to get the chocolate the perfect distance from all sides, and exactly centered. She finally placed it and it really did look like it was right in the middle. She might have a career in architecture.

"I'm glad you put your chocolate on fast enough," I said to Maci. "I thought the cookies would get too cold and the chocolate wouldn't melt!"

"Silly, Brynn!" She giggled, unwrapping another piece of chocolate and examining where to put it on another cookie. "I know how long it takes!"

"It's true," Syd agreed. "She has it down to a science."

"It's kind of scary," I said, watching her before looking up at Syd. "I haven't seen you in a couple of days. How are you?"

"Good. I've had a bunch of school work, and I've been spending time at Jax's."

I nodded, grateful that she hadn't been home, or suspected that I'd been avoiding her.

The kids continued putting chocolate on cookies. When they were done, we all helped Syd clean up, and left a stack of cookies in Tupperware containers on the counter for residents to grab on their way by. There was a standing rule for kids. One cookie a day. I had a feeling that rule was broken frequently when there was a lack of supervision.

"You want one?" Maci asked, holding a cookie out to me with one of *her* preciously placed chocolates on it. I knew that specific, perfect cookie wasn't offered lightly. Normally I would have said no to the empty calories and sugar, but it was hard to resist such a cute salesperson. If I baked for a living, I'd take small, adorable children with me to every event to hand out samples.

"I would love one!" I said, a bright smile on my face. "Thank you, Maci!" She handed me the cookie and I took a small bite, then closed my eyes like it was the best thing I'd ever tasted. Truly, it was right up there. Syd could bake well enough to have her own cooking show.

Maci beamed, and then Todd came up with the idea to play a board game in the play room, and they all went running in there, cookies in hand.

"That should keep them occupied for a little while," I said.

Syd nodded in agreement. "I'm going to sit for a while. I've been on my feet all day."

I followed Syd into the living room, decorated in warm butterscotch tones, and sat down on the dark brown microfiber sofa. I'd had to clean spills off that sofa frequently, and every time, I'd wondered why entire houses weren't made of the stuff. Nothing seemed to stain it.

"How did things end last night?" she asked. "I got some interesting texts from you."

I'd had a bad night, and had resorted to texting her a few times during my date. It wasn't something I did frequently because I thought using my phone on a date or in a social situation was horrible manners. It was the equivalent of flat out telling someone they didn't interest you enough for you to pay attention to them. If that was the case, I usually had no problem expressing that with words. But I'd felt bad for the guy. He wasn't an asshole. He'd just been nervous and had too much to drink. He'd passed out on his couch and I'd driven myself home. Luckily I'd seen where the night was headed way back at dinner, and had limited myself to one glass of wine and a lot of water.

"*Another* bad date?" Syd asked, eyes wide.

I sighed, grabbing a handful of dried fruit and nuts from a bowl on the coffee table in front of the couches. "He had whiskey dick."

Syd blinked, then stared at me. "Is that a new STD or something?"

I rolled my eyes and laughed. "It's a good thing you have me around. You're more innocent than a nun."

"I think I'm offended."

"I think you're lucky Jax doesn't drink often." He had a reason for that, and I didn't blame him. "It's when a guy drinks too much and can't get it up."

Syd's mouth fell open. "That really happens?" she asked. "I thought it was a myth."

I shook my head and popped another nut. "Oh no. It's real. And exceptionally disappointing."

She finished off the cookie she'd brought with her from the kitchen. "Was he equipped in the size department?"

I lifted one shoulder. "I couldn't totally tell because of the whiskey dick. He seemed to be adequate. You can do a lot with adequate if the guy has skills, but I don't know any of his talents thanks to W.D."

She shifted on the couch, crossing her legs under her. "I'm sorry, B. I assume you won't be going out with him again?"

I shook my head. "Probably not. He seemed nice, but I wanted sex, not a project."

"What about the guy a few nights ago?" Syd asked. "The guy who looked like Thor? You were pretty excited about him."

I sighed, my expression crestfallen. "Another cocktail weenie, and no other skills to speak of."

"What?" Sydney grabbed some chocolate from her bag and threw me a piece. I wasn't even going to turn her down. Just thinking about my dating life could make me an emotional eater. "Again?"

"Again," I said, popping some of the delicious dessert into my mouth. "I'm telling you, it's an epidemic. I've seen so many small dicks during the past few years."

"How does this keep happening to you?" she asked.

I shrugged as the coconut oil melted with the chocolate in my mouth. Organic chocolate truffles. I couldn't ask for more. "It can't only be me. I'm sticking with my theory about the hormones in milk causing the problem."

"I haven't heard about it from anyone else."

"It's not really a topic most people speak up about…unfortunately." Unless you're Mistress A, I added in my head.

She blew out a breath. "That really sucks for you. And it sucks there's nothing they can do to fix it," she said, thinking for a few seconds before continuing. "I mean, if I want bigger boobs, I have a lot of surgery options. If a guy wants a bigger dick, he's pretty much screwed, unless he wants one of those implants, but there can be all kinds of complications with that." She shuddered thinking about it. "I'm pretty sure size is genetic. So, if you end up pregnant by a cocktail weenie and have a boy, he might have a cocktail weenie too. Can they do genetic testing for that so you know what you're sentencing your potential kid to?"

I laughed at the amount of thought she'd put into it. "I don't think it's something they test for, but you kind of don't need it when you can get a basic idea from seeing a dude naked."

"True," she said. "So Thor's out, do you have someone else lined up for your next conquest?"

I shook my head. "I'm kind of over it right now." Truthfully, aside from the disappointing dicks, I hadn't really been interested in dating much lately. I knew why, and didn't like the reason. It started with the letter 'C', and certainly wasn't something I was about to admit out loud and especially not to Syd, who would likely make it her mission to set us up.

"What did you do today?" I asked, changing the subject. I was curious why she'd been on her feet all day.

"Mock trial competition training. They always stress me out."

I shook my head and smiled. "I don't know why. You always win."

A determined look settled on her face. "A win is never guaranteed. I have to work at it every time."

That was a good perspective for a potential lawyer to

have. And probably a good motto for life in general.

"What was the mock case about?" I asked.

"A disagreement between an employee and company over whether their insurance should have to cover birth control."

"I hope you got to argue for the employee."

She frowned. "I didn't."

"See," I said, shaking my head, "that's why I couldn't be a lawyer. I'm too much of a principle person. I wouldn't be able to argue for the other side—at least not convincingly. Who were you up against?"

"Cade."

My throat dried and my heart stuttered. For a moment, I thought it might come to a complete stop, and there were serious discussions going on between my brain and blood vessels to keep everything moving. Once they got on the same page, I was able to croak, "Cade?"

She screwed her nose up into an angry face. "We won't find out who argued it the best until next week, but I have a feeling Cade might have won."

"Didn't the Supreme Court already rule on that?"

"Yeah, but not in this context. The Supreme Court said small, closely-held companies with owners who all have the same religious beliefs could opt out for religious reasons. In this case, the employee was arguing that the small company was opting out because they just didn't want to pay. The employee said the company owners had no religious affiliation, and were using the religious argument as an excuse to not offer comprehensive health care."

I narrowed my eyes, my feminist side immediately annoyed at the company. "That would be frustrating. It would be hard to make a case for the company. Plus, it's difficult to argue against women's rights and not look like a douche pickle."

A muscle worked at her jaw. "I felt the same way." She was quiet for a few minutes, worrying her bottom lip before continuing, "I hope I'm not losing my touch. That's what I was concerned about when I started dating Jax. That a relationship would take up too much of my time and I'd lose focus on school."

That was the understatement of the year. She hadn't just been worried about it, she hadn't even wanted to start the relationship, and then she'd almost sabotaged her potential relationship over it. "You're not losing your touch," I said, leaning over to put my hand on her leg in a comforting gesture. "That would be a difficult case for any lawyer to make. If anyone could do it, it's you."

"Thanks, she said, absently tracing the checkered pattern on one of the couch's pillows with her fingertips. "Plus I was up against Cade, and he's a beast."

Totally inappropriate thoughts of Cade in beast mode immediately flashed in my head and a shudder ran all the way through me. I pushed the image from my mind and tried to focus on Syd. "You think he's as good as you are?"

"Yeah," she conceded. "It's one of the reasons I like arguing against him. He's smart, and helps make me better. It's why I study with him too."

That "study" bit of information would have been good

to know long before Syd introduced us at the coffee shop.

"I went to lunch with him after the mock trial and he had some really perceptive thoughts about my arguments."

"That's good!" I said. "Having a peer you can learn from is always a good thing."

Syd took a drink from her water bottle, and then glanced over at me. "He asked about you."

My heart did the almost-stopping thing again. My internal organs were really going to have to figure this shit out. They couldn't just choose to take a little rest every time Cade's name was mentioned. "He did?" I asked, trying to sound nonchalant. "Why?"

"He asked if I was still rooming with you, and how you were doing."

I pushed my brows together, wondering why. "That's weird. I haven't seen him since you introduced us at the coffee shop in the middle of November." Not for lack of trying. I'd been hoping to run into him like I used to hope to run into a donut truck crash.

"I think he assumed I'd moved in with Jax."

I crossed one leg over the other. "You pretty much have. I feel bad you're paying rent."

"We've only officially been together for a few months. Moving in is a big deal and I'm not ready to take that step yet. I told Cade I'm still living with you, but spend a lot of time at Jax's apartment. That way we can both have privacy."

"And I appreciate that," I said, sincerely. "It's nice to be able to walk around naked without worrying about offending you or your boyfriend."

She rolled her eyes.

"I'm not kidding." I really wasn't. Naked made me happy. I was a pant hater, and I'd go without clothes all day if I could.

"I know. I'm certain I've seen your boobs more than any other person on the planet except yourself."

I laughed. She was right about that.

"But," she said, her eyes flashing with mischief, "I can guarantee Cade wouldn't mind walking in and seeing them too."

"W-w-what?" I stammered out. "He said that?"

Syd studied me and my reaction. I didn't often get thrown by people or words. I was usually the one doing the shocking, not the other way around. "No, he didn't. But the two of you seemed completely enamored with each other on the day I introduced you at The Grind. You both acted like I wasn't even there. It was out of character for Cade, and definitely for you."

I lifted my shoulders, trying not to give anything away. I was still shocked I'd managed to make it through that formal introduction without ripping Cade's shirt off. I shook myself out of the memory. "He's attractive. That's all it was."

She gave me a doubtful look. I'd been worried about her finding out my Mistress A secret; now I was worried about her prying the Cade info out of me too. I shifted on the couch, trying not to make it look like I was squirming under her attention—because I absolutely was.

"Would you go out with him if he asked?"

"No," I answered immediately. "I wouldn't."

"Why not? You've never been particularly selective before. How do you know he wouldn't be good research material?"

That was the problem. I was worried he would be, and that one time wouldn't be enough. Or that we'd get down to business and he'd have no clue what he was doing. I mean, I'd written a Mistress A post about that very subject. Most men failed in the expertise department of sex. I kind of liked having him as a fantasy, instead of knowing for sure. Syd was right, though—our chemistry had been off the charts, and I hadn't been able to stop thinking about him. Why was I being so bi-polar about this? Usually I made a decision and stuck to it. What the hell was my problem?

I needed an excuse to give her, and grabbed at the first one I could think of. "He seems way too buttoned-up for me. Probably a missionary-only type."

"No way," Syd said, pointing at me. "You can't make that call based on *one* meeting!"

"Come on. I've been with a lot of guys. I know vanilla when I see it."

"Just because he wears button-up shirts and a suit occasionally doesn't mean he's like that in his personal life too."

I lifted a shoulder. "Kind of seems that way."

"You don't even know him."

So, there was that. And she was right. In my fantasies, he was buttoned-up as well, but only long enough for him to push his lips into mine as I ripped his shirt off and wrapped my legs around him, the shirt a casualty on the road to the bedroom…or couch…or floor, or countertop…any surface would do, really. "That's true. And he does have a nice ass."

She winged a brow. "I didn't realize you'd noticed."

I snorted. "He's a dude. I always notice."

She laughed.

"And he's hot. When I saw him, my panties tried to take themselves off."

She snorted this time. "Since when do you wear panties?" she asked, genuinely perplexed.

She had a point, but still. "I wear them…occasionally."

Her eyebrows went up like she seriously doubted my ability to put on undergarments. I rolled my eyes. "I also trust your judgment. You like the guy, so he must have some merit."

She threw a pillow at me. "Everyone has some merit."

I shot her a disbelieving look. "I could name twenty guys off the top of my head who definitely do not."

"You're just cynical."

She was right about that. I'd been treated horribly in the past. There weren't many people in my life I trusted because of it. "Guilty as charged, Prosecutor."

She sighed, knowing she wasn't going to win this argument…yet. I had no doubt it would be revisited—frequently.

Maci came running into the room with her favorite book and plopped down between Syd and I. "Read me a story, pleeeaase!" she asked, holding the book about a princess with pink hair up in the air for one of us to grab. Syd got to it first, and we took turns reading the different characters in different voices. Maci squealed in delight, and my heart was lighter knowing I'd made her day better, even if my mind was somewhere else.

# Three

## Tips and Tits: The Word from Mistress A

### To-Do-Me List

*We all have a list of places we want to have sex. I call it Bucket List Diddling. And if you don't have one, you should make one. On that count, I'm here to help. Here are five that I think should be in your top five!*

1. *The beach. Is there anything hotter than having sex in the tropics, a warm breeze blowing through your hair while water rushes around you? Just be aware of the sand because it can get in some uncomfortable places…and don't get too close to a strong wave, or your sexy times will end with a sea rescue.*
2. *Outside under the full moon. A full moon is beautiful, peaceful, and perfect for a summertime sex session! The moon brings out something animalistic in all of us. That primal force combined with*

*sex makes for an excellent partnership.*

3. *A vineyard.* Not in *the vineyard, though you could probably figure out how to make that happen if it's your thing. But a lot of vineyards also have hotels or bed and breakfasts on-site or nearby. Hello! Wine, a soft bed, the country…it's the perfect setting for romance…and a go-to overnight date for any love-related reality show. But there's a reason for that—because it's damn romantic!*
4. *A gigantic bathtub. One of those free-standing ones made for guys who can bench press a small car. The space will give you plenty of room to move around as warm water laps your slippery skin. The thought of your guy naked in the tub, with you wearing nothing but bubbles, should make you weak in the knees.*
5. *The car. I'm not saying the backseat of an old beater while parked in a dark parking lot, hoping you don't get caught. I'm talking about an SUV, or at least something with a bench seat. There's something intensely hot about not being able to wait to get home, and just pulling over on the side of the road. It's quick, dirty, and will leave you gasping for breath.*

I walked up the shoveled path to a cute, sage green bungalow with black shutters. The street was lined with cars and I'd had to park almost a block away. It was a good thing I'd worn my favorite skinny jeans, fur lined black boots, a black sweater and heavy coat to trudge through the snow and twenty degree temperatures. I'd have to take the coat off inside and it would probably be hot as hell in there, but the sweater had sleeves that pushed up easily, and the neck was cut low enough that it would help me cool off. I could hear voices coming from inside the house. Apparently the small gathering I'd been told about had turned into a full-on college party.

I dropped the house warming gift—one of my favorite candles with a wood wick that sounded like a real fire—off on the table, and made my way through the various groups of people. I saw Syd and Jax standing by the drinks, helping to serve people, and wandered over to them. "There's my favorite sexy couple," I said, grabbing a plastic red cup and pouring myself a glass of water with lemon.

Jax's lips slid up into his notoriously charming grin. "You're my favorite of Syd's friends, you know that?"

"I better be," I said, taking a sip. "I'm her best friend, and she'd know nothing about sex without me."

Jax's grin stretched. "I probably owe you some chocolate or something as a thank you."

Syd rolled her eyes. "You're both full of yourselves."

Someone bumped into me and I looked back to see my friend and occasional hook up buddy, Collin, leaning over my shoulder. His lips were turned up playfully. He'd been a basketball player at Easton, and president of his frat before we'd graduated last year; now he was getting his MBA. "There's the hot girl I've been looking for."

I gave him a wink. "You know how to get a girl's attention."

Collin was fun. We'd been friends for years, and booty-call buddies for almost as long. He had the right equipment, and he knew what to do with it. Every time I got disappointed during my big dick research, Collin was always there to make up for the other guys' shortcomings.

But it never went any further than sex. Because I didn't do relationships, and neither did Collin. We were both far better at casual sex than anything else, and didn't want to ruin a good thing.

I was surprised to see him at Courtney's housewarming party. Collin was my friend, and kind of Syd's friend. I didn't think he even registered on Jax's buddy list. Their relationship had started out rocky several months ago when Jax punched Collin in the face and broke his nose for letting Syd and I wander out of a Halloween party drunk without taking our keys.

Collin peered down into my glass. "You should live a little and have something with sugar."

I punched him in the shoulder. "I have cocktails all the time!" My tone came out more defensive than I'd intended. I tried to recover, explaining, "I'm driving tonight."

"If you weren't," Collin said, his eyes twinkling mischievously, "you could enjoy a panty dropper."

I laughed so hard, I almost spit the water I'd just taken a sip of out on him. "That's a new line."

"It's very, very tasty," he said, attempting a convincing tone.

I narrowed my eyes, thinking of all the times Collin and I had hooked up. I couldn't even begin to count them. "I believe you've tasted it before."

He gave a shit-eating grin. "Many times. But I was talking about the drink."

"I definitely didn't think you were talking about alcohol," Syd said, handing a girl I'd never seen before a drink. I assumed she was one of Courtney's friends from Mom to Mom.

"A friend of mine was traveling in Belize and tried it there," Collin said. "He said it was fantastic. He also won the chicken drop lottery, so he had plenty of money to buy a lot of panty droppers."

"We're still talking about the drink, right? Not girls' panties?" I asked.

Collin shrugged, grabbing some soda from the table and refilling his glass with it before adding some rum.

"Chicken drop?" Jax asked, curious.

"Yeah," Collin said, taking a gulp of his concoction. "He said there's this numbered checkerboard on the beach outside of a bar. You buy tickets and get your numbers. They let a chicken loose on the board and if it shits on your number, you win."

"That's…odd." Syd said, confusion clouding her face. Syd liked things to make sense. Paying money to bet on where an animal pooped was not in her realm of logic.

Collin threw back the rest of his drink before starting to make another. "It's something to do, and it goes to a good cause. If no one wins the lottery, the money is donated to an animal shelter. Most people who win also donate their winnings."

"But not your friend," I pointed out. "He used it to get himself and everyone else drunk."

Collin grimaced. "He's not a stellar human, it's true."

Jax had noticed Syd's reaction to the poop drop. He liked taking Syd out of her comfort zone. She'd almost broken up with him over a camping trip a couple of months ago. His eyes sparkled as he said, "Belize sounds interesting, and I bet it's warm and bikini friendly. Maybe we should visit, Syd?"

"I've been to your version of 'bikini friendly', and it involved a tent." Syd's eyes were narrowed, but her tone was teasing.

His eyes darkened. "I made up for it."

Syd blushed, but added, "You definitely did."

I took pity on her and changed the subject, asking Collin, "How did you find out about the party tonight?" I still wasn't sure how he'd ended up with an invite.

"Collin has party-radar," Syd said, taking a drink of her own mixture. It looked like soda of some kind, and I guessed she wasn't drinking. She wasn't a huge alcohol fan, which used to be good for me because it meant I had a babysitter when I decided to go out. That didn't happen much anymore though—she was usually with Jax, and I usually went out alone, and drank a lot less. "I'm surprised he hasn't created an app. If there's a party happening on any given night, Collin's aware of it."

"That's a good name for an app," I said. "Any Given Party."

"I think he should call it Party Dropper," Jax offered.

I pointed at him, and smiled, nodding my head. "Excellent suggestion, Blue Eyes."

Jax grinned, and Syd shook her head. "I can't believe you still call him that."

I pushed my brows together. "I can't believe you don't. They're the color of a goddamn jewel."

Syd rolled her eyes, but glanced up at him with an

expression so full of love that I couldn't tell if I wanted to hug them both, or run away screaming. That level of love and commitment was terrifying.

"The app's not a bad idea," Collin agreed. "But I'm not a party crasher." I eyed him doubtfully. We all knew that wasn't the case. He'd practically majored in alcohol and poor decisions. "A girl Courtney works with invited me."

"Ah," I said. "That makes more sense."

"What's that supposed to mean?" Collin asked, leaning against me and looking wounded. "It sounds like you're insinuating I couldn't get an invite on my own."

"With 'panty dropper' on your resume, I'm sure you appeal to a specific clientele," I said.

"I've dropped your panties many times," he said, apparently completely unaware we were in a room full of people with ears. "At least, the times you've actually been wearing them."

Another girl might have blushed. I was not that girl. "Tonight's not one of them."

Syd groaned. "I'm not sure I wanted to know that."

"It seems I've stumbled into an interesting conversation." The voice was deep, male, and one I recognized with absolute certainty. It had been branded into my mind from the first moment I'd heard it. My heart started to race, and I slowly turned to confirm the face belonged to the voice I thought it did. My mental-branding abilities had not failed me. He was wearing jeans that hugged every part that mattered—all of them in Cade's case, and a cobalt blue sweater that made his gorgeous pale blue eyes even brighter. His cheekbones were sculpted and drew my gaze down to his jaw that had surely been carved by goddesses. He had the fullest bottom lip I'd ever seen, and a skin tone that looked like he'd been on a beach even though it was the middle of winter. Despite barely knowing him, a primal part of me seriously considered lifting up his shirt and licking his stomach. I didn't even care who was watching. I realized I was staring and my eyes snapped back up to his face. He met my gaze, and it was suddenly clear he'd been assessing me in the same way I'd been measuring him. Electricity sparked between us, and I was immediately uncomfortable with it. Chemistry was one thing…this felt like something more, and had felt the same way every time I'd seen him. I wasn't prepared for it to continue happening each time we saw each other, and definitely not okay with it.

"Cade!" Syd said, breaking mine and Cade's eye contact. Her face lit up. "You came!"

He slowly shifted his gaze from me, giving his attention to Syd. "Wouldn't have missed it."

Wouldn't have missed it? Cade got invited to Courtney's housewarming party, and Syd didn't think I might need to be advised about that? Especially after our conversation at CARE earlier? She had plenty of time to tell me! What had she been thinking? Maybe I led her to believe a warning wasn't required, but come on! She was my best friend and knew me better than that. She could have at least mentioned it during the whole you-have-chemistry-with-Cade speech.

Jax did the dude head nod in Cade's direction. "I heard you were quite an opponent."

Cade tilted his head. "Syd did a great job. She's her worst critic. I was just glad I didn't have to argue her side."

"Do you want something to drink?" Jax asked, motioning to the table.

"Sure. Something strong."

"Make him a panty dropper," Collin suggested.

Cade leaned against the counter, the veins in his forearm standing out against ropey muscle. "I've never had a problem in the clothes dropping department," he said, his gaze sliding to mine.

My heart sped up even more and I was rather worried about my blood pressure.

I liked sex. I was interested in sex. Nothing else. So the fact Cade had gotten under my skin before I even knew his name frustrated the hell out of me. No man had done that in years. I'd made sure of it. We had an intense connection from the first moment we saw each other. Chemistry. That's all it was. I took a deep breath and repeated that to myself again. Chemistry. Nothing more. I just needed to forget about him, or get him out of my system. The problem was that I wasn't sure which option I wanted. Actually, I wanted both of those things: to get him out of my system, and then forget him. But I was worried I wouldn't be able to do the forgetting part after the getting part. That was my current quandary.

"I don't even know what's in your fabled panty dropper," Jax said to Collin. He grabbed some alcohol and poured it into a cup with soda instead, then handed it to Cade.

"Pineapple juice, orange juice, cranberry juice, vodka,

triple sec, coconut rum, schnapps, gin, and delicious regret."

"I feel tipsy even hearing the list of ingredients," I said.

"I can think of worse things than tipsy sex on a beach," Collin said, wiggling his eyebrows.

Syd shook her head. "Beach sex is tricky. Sand. *Everywhere.*"

Collin grabbed a cookie off the table next to the drinks. "Clearly, you don't read Mistress A. Beach sex is on her To-Do-Me list."

I looked away, trying to make myself seem inconspicuous. I knew exactly what Mistress A's To-Do-Me list was because I'd written it. I'd been working on my poker face lately, but I still got nervous every time Mistress A was brought up in conversations I was part of. What if I slipped and said something I shouldn't, and someone figured out my secret identity? It was a scary thought. I didn't want it to affect my life, school, or volunteer work. The reality of it was that could very well happen. Only people I trusted completely could ever know I was Mistress A.

"Not true," Syd said. "I saw that blog post. And based on her suggestions, I'd be worried about getting arrested for indecent exposure."

Jax grinned. "You're almost a lawyer. I'd be fine with that."

Syd gave him a look. "I'm in my first year of law school. That hardly qualifies for 'almost a lawyer'. Not to mention that it would be tough to represent myself if I was the one caught fornicating."

"Who even uses that word?" Collin asked, giving her a dumbfounded look.

"Lawyers," I said.

"Good thing you're such good friends with Cade then," Jax said. "He'd get us out of it."

Cade's lips stretched, slow and sexy. "I'd have you out of the cell in no time."

My mind abruptly wandered to a memory of Cade and handcuffs. I shut it down immediately.

"Who's this Mistress A, anyway?" Jax asked.

"You haven't read her posts? She has a sex blog," Syd explained. "She gives advice."

Jax pushed his brows together. "Lots of people give sex advice. What makes her so special?"

"She's witty, and no topic is taboo," Collin said. "Her blog's been up for a couple of months. But the thing that makes her especially popular here is that she's referenced the Winchester area and Colorado in some of her posts, so there's speculation she's local. Everyone's trying to figure out who she is."

A knot formed in my stomach. That concerned me. I was prepared for speculation, and had taken every precaution possible, but there was still a chance word could get out. When I'd first started, I hadn't considered there would be so much interest in my identity. I'd let a few minor things slip about Winchester and Colorado that people had latched onto. They were references that could easily be explained away, like a post I did during a blizzard that listed ways to make snow sexy. But people had made connections, and the connections had turned into theories.

No one had proven any of them yet and I'd been much more careful since, but it still made me nervous.

"That," Cade said, "and unlike some sex advice columnists who are just going off of personal experience alone, she actually seems to be educated in her responses."

My mouth started to gape and I quickly picked it back up. Cade Brett, buttoned-up attorney to be, read my blog? I mean, it was out there. Right on the internet for Zeus and everyone, but still, I hadn't really considered the star of my current fantasies would be reading the things I wrote. I was slightly embarrassed at the level of intimacy, even though I shouldn't have been because the blog was public, and no one knew it was me. However, I was putting myself out there and people would read into it a thousand different ways that I couldn't control. I'd made peace with their likely erroneous opinions about Mistress A and her sex life. It's not like I'd actually tried everything I advocated—but I made sure to research and get educated on the subjects I wasn't familiar with before offering advice or opinions. I'd intended the blog as a helpful, fun tool to improve people's sex lives. I hadn't considered I might be giving tips to the guy I wanted to climb like a tree. I shook the feeling off. There was no reason to be embarrassed, or feel weird. Nothing had changed, except I now knew Cade was reading my posts. He'd clearly been reading them for a while and the world hadn't ended.

"You read Mistress A?" Collin asked.

Cade nodded. "I like to stay educated. Learn new things."

Syd's brows went up ever so slightly, her gaze straying to me. Her look practically screamed, "He's up for learning new things!" I rolled my eyes, but inside, my stomach was doing somersaults at the thought of a guy who knew what he was doing in bed. It was like accidently tripping over a wish-granting genie.

"I think she's a goddess, and wish I knew who she was so I could thank her personally," Collin said. "She's helping to make my extra-curricular activities much more adventurous."

"You don't need any more adventure," I said.

He pointed at me. "Satisfied customer, right there."

I glared at him. "You need to refresh your memory and read her post on how not to be a dick nugget."

Collin grinned. "You love me."

I shook my head in mock exasperation and noticed Cade had been watching our exchange with interest.

"So," Cade said, motioning between Collin and I, "you two are dating?"

Syd burst out laughing.

Cade looked at her and raised a brow.

"No," Syd said. "They are *definitely* not."

Collin lifted a hand to his heart, faking offense. At least, I *thought* he was faking.

"Unless I misheard earlier," Cade said, his eyes holding mine, "he's seen your panties."

I shrugged. "We have a history," I said by way of explanation. I didn't see any reason to go into details about that history, or my booty call list. Yes, I had a list. Collin was just my preference. And none of those things were anyone's business but my own.

Cade eyed me like he was appraising me again, and trying to figure something out. He already had way more knowledge than I wished he did, and I wasn't in the mood to give him more. I decided the best course of action would be to change the subject. I was using that tactic a lot tonight. "How are you doing, Cade? Syd says you're her favorite study partner because you're almost as good at arguing as she is."

Syd shot me an annoyed look. "I said you were better than I was."

"I'd agree with Brynn's statement," Cade said, taking a sip of his drink. "This is great, by the way. Thanks, Jax."

"What kind of law do you want to specialize in?" As a first year law student, I knew that he was just taking electives, but wondered if there was a type of law he was interested in.

"I want to work in health law."

"Helping the doctors, or the patients?"

"The patients, preferably," he said, taking another sip of his drink. "What about you, Brynn? I know you're getting your Masters degree. Syd told me about your research."

I shifted my gaze to Syd, trying to ascertain exactly how much she'd told him, but she was busy getting someone another drink. I turned back to Cade. "She did?" I'd learned shorter responses were best when trying to figure out what a person actually knew. If she'd told him all the details, it wasn't very best friend-y of her. But she probably thought it didn't matter. It's not like I kept my enjoyment of carnal activities a secret. Still, for some reason I couldn't put my finger on, I kind of didn't want Cade to know.

"On sex among college students," he clarified.

A flood of relief swept over me. So Syd hadn't told him my original topic of interest, and what had really driven my research—my quest for large penises. "Oh. Yeah."

"That's an interesting topic."

I nodded. "I'm studying to be a sex therapist."

"I heard that too."

I glanced at Syd, sending her daggers with my eyes before turning my attention back to Cade. "Is there anything Syd *didn't* tell you?"

He looked contemplative. "She didn't tell me if you have a boyfriend."

Wow. That was direct. I liked it…more than I should have.

I inhaled a little more rapidly than I'd intended. Cade noticed, one corner of his mouth going up. "No. No boyfriend."

"She's not really the relationship type," Syd said helpfully as she came back over to us.

He eyed me speculatively. "I've gathered as much."

Syd's brows pushed together. "But this is only, like, the second time you've ever even spoken, right?" Syd said, her eyes going back and forth between Cade and I.

"Yeah," I answered immediately, sending him a warning glance. It was the second time—if you didn't count our encounter in October.

Cade's eyes narrowed as he caught my gaze and held it. I didn't like being under his scrutiny any more than I liked being under Syd's. Damn lawyers.

Cade licked his lips. "So we're going to pretend that was the first time we met?" Cade asked, right in front of Syd, Jax, Collin, and whatever deities existed. "That's what's happening here?"

My breath was staggered as I remembered back to both times I'd spent with Cade before tonight. He threw me off my game, and I didn't get thrown. Not by men, school, conversation topics…nothing. Except this damn guy. I didn't like it. But I didn't want him to know that either. I pulled my lips into a sweet smile and pretended like I'd totally forgotten our first encounter. "We met at the coffee shop. Syd introduced us and I thought you were really nice." It wasn't a lie. That's when I'd actually found out who he was. Before that he'd just been the mystery man I couldn't get out of my head, or my fantasies.

A smile played across Cade's lips, his dark pink tongue running over them. His head went down in a nod of assent. I thought I might be getting my way, and he was going to let me off without pushing me on my omission. I was wrong. "I'm not talking about that time, B. And we both know it."

B? What the hell? He wasn't authorized to give me a nickname. I barely knew him!

"What time *are* you talking about?" Syd asked, looking at me with curiosity before settling her attention back on Cade.

My eyes went wide as I feigned innocence and lifted my shoulders. I wouldn't have a problem discussing October if we'd been in private, but I wasn't comfortable letting everyone else in on the conversation.

Cade's eyes narrowed, the knowing grin never leaving his face. "Apparently I wasn't very memorable. I'll have to work on that." He held my gaze and the look he gave me was part threat, part promise. The lower half of my body responded immediately; I'd never been so upset at my ovaries. My chest tightened at my warring emotions. I'd met guys like Cade before. He was walking devastation and I couldn't help wondering how many hearts he'd destroyed. I wouldn't let mine be one of them.

Syd watched the interaction with interest, analyzing every word and action. "I need to check on Courtney. Brynn needs to help." She grabbed my arm and pulled me away, through the house until we got to Paige's quiet, unoccupied bedroom. She dragged me in and shut the door. "Have you slept with Cade?" she hissed.

A look of deep offense crossed my features, a line forming between my eyes. "I sleep with a lot of guys, Syd, and I don't apologize for it, but I take umbrage at the insinuation that you seem to think I've slept with *everyone*." I was impressed I'd managed to answer the question without really answering it.

She lightly punched my shoulder. "That's not what I said. And you know I'd never judge you anyway. I love that you are who you are, and give zero fucks what people think. But he seems to think you met before the coffee shop."

I shrugged a shoulder. Not willing to admit that was the truth, not even to my best friend. Relationships were messy, and I'd thought about him way more than I was comfortable with since that day.

Syd blew out a long breath. "It's time for the honesty train, Brynn."

I lifted my brows. "Honesty train? Did you just make that up?" Really, I'd given her the honesty treatment a few times when she needed some sense talked into her about Jax, so I couldn't fault her for doing the same. I decided to try being open minded.

She waved off my comments. "Here's the thing, Brynn. You and Cade have *a lot* of chemistry. Like, more chemistry than I've ever seen you have with *anyone*."

I leaned against Paige's pale pink dresser, crossing my arms over my chest as I prepared to listen to the rest of her lecture.

"I'm not kidding! I already told you I felt it that day at The Grind, but didn't want to push it so I didn't say anything. Then earlier when we were talking about him at CARE, you were acting weird. And when I asked Cade if he wanted to come tonight and he asked if you'd be there—"

"—He asked about me?" I interrupted. I immediately chastised myself for seeming overeager, but I really did want to know what he'd said.

Syd's lips curved up, slow and knowing. "He did." She folded her arms across her chest, mimicking me. "And I thought you didn't care."

I reached down, picking at a thread on my shirt. "I don't. What did he ask?"

Her smile spread wider, knowing she'd hooked me. "He asked how long we've known each other, and what your story was."

"What did you tell him?"

"That we met freshman year of college, have been best friends ever since, and you're basically my girl soul mate."

I smiled at that. "It's true. If you ever try to claim someone else as your girl soul mate, I'll go caveman on their ass and club them over the head with something really hard."

"Right back at ya."

God, I loved Syd. She was my rock. My kind, moral compass who supported my dreams and encouraged me to make them even bigger.

"I told him you're getting your Masters in psychology and studying sexuality."

"Thank Thor you didn't tell him I was researching dick sizes."

"Thank Thor I convinced you to change the title."

Also true. "You're an excellent best friend."

"I know." She checked her makeup in Paige's mirror, wiping a finger under each eye, and reapplying some lipstick. "He also asked if you were seeing anyone."

My breath caught in my throat. He'd asked that a few minutes ago too, but I wanted to know what Syd had told him, and how he'd reacted. "What did you say?"

She finished with her lipstick and put it back in her bag. "I said if he wanted to know, he should ask you. And that he'd have to define "seeing"."

"Ha ha."

"It's true though. You "see" a lot of guys, you just generally don't see them naked more than once."

"I do if they have skills."

She tilted her head to the side in acceptance. "You have hook ups, and occasionally repeated hook ups—like with Collin, but seeing someone, as in a relationship? No. That's not your standard operating procedure."

"What did he say back?"

"Not much. I think he was just gathering information. Probably forming a plan of attack for your lady parts."

I could actually feel the heat rising in my cheeks. I don't blush, dammit! What was this guy doing to me? "That's ridiculous."

Syd noticed my crimson cheeks and her mouth fell open forming a shocked 'O'. "Holy shit! Do you *like* him, Brynn?"

"Define 'like'," I said, my tone mocking.

She gave me a hard glare.

I sighed. "No. I don't do relationships. You know that."

She stepped back, giving me a visual analyzation that felt like she was taking me apart. If anyone could do it, it would be Syd.

"Maybe it's time for you to reconsider that rule."

# Four

## *Tips and Tits: The Word from Mistress A*

### Don't Do Douches

*Let's be clear: douches are what we call people, not something we use. Years ago, someone who didn't have the common sense that the goddesses gave baby maple trees came up with the idiotic idea that vaginas needed to be cleaned after sex. I'm sure it was a man, and I could probably write an entire novel on the topic: "Dumbass shit that dudes have advised women to do." Your lady parts are not supposed to smell like a flower scented room deodorizer. I'm a germ-freak, and spread Clorox around like candy, but if there's one thing that doesn't need to be pressure washed, it's your vagina. Vaginas are excellent at self-cleaning, and using douches actually changes the PH of your body, making it so you're more prone to yeast infections. If you don't want to end up in the feminine product aisle itching your nether regions like crazy, stop douching.*

I walked down the steps of the psychology building, putting my head down as the wind bit at my exposed skin. I needed a coffee and some quiet time to get homework done, and reread the chapter that we'd just finished discussing in class. Well, that other people had been discussing; I hadn't been paying much attention. My mind was infuriatingly occupied with a tall, muscular law student.

I went to the commons area and ordered a skinny latte with sugar free vanilla. I added some cinnamon so I could pretend it was a cinnamon roll, and found a private, unoccupied alcove by the massive floor-to-ceiling windows. I dropped my bag next to the overstuffed chair, and settled into it, crossing my legs. I held my coffee with both hands, sipping it slowly as I watched people hurry from one building to the next, trying to get out of the cold.

My thoughts strayed again to Cade. During the middle of my professor's lecture on the sexual revolution, I'd firmly decided it was absolutely *not* time to start reconsidering rules, or wanting relationships like Syd had suggested. The level of discomfort I was feeling from the entire Cade situation was becoming a serious frustration.

I'd left Courtney's party last week even more conflicted about my feelings. Cade had arms like a bodybuilder, and the face of a man who usually only shows up during dreams. Naughty ones. Plus, he read Mistress A. And he'd mentioned that Mistress A knew what she was talking about—which I did—and that also meant he had to have some level of education on the subjects I'd highlighted.

He'd intrigued me, repeatedly. I wanted to know his history, and more about him. But…that didn't mean I had to have a relationship with him. A sense of relief washed through me at the realization I could get to know him and even have a friendship with him, but nothing more. I could do friends. I had a lot of guy friends. There was no reason Cade couldn't be one of them. And maybe he would even turn into a friend with benefits, like Collin.

Now it was just a matter of deciding exactly how to do that. I could ask him to hang out. Maybe meet up for coffee? That was non-committal. It was coffee, not an entire meal. I already knew he liked coffee, and friends had coffee a lot. Yes, I nodded to myself, coffee was a good plan. I'd figure out a time when Syd was going to be with him, and conveniently run into them. Then see where things went.

My mind started to wander as I sat there, sipping my hot drink, staring out the window, and daydreaming about how the whole thing would play out: what I'd say, what he'd say, what position we'd end up having sex in.

My thoughts were jolted out of The Sultry Saddle when a group of girls sat on the couches on the other side of the alcove I was in. There was half of a wall separating us, but I'd seen them walk up, and could hear them clearly.

"Did you see his post about the cold weather?"

A chorus of giggles erupted. "Snow isn't just for snowboarding."

"He was so right! My boyfriend tried some of his tips

for playing with different temperatures and it was amazing! Hit the 'best sex of my life' list for sure."

I wasn't trying to eavesdrop, but they were being loud and my ears perked up at the conversation. Sex, and temperature play? I'd done a few articles on that myself. What were they talking about?

"Really?" Another voice said. "I'm totally going to try it then."

"I like him almost as much as Mistress A."

I caught my breath and almost dropped my coffee. I sliced my head in the direction of where they were seated, trying to hear them better. I was glad the wall blocked me from view.

"It's nice to get a male and female perspective. I follow them both on all of their accounts so I know as soon as something is posted."

Follow us both? A male and female perspective? Who the hell were they talking about?

"People think Mistress A is from Winchester. I wonder if he's local, too?"

Another voice, "Maybe they're working together. It would make sense."

"Totally! They're both so similar. It would be smart to team up."

No, no, no, no, no…there was no teaming up going on. Who the fuck was this guy, and why the fuck had he stolen my fucking idea? My blood felt like it was set to boil and I was inching my way up to a full-blown explosion. I was pissed!

"I just want to know who Master Z is so I can date him

myself. I think the man knows more about my girl parts than I do."

My mouth fell open and I immediately grabbed my laptop out of my bag. I typed Master Z into the search engine and had a slew of results within seconds. I scrolled down until I found what looked to be the right website, and clicked the link.

The site came up with a warning about adult content. I was familiar with that particular screen…because I had it on my own damn site! After accepting there would be adult content, the screen turned black and the image of an ornate four poster bed appeared with white tangled sheets that had a shine to them like they were some luxurious fabric. A dude with a goddamn eight pack, his face darkened out, stood in the corner of the room, half of his body in shadow, but a hint of a tattoo peaked out down his side, over his ribs. The words "Master Z" faded across the top of the page in an elaborate script, with a subheading that read: Alpha Answers. Then a menu popped up beckoning the user to choose their next location. Bed, couch, kitchen table, blankets by the fireplace, bathtub, and pool were some of the options.

The next seventy-three words out of my mouth contained the word 'fuck', or a variation on it. My blog was awesome! But his user interface was much fancier, and clearly catered to a specific clientele: women.

I clicked on "kitchen" and got a list of posts that had to do with sex in the kitchen—tools, foods, best surfaces to use. I clicked off that and went to blankets by the fireplace. That gave me a list of blog posts that had to do with sex in cozy comfort. I took a deep breath and tried to push my initial emotional reaction out of the way…at least for the moment. From a business perspective, his posts and branding were smart. I saw the first one, the post about temperature play that the girls had been talking about. They were still talking, but the topic of discussion had moved onto a group project instead of sex advice and whether Mistress A or Master Z was better at it. It took all of my restraint not to stand up and tell them Mistress A was obviously better…not that I was biased or anything. No one knew girl parts and what girls wanted like another actual girl. When it came to women and their motivations, men spent most of their time guessing…if they put in any time at all. Most dudes would take the easiest path possible to get what they wanted.

I read through the post.

## Alpha Answers

### Snow Isn't Just for Snowboarding

*It's cold outside, which means this is the perfect time to warm up in the house with your favorite naked partner. Nothing gets you warm faster than taking off your clothes, so get down and dirty, then grab some snow from outside (put some clothes on first unless exposing yourself gets you off, then by all means, go out there naked) and use it to cool off. You can do this in any number of ways, but I'm a fan of packing the snow into a little ball, and using it to tease your lady's nipples. Circular motions work well, but try different things and see what she likes. If your foreplay was stellar—and it should have been—her body will be ready for anything, and the pleasure/pain combo of the cold on her nipples by the heat of the fire will make her even hotter. When you're done with the snow on her nipples, take your cold hands and use them on her clit before pushing them inside her. She'll be screaming for more in no time.*

What. The. Fuck?!? Number one, the dude was boring. His posts weren't nearly as entertaining as mine. Number two, he'd absolutely stolen my idea and copied it to almost to the letter: short posts with non-mainstream sex advice. And he'd used the name Master, the counter to my Mistress! This was not a coincidence. I felt certain he'd copied my blog, and even wondered if the copycat asshat was someone I knew…someone who had figured out that I was Mistress A. I started scrolling through other posts, though there weren't many. His blog had only been active for a few weeks. Mine started over two months ago!

Who the fuck was Master Z? And who the fuck did he think he was taking my idea and using it to profit for himself?

I made the mistake of scrolling through the comments section. No one should ever read comments. It just makes you stabby, especially if you're included in the topic of said opinions.

*Who's Master Z?*

*I'd like to meet him!*

*I want to be fucked by him!*

*Maybe Mistress A and Master Z know each other?*

*Master Z is way hotter than Mistress A!*

I exited the screen because I could literally feel my blood pressure rising even more, and it was already at dangerously high levels. I didn't want my laptop to end up as collateral damage. How the hell did they know who was hotter? No one had seen photos of either one of us!

I slammed my laptop shut and shoved it in my bag. I was not happy, and needed to figure out what to do about it.

I'd been waiting hours for Syd to get home, and that had given me plenty of time to read through Master Z's blog in its entirety. Like I said, it was only a few weeks old, so it didn't take me long. His posts were all similar to mine, discussing various elements of sex from positions to porn, and giving advice from the "male perspective." I refused to call him alpha, even if he thought he was.

I was still pissed. Way pissed. But now I wanted to know who the hell he was, and where he got the nerve. I considered emailing him immediately, but I thought better of it. I was too worked up and would probably say something I shouldn't, or out myself in the process. It was clear he was keeping his identity a secret as well.

The door opened and Syd came up behind me. "Hey! How was your day, did you—"

Her voice trailed off as she noticed my screen.

"Who's that?" she asked, pointing at the shirtless dude on my screen.

"Not who he claims to be, I'm sure," I said, turning to look over my shoulder at her. "I'm sure it's a stock photo."

She plopped down on the couch next to me, reaching over and scrolling down. "Is this another sex advice site?" She studied it as she scanned the page. "It seems a lot like Mistress A's."

"It is," I said, trying not to growl.

I needed to talk to someone about this. Syd was the obvious choice, but I had to do it in a way that didn't give my own secret up. I was still pretty upset though…upset enough that I wasn't sure I could talk about it calmly.

Syd kept scrolling. "Ha! Alpha Answers. That's kind of catchy."

I took a deep breath. "I think Tips and Tits is more clever."

"I like Mistress A a lot too, but I think having a male perspective is a good idea." She paused as she read a couple of his posts, then took a moment to look at another pic of the faceless dude wrapped in some sheets. She had a real-life perfect dude with a face she could be looking at, so I wasn't sure why she was so interested in this stupid faker. "I wonder if they're working together. Seems like that would be a good partnership."

I pursed my lips and tried to calm down. "If they're not, I bet Mistress A is pissed that someone stole her idea."

Syd shrugged. "I bet she's not. She seems pretty open to all things sexual, and would probably welcome a male point of view. I've only scanned a couple of his posts, but he seems to know what he's talking about. They should work together if they're not. They both seem to have the same goals."

That was a cute way to look at it. Like a Mistress and

Master who were both alphas in their own rights could manage to be friends and not kill each other, let alone collaborate and work together. It was a ridiculous suggestion—by every person who had suggested it, and so far there were many.

"I'm curious to see where this goes," Syd said.

"What do you mean?"

"They're going to have to address the situation. Tell people if they're working together or not."

I'd been so caught up in my anger that I hadn't considered the next steps, or addressing the rumors. People were already speculating: the students I'd heard earlier, and now even my best friend. Every one of them was making the connection between Mistress A and Master Z. I wrinkled my nose, annoyed I was going to have to make a statement of some sort and deal with this. I hated that he'd taken my idea and basically just written it from a guy's perspective. I hated coattail riders. But I couldn't stop him from doing it, so it was better to deal with it and move forward. Maybe acknowledging the situation would help us cross-promote and get other readers.

Syd stood and started up the stairs to her room. "I wish I could stay and read more, but I have a date with Jax tonight. Maybe I'll tell him about the snow post." She flashed me a conspiratorial grin.

"Make sure you use clean snow," I mumbled. Syd gave me a funny look, like a germ freak would use anything but the cleanest of flakes.

"I'd be surprised if there's anything Master Z knows

that Jackson West doesn't," I added, my eyes back on the laptop.

"I don't know about that. We tried the popping candy blow job suggestion from Mistress A. Jax was a fan."

I laughed, glad Syd and Jax were benefiting from Mistress A as well. "I imagine most guys would be. And really, guys aren't the difficult ones to please. I hope men are reading Mistress A and learning things. All women deserve a partner who understands how to satisfy them."

Syd eyed me for a few seconds. I knew that look…it was one she used when she was trying to figure something out. I quickly ran over everything I'd said, picking it apart. I'd used innocuous, general statements that anyone could have made. "I couldn't agree more," Syd said. "Speaking of that, Cade mentioned that he enjoyed seeing you the other night."

My head shot up. "When did he say that?"

"After class today."

My heart started fluttering and my thoughts were all over the place. He'd asked about me? Again?

Syd started to laugh. "You look like someone just caught you eating an entire cake."

I made a face. "That's ridiculous. You know I don't eat cake."

"But if you did, and someone caught you, you'd look like you do right now. Abstract horror."

I lifted a shoulder, seeing no reason to lie to Syd about my feelings. "Because I think he's hot, and he's not like most guys I've dated."

"Meaning he's not someone you want to just hook up

with and never see again," she said. It was part statement, part question.

"That, and I'm not sure what he wants. If we both only wanted sex, it would be one thing, but I can't get a read on his intentions."

Her brows went up. "I think that's a sign you need to get to know him better."

I frowned. "That's *way* out of my comfort zone."

"You have other guy friends. How is it any different?"

I thought about it for a minute, trying to figure out what made Cade different from someone like Collin, or Jax, or any of my other friends with penises. Maybe it was the attraction, or the mystery. My mind wandered back to the first time I'd seen him and my body reacted immediately. I squirmed in my seat and tried to make it look like I was only adjusting and not trying to reposition the seam in my jeans. "I'm not sure…it just is."

Syd shook her head. "Well, you're going to have to figure it out eventually."

I lifted a shoulder. "Maybe I won't. I can pretend we never met."

She started to laugh and through her giggles said, "Oh Brynn, you don't know Cade at all. He's interested in you. He's not going to give up that easily."

I pressed my lips together in part worry, part anticipation. Syd climbed the stairs still chuckling, and a ball of nerves formed in my stomach. I was kind of looking forward to the chase.

# Five

## Tips and Tits: The Word from Mistress A

### Clitor-what???

*One stormy night, I was hanging out with some friends in their college dorm. They lived on a floor with forty girls. Of these forty girls, none of them were aware of an essential part of their own anatomy: the clitoris. This revelation came when one of the girls obtained a copy of* Penthouse Letters *and everyone sat around the dorm's living area, reading stories and being scandalized. When one of the first stories mentioned a clit, all of the girls started murmuring questions about what exactly it was. I'm chalking this misinformed travesty up to a serious lack of sex education in schools—damn abstinence only education helps no one—and parenting fails, because all things regarding sex, pleasure, and the human experience should have been explained in both school and at home. Men should have a clit course because it's a big part of giving their partner pleasure. Women should have one because it's a part of their bodies, and a big part of giving themselves pleasure. The clitoris is the equivalent of the head of the penis, only with WAY more nerve endings. While there are different types of orgasms, penetration orgasms are harder for many women to reach. However, with a little stimulation, clitoral orgasms can happen much more often, and can be done apart from, or at the same time as penetration. Your partner should know what they're doing in this area. If they don't, feel free to take matters into your own hands, literally. Every woman is different when it comes to the clitoris, so take some time and find out what you or your partner like the most. I'm sure your partner will be happy to assist your research. If they're not, they don't deserve access to your panties.*

## A Special Word from Mistress A

*It has come to my attention that a certain male blogger (I'm assuming he's male since he's calling himself 'Master', but I really have no idea) has taken it upon himself to copy my blog, and dole out carnal advice of his own. Imitation is the best form of flattery, and I certainly don't mind a little healthy competition. I think the more places readers are getting informed, the better. Everyone has different experiences and things to offer—just like during sex—and a male perspective (assuming this 'Master' is actually in possession of a penis), could give you useful information. But I've heard inaccurate speculation that I might be working with this particular "Alpha" to bring you content. I've even had people suggest we're in a relationship in real life. Let me be perfectly clear: I have no problem with multiple partners when it comes to sex, but when it comes to business, I have none. Mistress A is her own woman, and I love doing things solo.*

The school library was crowded and it had taken guerilla tactics to obtain a quiet space alone. I'd waited outside the line of rooms, wandering by every five minutes, eyeing the windows as I passed for signs of someone getting ready to vacate. My ministrations had paid off, and I'd finally gotten a quiet area to do some work.

I was researching sexual deviants, and what exactly defined a deviant. Was someone who liked to be spanked a deviant? What if they liked to be spanked with a kitchen spatula while wearing a tutu and singing 80s rock? What were the levels of social acceptance in a society where sex was so readily available? From a scholarly perspective, I found it fascinating. The lines were blurry at best, and as a potential therapist, I felt like it should be a question of where those lines resided for each particular person.

As for me, I'd try just about anything once with a willing, adult partner. I liked sex to be exciting, and surprising. Considering my history, surprise was difficult to come by. It was well-established that I liked to be in charge…also a result of my past.

Syd had texted about thirty minutes ago saying she was going to The Grind if I wanted to meet her there. I'd been working for hours and could use the break, and some Syd time. I just needed to get to a good stopping point. I was taking some notes when I heard the door to my study space open. I startled at the noise and looked up to see Collin saunter in with a sucker in his mouth. He sat next to me, leaning back in the chair and into me so his shoulder was almost touching mine. He propped his foot up on the edge of the table. "Hey, hot stuff."

I laughed, gesturing to his foot. "Make yourself comfortable."

He pulled the sucker out of his mouth with a pop. "I'd be more comfortable if you were naked."

"Me too," I agreed. "I hate pants."

He put the sucker back in his mouth, the bump visible behind his cheek, and clapped his hands together. "Great! Let's take care of that." He moved toward me.

I giggled as I pushed him off. "You're ridiculous. Do you know how many people are walking by, checking out these rooms and trying to commandeer one? Everyone would see us."

He gave me a look. "You've never been shy before."

It was true; I wasn't above public sex. There was a danger factor to it that made the sex even more mind-blowing. But I still tried to be cognizant of where I was and the percentage of risk that we'd be caught. "I'm not shy, but I also don't want to get kicked out of school…or my study space."

His eyes flashed, his devious intentions almost visible. "I could make it worth it."

I grinned. "I don't doubt you could. And I'd enjoy it at the time, then regret it later."

He made a dissatisfied noise, rolling the sucker around in his mouth. It smelled like cherries and spun sugar, and had turned his lips a shade of bright red.

"Does that have gum in it?" I asked.

His lips tipped up as he nodded slowly. "Perfect for

blowing."

I rolled my eyes. Everything was innuendo with Collin. It was one of the things I loved about him though, and why he made such a good hook up buddy.

"What are you doing here?" I asked.

He leaned back on the chair again. "Looking for a room to work in. My roommate is busy in ours, and I need to get this paper on macroeconomics done before my date tonight."

"Hot girl?" I asked. It was a redundant question. He was Collin, and it was a girl, of course she was hot.

He smiled. "The hottest."

"Someone from school?"

He nodded. "You probably know her. Alison. She's on the dance team."

I paused and then turned sideways, giving him a considering look. I did know Alison. Most people on campus did. She had autism, and was one of the sweetest girls I'd ever met. Her parents had been reluctant to let her go to college on her own, but the campus had rallied around her and she'd become everyone's little sister. I had no idea Collin had any sort of friendship with her. "I do. I didn't know you knew her well."

"We go out sometimes," he said, taking another drag on his sucker. "We're buds."

Occasionally, Collin let his playboy façade drop, and people could get a glimpse of the real man. He was smart, strong, and had more character than the majority of men I'd ever met. This was one of those times. "That's really cool of you. I'm glad, Collin. You're an exceptional human."

He sat up, putting his elbows on the table. "You're going to give me an ego."

I smiled. "In this case, you deserve it." I started packing my stuff into my bag. "I have to leave to meet Syd, so you can have my room."

His bottom lip jutted out. "I'm sad to see you go."

I lifted my eyes to the sky at his fake sorrow. "The people who have been walking by trying to get my room aren't. They're going to be pissed when they realize you've hijacked it instead."

"I'm fine with that," he said, unapologetic.

I laughed and grabbed my stuff, giving him a half hug. "Have fun with Alison."

"Always," he said, as I walked out the door.

On my way to The Grind, I started thinking more about Collin. I loved that he was spending time with Alison, and making her feel good about herself. The fact that I'd known him for years and had no clue about his regular dates with her also said a lot about who he was as a person. It's rare to find someone who is kind for the sake of kindness, and not for the opportunity to be recognized for it.

I liked Collin a lot. The sex was great, and I loved him as a friend, but it had never gone beyond that. Maybe because I didn't like relationships and hadn't let it. Collin never pushed, and seemed fine with our arrangement, but

I wondered if he ever wanted something more. We had chemistry, but I didn't really have feelings for him. Then again, I didn't have relationship-y feelings for most guys. The only one in recent years was Cade, and I still wasn't convinced those feelings weren't just hormones. As I thought about Collin though, I also remembered one of Master Z's posts involving candy. It had mentioned suckers just like the one Collin had been licking. I hadn't even considered that Collin might be the mysterious blogger, but it would make sense.

That line of thought was jarring. Truly, any guy on the planet could be Master Z, and it could just as easily be a girl pretending to be a guy. I had no idea. But now, literally everyone I knew was hitting my suspect list. Collin included. He certainly knew what he was doing, and could speak, or write, eloquently about it. He was also well-versed in topics surrounding Mistress A. We'd discussed her blog the other night.

Yes…I was keeping Collin on my potential Master Z list. Right at the top.

I pulled open the door to The Grind, the cold air following me inside, and searched the room as I started to take off my gloves. My eyes fell on Syd and I froze. She was sitting at a table with Jax…and Cade. She saw me and motioned me over, her eyes bright with conspiracy. Her movements caught the attention of Jax and Cade, who both turned in my direction. Jax smiled. Cade's brows went up with the corners of his lips, his greeting more of a challenge than a hello—Thor help me, I liked it.

I muttered a string of swear words under my breath and

made my way to the table.

"Hey," I said, flashing my brightest smile and sitting in the one empty chair—next to Cade. "I didn't know the guys were going to be here." I gave Syd a look that said she should have warned me. She returned my look with one that said she knew I wouldn't have come if she had—she was probably right. I had no doubt that she was playing matchmaker after our last conversation where she was convinced I needed to get to know Cade better. I stifled a groan.

"I had a break from work," Jax said.

"And we needed coffee after our last class," Syd said, gesturing to Cade.

"Were you debating today?" I asked.

Syd shook her head. "No, it was a lot of legal cases and reading. We both wanted to fall asleep at our desks."

"That does sound pretty boring." I looked to the counter to see how long the line was. It wasn't bad, and after the Cade ambush, I needed a drink, preferably one with alcohol. "Speaking of coffee, I need one too. I'll be right back."

Cade stood. "I'll get it. Skinny latte with a little sweetener, right?"

I narrowed my eyes. "Yeah, but how—"

"Syd told me."

Of course she did. I shot her a glare.

"I can get it," I said. Not wanting him to feel like he needed to buy my drink. We weren't even on a date, and I could afford my own coffee.

"I'm already up," he said, and was across the room

before I could even get out of my chair to follow.

I scowled at Syd across the table.

"What?" she said, putting her hands up in front of her in a defensive position.

"Are you kidding me?" I hissed. "He knows my coffee order? What else have you told him? My preferred method of birth control?"

"Not yet." Her tone was totally serious.

Jax started to laugh. "Not funny, Blue Eyes," I said, pointing at him.

"It's a little funny," he said.

"It is," Syd agreed.

"You," I pointed at her, "don't get to have an opinion. Freaking Judas," I muttered, looking around the room like I was trying to make sense of a universe I didn't recognize. "My best friend is a damn traitor."

"No, your best friend is trying to help you."

I made a face, still annoyed at Syd, but surprised with Cade as well. Frankly, I was shocked he'd taken the time to ask, let alone remember, my coffee order. It seemed like a trivial detail that would take most men months and a committed relationship to learn…if they even learned it then. He'd obtained the information before we'd even been out on one official date. It was flattering…and slightly unnerving. My past was full of men who'd only wanted to use me for sex. I wasn't used to guys who remembered seemingly trivial details for me, or were genuinely kind. A lot of that was my own fault. There were plenty of nice guys out there who had wanted to be let in, but I hadn't allowed them. I still wasn't sure why Cade was different.

Cade came back and handed me my coffee. "They were fast."

"Thanks," I said as he held it out to me. I reached up, my fingers brushing his as I took the cup. The spark was there again, arcing between our hands. My eyes fluttered to his involuntarily. He was looking at me too. I held his gaze as I brought the cup to my lips and took a sip. It was like he'd taken a Brynn coffee ordering class. It was exactly how I liked it.

"How is it?" Cade asked.

I licked my lips to catch any errant foam or milk that might have escaped. "Sweet, but not too sweet. Perfect."

Cade's eyes darkened as he watched me, and I had the distinct impression that he wished he was licking my lips instead. So did I.

Syd's voice jolted my attention away from Cade and his high levels of testosterone. "She likes her coffee like she likes her men," she said, paraphrasing *Airplane*, an old movie we'd watched one night on cable. It had a lot of silly, quotable lines. "Hot."

I gave Syd a look. "Funny. That's not even the line."

Syd lifted her own coffee in acknowledgment. "But it's true."

I did not want to get on the subject of how I liked my men with Cade sitting right there listening in. Though I was sure Syd would tell him almost anything he wanted to know in her bid to be the Easton University matchmaker. Supreme Court justice wasn't a high enough goal for her, apparently. I switched subjects, "Are things slow at the garage today?" I asked Jax. He worked at Red's Garage, a service station and mechanic shop across the street from The Grind. That was how he got to know Syd—because her '69 Camaro constantly needed work. Old cars are a lot of maintenance.

"Yeah, it hasn't been too busy. I'm off in a few hours."

"Then you can go home and work on Syd's car instead. Good hell, she was lucky to find you. You're saving her a fortune in repair bills."

His lips slid into a grin. "She pays me in other ways." He winked, and Syd's face flamed. Everyone except Syd laughed.

Now it was Syd's turn to change the subject, "What were you working on today, Brynn?"

I took another sip of my coffee. "A paper about sexual deviance."

Cade's brow went up. "That's an interesting subject."

I smiled slowly. "Sex is always interesting."

Cade eyed me from across the table. "I've always felt the definition of deviant is rather subjective," Cade said. "It depends on the person, and their preferences."

I stared at him, wondering if he could read minds since that was almost my exact same opinion on the subject, and the argument I was putting forth in the paper.

"It's true," I agreed. "And sexual norms and ideas are culture based as well. Even talking about sex in some places can get you thrown in jail. But in others, sex is sold in window displays like clothes. A lot has changed in recent years. Ten years ago people weren't as open to talking about sex as they are now, and things that were shocking, like nudity on primetime television, are now commonplace. Yet there are still states where blow jobs are illegal."

Jax's lips pulled back in distaste. "Remind me never to move to any of those places."

Syd blushed again, and I felt a little satisfied at her embarrassment considering the position she'd put me in today with Cade.

"Me either," Cade said. "Though I imagine they have a difficult time enforcing that one, especially if it's done in a private location."

"The cop would probably give them both a high five, or pretend they didn't see it even if it was in public," Jax rationalized.

I laughed. "Some people don't like to have sex in private though." I leaned against the back of my chair and crossed my legs. "My perspective is that as long as you're doing something that can get you off with a willing partner, there's nothing wrong with it, but there will always be a subset of the population somewhere who considers any given sexual act to be aberrant. The fact remains that we're all a little deviant in one way or another."

Cade's eyes darkened and my stomach immediately clenched, desire pooling. I wanted to know what was running through his head to make him look at me like that, and what the hell was going on with my hormones to make me respond so quickly to a simple expression. "I agree completely," he said.

His voice lingered and the air became electric again. I

had the sudden realization that the exhibitionism we'd just been discussing was happening right at our table. I mean, our clothes were still on, but the electric feeling cascading between us was one I could only compare to sex with an exceptional partner—except the feeling with Cade exceeded that, by about a thousand volts. The chemistry was palpable, and I'd be surprised if everyone else in the area didn't notice it as well.

Syd coughed, confirming that she was indeed aware of the connection, and breaking the spell between Cade and I. "I thought you'd be working today," she said to me, her brows pressed together in confusion. "Did you switch your schedule around?"

This was a conversation I'd been wanting to have with Syd, but not one I wanted to have with Syd and an audience. Normally I would have been at work, but I'd quit my part-time job doing office work for a local psychologist a few weeks ago. Mistress A was a full-time job in and of itself. I'd meant the blog to be a fun little resource for people to read when they had time, but it had turned into something much bigger. Responding to emails, blog comments, posting on social media, scheduling interviews, etc. all took up far more time than I thought it would when I'd started the blogging endeavor. That coupled with school, left me no time to get anything else done.

I'd read about earning money from blogs, and put ads on my site soon after I started Mistress A. When the blog gained popularity, my ads started paying me. A lot. Like, I was making enough to cover all of my expenses and then some. If my readership stayed like this, or kept increasing, I'd easily have enough money to pay off my student loans, and do pretty much anything else I could ever want. I couldn't tell all of that to Syd without admitting to being Mistress A, and I couldn't do that…yet. So I needed another explanation.

"I quit my job a couple of weeks ago."

Her jaw dropped and she practically yelled, "You what?" Syd didn't like being left out of the loop, so I knew this would upset her. "Why? And why am I just hearing about this now?"

I shrugged it off like it was no big deal. "I've been so busy with school that telling you slipped my mind." School, and the blog…and Cade, as much as I didn't want to admit it. But I didn't need to go into detail. "That's why I quit. I needed more time to get stuff done."

"But…" she sputtered, her eyes going from me, to Jax and Cade, and back to me again. She decided to press forward with her question despite our audience. "Are you okay with that? Can you afford to quit?"

I nodded tentatively, wishing we were having this conversation in private. Jax I didn't care about, Syd would likely tell him everything I said anyway, and I knew that…that's how couples worked. Even if you were best friends with someone, their friendship with their partner should always come first, and they should share things and confide in each other. I was fine with that as long as I trusted both parties, and in this situation, I did. But I didn't know Cade well enough to confide in him. I came up with a cover I hoped would hold. It was true, it just wasn't the whole truth. "I have some money saved up."

I absolutely had some extra cash, so I wasn't lying; but the fact I'd been getting it from the secret blog I wrote was information I neglected to offer.

Syd was watching me with far too much interest. "Enough to make it through the rest of the year without an income?"

I tilted my head to the side. "I have student loans as well." Also not a lie.

"You've had student loans before and still needed a job."

Damn Syd and her stupid cross-examination. I scrambled for a plausible explanation. "I knew grad school would take up more of my time, so I've been saving for a while." That seemed open-ended enough. Syd was skeptical about everything though, and had a bullshit meter as good as mine.

She narrowed her eyes, and I had no doubt we'd be revisiting this conversation later.

"I need to get back to work," Jax said, standing and picking up his coffee cup. He leaned down and gave Syd a thorough kiss. Her inhale after he was done was rattled, and they both looked completely in love. I held back a sigh. I'd had a lot of kisses in my life, but none that had left me breathless. Syd got it every day, multiple times. I didn't like relationships, but some aspects were extremely appealing. The long kisses and lingering looks were both high on my envy list.

I moved my gaze away, trying not to stare, and ended up looking right at Cade, who was also looking at me. It seemed he'd noticed me noticing Jax and Syd, and clearly, he'd noticed them as well. It was hard not to. Everyone at our table was thinking of kissing, but only two of them had actually been engaged in the act. My eyes went over Cade—not a hair out of place, mouth parted slightly, and shoulders broad enough that I was certain every lawyer-y suit he owned must need massive amounts of tailoring, if not a special cut—and I seriously considered adding two more people to the kissing participant list.

"I'll see you later," Jax said to Syd. The words came out like a promise of exciting things to come. I envied that too. "Have a good day, Brynn and Cade."

"You too," Cade said.

"Bye," I said, and watched Jax walk out the door.

Syd was watching him too, and looked positively smitten. "You're adorable," I said.

She blushed. "He's good to me."

"I'm glad you got rid of your ridiculous 'no dating until I'm a Supreme Court justice' rule," I said.

"That was a rule?" Cade asked, eyes wide with curiosity.

"For a while," Syd confirmed. "I didn't want dating to get in the way of law school."

"Then he told her he was better in bed than a werewolf, and she saw him without his shirt," I said, over the rim of the coffee cup I was holding. "The Supreme Court took a backseat."

Cade laughed. "If anything, he'll help you get there faster," he said to Syd. "A supportive, loving partner can make all the difference."

"I agree," Syd said, pulling a cookie from her bag and

unwrapping it. "And I'm glad I changed my mind too. Now we just need to get Brynn to change hers."

"Not happening," I said, shaking my head.

Cade looked at me with confusion. "You date, right?"

"Yeah. Date," I said. "But I don't do relationships."

He raised his brows, waiting for me to expand. I didn't feel the need to. Syd did it for me. She's dependable like that. "Brynn thinks relationships are messy."

Cade shifted his head to the side in concession. "Some are," he said. "But life is messy. Experiences are messy. There's no point to life if you're not living it."

"I'm living," I defended, "just not dating the same guy repeatedly." I gave him a mischievous grin. "I get more experiences that way."

"What about Collin," Cade asked. "You seemed to have a history with him."

I shrugged. "Hook ups. Nothing more. We've never been monogamous. But we're friends. Friends with benefits can work, as long as no one catches feelings."

Cade watched me closely, an analysis happening behind his eyes. I recognized the look because it's one I gave people when I was trying to figure out what was screwed up in their tiny little brains, and how I could help them. I didn't appreciate the look being turned on me.

"Go out with me," Cade said. It wasn't a question, more of a command. I didn't do commands well…at least, not outside of the bedroom…sometimes not inside it either.

Now it was my turn to look at him like he was crazy. What in the…where did that come from? "I'm sorry, what?"

"On a date. You and me."

I shifted my eyes to Syd to confirm this was really happening. She was suppressing a smile. I'd just told Cade I didn't date. So…why was he asking me out on a date? Did he think I'd be an easy lay? I mean, it was Cade, and he'd been on my to-do list for a while so I couldn't say I wouldn't be, but why? What were his motivations? He didn't seem like the type to use a girl. He definitely seemed like the "settle down, want more, it probably involves rings and suburbs" type. *So* not the kind of guy I spent time with. Their expectations were far too high. "I told you, I don't date."

"Make an exception."

My brows shot up and I couldn't believe his nerve. "You're kind of bossy."

His lips slid up slowly in a way that promised a plethora of other interesting things he could be doing with them—and my mind was cycling through them all, with visuals. "You have no idea."

My jaw dropped slightly and all I could do was stare at him. I had no words.

He leaned into me, still holding my eyes. Inches from my face he said, "I dare you."

I watched him for several minutes, part fascinated, part annoyed. But the fascinated part of me eventually won out. I'd been wanting to spend more time with him to get to know him better anyway. I wanted to develop a friendship, and hadn't known how to implement that. He'd just taken the first step for me. Spending more time with him would let me find out what other surprises he was hiding. "Okay, Counselor Cade. I accept your date dare. Let's make a plan to get coffee sometime." Coffee was a big deal for me. Coffee meant spending a block of time alone with a guy and having conversation. It also meant I could drink my coffee fast, or take it to go if things were headed sideways. It wasn't a meal, but it was a commitment nonetheless.

He sliced his head once to the right. "We're already getting coffee." He pointed to my drink like I might have forgotten it existed. I didn't. I could smell the brewing coffee in the air, and was acutely aware of our location. Apparently though, coffee wasn't as big of a commitment for Cade as it was for me.

"I meant we could get coffee alone—without Syd." I glanced at Syd, who had been unusually quiet during mine and Cade's exchange. "No offense."

"None taken," she said, her eyes huge with interest as she watched Cade and I go back and forth.

Cade didn't even notice her. I turned my attention back to him and he hadn't taken his eyes off of me. "Dinner. Tonight."

Dinner? What the hell?! Dinner with a commitment fan like Cade was *so* far out of my comfort zone it might as well have been taking place on Mars. That was like skipping right over a dare, and starting at triple dog dare! I held his gaze right back as I answered, "I'm busy." I didn't have plans tonight, but I wasn't going to let him think I was available on such short notice.

"Tomorrow, then."

I didn't want him to think I was that available either. I didn't respond.

"I can keep going, there's the day after that, and the day after that."

I shifted my eyes to Syd for help. She was trying not to laugh. She wasn't kidding; Cade really was relentless. "You can't blindly throw out dates without even checking your schedule. Don't you have other plans?" Surely, his social calendar couldn't be that free.

"I'll cancel them."

My mouth gaped again. Cade was unlike any guy I'd ever encountered—and I'd encountered a lot. I picked my jaw back up and answered, "I'll have to check my calendar."

Cade motioned to my phone. "I can wait."

Holy warrior princesses! He wasn't going to let this go. I pulled out my phone and tapped on my calendar. There was a party tomorrow night, but I wasn't married to the idea of going. I'd rather get the date over with, and hopefully see his naughty bits and get him out of my system so I could stop constantly thinking about the infuriating man. "I can do tomorrow night."

"Great. I'll pick you up at seven."

My stomach did a flip flop and I couldn't discern whether it was the result of anticipation, or nausea—maybe a little bit of both. I glanced at Syd from across the table and she couldn't stop grinning. I was looking forward to crossing Cade off my list.

# Six

## Tips and Tits: The Word from Mistress A

### Oh, Oh, O-o-o-o-rgasm!

*After my post on the clitoris, I decided we needed to talk more about the O. This should, and probably will be multiple posts, because it deserves multiples, just like you deserve multiple orgasms. Like people, orgasms are various, and complicated. If you've never had one, look for my upcoming post on adult toys. If your partner is intimidated by toys and doesn't like making you writhe in pleasure, your partner doesn't deserve you and should be sent to some barren planet for people who hate bliss…with the Paleo eaters. But for this post, let's talk about girls who can come. That's right.* Come. *Nope, it's not a myth. Men are not the only sex equipped with the ability to ejaculate. Is it easier for guys? Absolutely. But my vagina-owning friends can accomplish it as well. I don't advise undertaking this particular O with a novice partner. The man or woman performing the task has to know what they're doing, and be capable of following instructions. I know, that knocks out most of the male population right there…have you ever seen a dude actually read an instruction manual? If you find one, he's a keeper. He'll absolutely need the directions for this task! In fact, I'd suggest taking one of the handy instructional O videos with you into the bedroom. This particular O has to do with the G-spot. I know, most of you are thinking your partner couldn't find your G-spot with GPS and black magic, let alone manipulate it with enough skill to make you ejaculate. But I assure you, the G-spot is real! So is the orgasm, and if you know how to do it, ANY woman can ejaculate. That's right. ANY woman. You don't need special skills, or witch training. Just the correct pressure and speed on the G-spot. In the past, a lot of people assumed that the liquid expelled was urine because the sensation makes a woman feel like they have to pee. It's not, folks. It's been tested. Totally different liquid. And it actually has the same prostate specific androgen as male ejaculate. If you need more of a tutorial, Google is your friend; some of the results have handy, and not so handy visual references. Or, if you'd rather not wade through the plethora of information (and believe me, there's a lot), you can click the link at the bottom of this post. Please be aware, that while not pornographic, the tutorial is probably not something you want to watch in public. Happy orgasming, my friends!*

I got up from my desk and stood in front of my closet, trying to pick out an outfit for my date with Cade tonight. If he was prompt—and I had a feeling he was—he'd be here in less than two hours to pick me up. Thanks to my orgasm post, I'd spent most of my day answering comments and questions. The post was getting more traffic than any other post I'd written. Apparently not many people were aware of female ejaculation, or thought it only happened in porn.

Spending all day answering questions about the big O reminded me that I hadn't had one in a while…at least not with a partner. The realization startled me and I grabbed my calendar to calculate exactly how long it had been since my last hook up. I went back a month…then two. I scratched my head, thinking that couldn't possibly be true. I'd had an orgasm more recently than two months ago, hadn't I? I rifled through the sex memory file in my head. Yes…I had enjoyed several climaxes, but they were all solo. I'd had some random dates that had seemed hopeful, but for one reason or another, my own pants never came off.

At one point, my continual dissatisfaction had elicited a desire to see what a guy was working with before I'd go out with them. I'd rationalized most men wouldn't actually send me the dick pics I was requesting, and those who did probably weren't guys I was interested in sleeping with anyway—unless they were incredibly well-equipped. My pic plan had been flawed from the beginning, however, when I'd failed to ask for proof of dick. Men were resourceful when they wanted to be, and it was exceedingly easy for them to find photos of large penises masquerading as their own to send me. Some asshats had even digitally added their face to the body of the real dick. After that, I'd required potential dates to send proof that the pic was real, and it was them…like a guy holding a calendar showing today's date. Unfortunately, that's also easy to alter with photo editing tools. I gave up on the idea soon after I implemented it.

I paused, thinking about my lack of partnered up sexy time in more detail. Several of the men I'd dated in the last three months, and normally would have at least given a chance to show me their skills, did not get that opportunity. I looked at my calendar again, trying to figure out why.

The last time I'd hooked up with someone had been before Thanksgiving. I clicked on calendar dates around that time, reading through my daily activities. I went through almost four days before I came to it: coffee with Syd at The Grind. I inhaled a rattled breath, making the connection. That was the day Cade had walked in and I'd finally found out his name. From then on, I hadn't been interested in anyone else. If I was being honest with myself—and I was always honest with myself—from that moment, and even before, when I'd first met him, Cade had been the star of every one of my fantasies. Technically, my orgasms hadn't been unassisted either; there was serious support going on, Cade just wasn't aware he'd been involved.

This kind of obsession over a guy hadn't happened to me in years. Years. I'd vowed it would never happen again. What the hell was wrong with my brain, and why wasn't it working in coordination with my heart like usual?

I put the calendar down and scanned my closet, organized by color. I picked out a sky blue tank top; semi see-through long sleeve grey sweater; ripped, faded skinny jeans; and a pair of grey boots that hit just below my knee. I thought it was attractive, but not rip-my-clothes-off sexual. I would have worn something showing more skin, but he'd given me no clues about where we were going for dinner, so I chose something I thought would work anywhere.

I threw the assembled outfit on the bed and was rummaging through my jewelry when my phone buzzed. I grabbed it, thinking it was a text from someone…maybe even a message from Cade. Instead, it was an RSS feed notification. I'd subscribed to Master Z's feed to keep tabs on him and his copy-cat ass. I clicked on the link to a new Alpha Answers, and started to read.

## Alpha Answers

*It has come to my attention that a certain female sex advice blogger (I'm assuming she's female since she's calling herself 'Mistress A', but who can really say since none of us have ever gotten a glimpse of her—much to my dismay) has her panties in a twist that I've been giving sexual advice. Last I checked, Mistress A hadn't cornered the market on sex, or the internet. Did I use her idea as a springboard for my own? Absolutely. I think Mistress A is brilliant, and talented, and she's doing a service to every uneducated sexual being on the planet. I certainly don't mind a little healthy competition: personally, I think it makes for better foreplay. In regard to the speculation that Mistress A and I might be working together or dating, I will agree with her on that point. We are not partners in business, or real life. Though I, too, have no problem with multiple partners, and think experiences are far more fulfilling when shared.*

*Truly, I'd like to take her out for drinks, dinner, and what I'm certain would be scintillating conversation. But it seems our Mistress A is not a fan of fraternization with those she views as enemies. Pity. Angry sex is fantastic sex. Should she change her mind, there's an open invitation for the two of us at a restaurant of her choosing, and I'd be happy to help her untwist her panties.*

I read the post.

Then read it again.

Then heard an angry, guttural growl and realized the noise was coming from my own mouth.

The nerve of the man knew no bounds! So what if he'd called Mistress A brilliant? He'd taken my exact post, made snarky changes, and called it his own. Again! He was a grade-A douche goblin. If he thought this was going to make me back down, he was sorely mistaken.

I was furious, and taking it out on my damn hair when Syd walked up the stairs.

"Whoa! You should maybe try not brushing so hard," Syd suggested, watching me from the hallway. "You might not have hair left if you keep that up." I was still seething. Untwist my panties. What the hell? He knew nothing about my panty situation, and never would!

I grumbled in response, grabbing the curling iron.

"Seriously, what's going on?" Syd asked, her tone full of concern.

I couldn't actually tell her what was going on, and that sucked hairy monkey balls because her advice would have been helpful. Instead, I went with a more broad explanation, "Bad day."

"Do you want to talk about it?"

I shook my head, wrapping another piece of hair around my curling iron. "Not really. I just hate dealing with asshats."

Syd nodded in understanding and didn't press for more information. I loved that she knew me well enough to know when to push. She glanced in my room and saw my clothes on the bed. "Are you excited for your date?"

I had been. Now I was preoccupied with Master Z, and kicking him right in the nuts with pointy-toed shoes. I shrugged, trying to put my focus back on Syd's question. "I want to get to know Cade better, and he's nice to look at."

She leaned her shoulder against the bathroom door frame. "Well, I know he's excited to go out with you."

I raised my brows as I released a curl.

"He mentioned it."

"He seems to mention a lot of things to you," I said, trying not to seem as distracted as I was. "He was pretty persistent."

Syd laughed. "I warned you."

I grabbed my makeup and touched up the light brown shadow on my blue eyes, then added bright red lipstick. Red was my signature color, and I'd found an exceptionally awesome brand of lipstick that didn't come off—through *anything*. The lipstick needed its own blog post. The color was topped off with shimmery glitter gloss that made my lips as irresistible as a Palantir Stone. Syd was one of the people frequently hypnotized by it. "I can never look away from that lipstick."

I waited a few seconds for the first coat to dry. "You need to try it."

She watched me apply the second layer, and then the third. "I'm not really a red person."

"Whatever," I said, my lips stretched to make sure the color saturated every part of them. I wasn't sure what the stuff was made of, but it seriously didn't move once it was dry. "It comes in other colors, too, but you could totally pull this off. Jax would love it, and the fact that he wouldn't end up scrubbing red marks off his whole body after sex."

"I don't think Jax even notices when I wear makeup."

I eyed her like she'd lost her mind. "Are you kidding? Guys *always* notice red lips. The right lipstick can make or break the mood."

She gave me a disbelieving look. "Guys *always* want to have sex. It doesn't matter what your lips look like."

Poor, Syd. She had so much to learn. "When I put on lipstick, it's to draw attention there. I want men looking at my dewy, full, sparkly lips, thinking of everything they want me to be doing with my mouth."

She snorted. "If you're trying to get Cade's attention, you've already succeeded."

"It never hurts to remind a guy. Plus, red's my thing."

She nodded in concession. "You do look gorgeous in it."

My curls had set while I finished my makeup, so I started shaking them out to get some volume and make the curls look like I'd just wrapped up a very productive hour or two naked. Nothing made my hair look as good as getting laid. I wished I could bottle the hair volume abilities sex provided. Some people call the look 'bed head'. I call it *Hustler* hair, and firmly believe it gives women special powers.

Syd folded her arms across her chest. "So, about this whole job thing…"

I groaned inwardly. I knew this topic would come up again, but I was hoping it wouldn't come up so soon. "What about it?"

"Are you sure it was a good idea to quit?"

I concentrated on applying my bronzer so I wouldn't have to look her in the eye. She'd be able to sense I wasn't telling the whole truth. "I needed the extra time for school stuff. It's not a big deal."

She pressed her lips together, trying to hold back what she wanted to say. I don't have that problem. I have a low tolerance for bullshit, and nothing bothers me more than people who don't take responsibility for their words and actions. I always say what I mean, and call people on it when I think they're being disingenuous. I'm blunt, honest, and the best friend anyone will ever have. Some people can't handle someone like me, and I'm fine with that. I don't like everyone, and certainly don't expect everyone to like me. Syd wasn't one of those people who couldn't handle the truth, however, and she had no problem with conflict. She liked me fine the way I was. "I'm just worried about you," she said. "I don't want you going into more debt than you have to."

Syd's parents were helping her with school so she didn't have to worry much about money. My situation was a bit different. My parents didn't have the income Syd's did, and really, I was twenty-three years old. I didn't feel like they should be paying for any of my expenses or schooling anyway. They helped when they could, and it made me uncomfortable every time. Now that I was in a position to completely cover things myself, I absolutely would.

My lips stretched into a genuine smile, touched at Syd's concern. She was a true friend. "I know. I don't want to either. If I thought it was a bad move, I wouldn't have done it. But I promise, I'm not going into any more debt. I'm totally fine."

She gave me a skeptical look. "The money you've saved is really enough to cover your paycheck?"

Again, I did my best to answer the question without a direct untruth. "Yes, it's plenty."

She watched me closely and opened her mouth to ask another question, then shut it. I'd known Syd for a long time, and was certain she wanted to ask where else I was getting money, and what illegal activities I was involved in. She didn't have complete proof though, so she hedged on saying anything. I could tell it was killing her. I grinned and gave her a hug. "You worry too much."

She blew out a long breath. "You don't worry enough."

I pulled my shirt over my head, bent over to rearrange my boobs in my bra for optimal cleavage display, and pulled on the blue tank top and grey sweater.

"I really wish I had your boobs," Syd said.

I looked at her like she was crazy. "Don't be ridiculous. You have great boobs! I'm certain Jax has never complained."

Her cheeks pinked and she ducked her gaze.

"Seriously. Women need to stop being so hard on themselves. Most guys aren't going to stop in the middle of having sex with a woman to critique her body. They see us differently than we see ourselves."

One of Syd's eyebrows went up. "You should take your own advice on that."

Syd knew my history, and she was right. The problem was that I'd taken my own advice on that particular issue, and felt like I'd been burned by it. Yeah, the guy wouldn't stop having sex with you, but he might not start in the first place…or he might do it, and then pretend he didn't know you. My self-esteem should have been higher, and I shouldn't have let any guy make me feel bad. But that's one of the reasons I started the blog—to try and help people in all areas of their relationships…including their relationships with themselves. The doorbell rang. "That's either Cade or Jax," Syd said. "I'll get it."

"I didn't know Jax was coming over."

Syd paused at the top of the stairs. "He was running errands and said he'd stop by on the way home."

I nodded as I took off the comfy cotton shorts I'd been getting ready in, and pulled my jeans on instead. I added the boots, and a chunky turquoise bracelet with blue and silver earrings. I took one last look in the mirror and started to walk out of the room, then stopped and went back to my desk. I flipped my laptop open and quickly pulled up my blog. I typed out a short reply in response to Master Z. I gave a self-satisfied smile as I hit 'post,' and then put the whole situation out of my mind for the time being. It wasn't fair to Cade if I was thinking about someone else all night. I couldn't get to know him if I was spending our entire time together feeling stabby about the asshat with a death wish who was capitalizing on *my* blog.

I went downstairs to meet Cade, who I could hear talking to Syd.

"She's probably going to want to put on a different outfit," I heard Syd mutter.

"Why would I want to do that?" I asked, walking around the corner and stopping in my tracks. I couldn't stop staring. He was wearing jeans, and a tight emerald green and black striped sweater with the sleeves pushed up on his forearms. His pants hugged his hips, the front of his sweater tucked behind a rectangle black and silver belt buckle. The deep jewel tone of his sweater did something to his eyes. They took on a more tropical quality, and definitely picked up more of the ocean hues than I'd seen in our meetings before.

Cade's gaze trailed over me, from the top of my head, down to my feet and back up. I felt his perusal like a shot of heat. "You look beautiful."

"Thanks," I said, tamping down the urge to blush. "Why do I need to change clothes?" I asked, my attention going from Cade to Syd.

Syd looked at me with big eyes. "Cade was mentioning something about blindfolds."

I gave Cade an intrigued look. Blindfolds? This night

might be significantly better than I'd anticipated.

He returned my look with a mysterious one. "I'm full of surprises."

"Clearly."

I heard someone come up the back steps, and Jax walked in holding a pizza and beers. Two of my favorite things that I rarely let myself indulge in. I often wondered if constantly obsessing about food made me miss out on happiness. The more I thought about it, the more certain I became. But I didn't know how to fix the problem. I envied people who could use food for both fuel, and joy.

Syd's smile grew and she moved over to help him. He dropped the food on the table, wrapping her in a hug and lifting her off the ground before giving her a serious kiss.

"Hey, sixty-nine," Jax said, using one of his nicknames for Syd. Her Camaro was also a '69, but I felt like Jax's reference had a lot more to do with sex than the year her car was born.

Syd held his eyes, her arms still wrapped around his neck. "Hey, sexy."

Jax looked over at Cade and I as he lowered Syd's feet back to the ground. "Hey."

I gave Jax the eye equivalent of a high five in approval of his greeting for Syd. She deserved to be treated with all the love and kindness in the world, and Jax did that for her. "Hi, Blue Eyes."

"Dude, I like you a lot," Cade said, shaking his head, "but I'm not calling you Blue Eyes, or sexy."

"I'd be concerned if you did," Jax said. "Where are you guys off to?"

"Cade's keeping it a secret," Syd said.

"That's brave," Jax said, taking some sauce, parmesan, and red pepper out of the bag he'd put on the table. "Brynn's not a fan of secrets."

"Really?" Cade asked. "We'll have to work on that."

What was all this "we" stuff? *We* wouldn't be working on anything. *We* were going to go to dinner, then get to work taking off *our* pants. At least, that was *my* plan for the night.

"It's a good thing you got here before I turned on the TV and a new episode of *House Hunters* started," Syd said to Cade. "You would have been stuck watching it with us until the end."

Jax nodded, a serious expression on his face. "She's not kidding. These two," he said, pointing back and forth between Syd and I, "are *House Hunters* nuts."

That earned him a glare from both of us.

"Once you see the first house, you can't leave until you see them all and know which one they decide to pick, and if they chose wrong!" I defended. A lot of times, they chose wrong.

"You do know reality TV isn't real, right?" Cade asked.

Now Cade was the one getting laser death glares from two sets of eyes. "I read somewhere that some of the people on the show purchase their house, but then go around looking at other homes for the sake of the episode, even though they've already chosen and bought the house they want."

Mine and Syd's mouths fell open simultaneously. Jax was doing a slight head shake and making a cutting motion across his throat at Cade.

"That's blasphemy," Syd finally said when her voice started working again.

"Seriously," I said to Cade. "If that's true, I'll have to question everything I know. I don't have time for that. Do not bash HGTV."

Cade put his hands up in the air in surrender. "Noted. As I learn more about your favorite TV networks, I will attempt to keep them out of conversations."

Syd and I both gave huffy little nods.

Cade's phone buzzed. He pulled it out and gave it a quick glance. Amusement sparked in his eyes, then he put it back in his pocket. "We need to go," Cade said. "But you two have fun watching people paint."

Syd grinned. "Oh, we will!"

Jax gave her a mischievous smile. "We'll be doing some redecorating, but it will have nothing to do with HGTV."

Syd gasped and punched him in the shoulder. "Jax!"

I laughed. "I'll make sure to text before I walk in the house." I grabbed my coat out of the closet and followed Cade out the door to his SUV. He had a newer SUV…something rugged and manly that looked expensive. I really knew nothing about vehicles, and only cared if the car worked, didn't need a lot of maintenance, and got me where I wanted to go. Syd was a car snob, and thought my lack of vehicular interest was pure insanity.

Cade opened the car door for me and I climbed in, buckled up, and felt my phone vibrating like a sex toy on crack in my purse. It had been vibrating since I picked my bag up, which meant my notifications were blowing up with comments on the post I'd just made. I thought I'd turned the notifications off. I pulled my phone out to put it on Do Not Disturb, and grinned as I saw my blog post flash on the screen. It was going to be a good night.

## A Special Word from Mistress A

*Alpha:*
*I don't wear panties.*

# Seven

## Tips and Tits: The Word from Mistress A

### Commando, or No No?

*Sometimes I go clothes shopping, and forget I'm not wearing panties. There's little as frustrating as getting to a store that has what looks to be the Holy Grail of jeans—the ones that make your ass look perfectly perky, and your legs long and lean—and then not being able to try them on because you forgot a key component of your outfit. It's not that I don't like a good pair of panties. They're perfectly fine for looking pretty on the way to sexy times. I see their purpose. I just choose not to wear them on a regular basis unless I have to. The undergarment debate has been going on for years. Kitty Fisher is someone you've probably never heard of, but, like some reality TV show stars, she was quite famous for being famous. Also like some reality TV show stars, she got that way after a bit of clumsiness showed off her lady bits. Around the year, 1760, Kitty was riding a horse and fell off the animal. In a most ungraceful dismount, she went tits over teacups onto the ground. In the tumble, she revealed to the goddesses and everyone that she wasn't wearing any undergarments. Quite a feat when you consider the sheer amount of clothes women had to wear at the time. Every woman has a panty preference. Some like grannies, others favor boy shorts, bikini, or thong. And some prefer nothing at all. Some women change their mind depending on the time of the month. Just look at the popularity of period panties! As far as what the best method is, it really comes down to personal preference, but scientific studies back up the commando theory, at least for part of the day. People who sleep naked have better sleep quality, and women who sleep naked have fewer lady bit issues. You need to give your skin, and all your parts, a chance to breathe. In my opinion, it's all about comfort. So, be like Kitty: wear what you want to wear…just make sure you have the proper attire the next time you're riding a horse, or trying on pants.*

"So what's this about a blindfold? I didn't realize we were already at the BDSM stage." I was even more curious about Cade now. What did he have planned? He knew I didn't date, yet he'd asked me on one. Did he think we were going straight to sex? Not that I'd mind the sex, but I'd be lying if I said I wouldn't be disappointed at not having time to sit, talk, and get to know him first. I hadn't done that with someone I actually wanted to get to know in a long time, and having it offered made me realize how much I'd missed that part of the dating process. Most of the guys I met were ass monkeys. Cade was different. I was good at reading people, but Cade had an air of mystery around him that made it hard to put him into any of my preconceived man-boxes. I truly wanted to get to know him better, and unravel what it was about him that made me so ensorcelled.

We were driving into downtown Winchester. It wasn't a huge town, and I couldn't imagine we were going anywhere I hadn't been before.

His hand was draped lazily over the steering wheel, left leg resting against the door like he was in an ad for temptation. "I figured we'd already done handcuffs, blindfolds seemed like the next logical step."

I inhaled a rattled breath at the reference to the first time I'd seen Cade. The time I tried in vain to not think about. It was impossible. I replayed the meeting in my mind on a regular basis. But I'd firmly agreed not to think about it tonight, or discuss it! Cade didn't seem to be under the same gag order. "You're not the type to hold back, are you?" I asked.

He shook his head. "No. Not at all. And I don't get the feeling you are either."

I folded my hands into my lap, trying not to fidget. "You're right. I'm not."

"Then why did you pretend we'd only seen each other one time when we were in front of all of your friends the other night?"

I shrugged. I'd been trying to figure that out for myself as well. Maybe it was because I wanted that memory for myself. Or maybe I just wasn't ready to deal with how he'd made me feel, or the fact that he was the first man to make me infatuated in years. More than anything, I thought it was because despite Mistress A's public persona, I liked my privacy and didn't want everyone knowing—and asking—about our history. "I'm not sure," I answered honestly. "You kind of left me standing there speechless. It threw me off my game. A guy hasn't done that in a long time."

His lips slid up slowly. "I didn't realize I'd made such an impact."

I scrunched up my nose, unhappy about admitting that. "Most men don't nail that whole impression thing, so congratulations. Any other girl and your approach might have gone sideways."

He laughed, a low, masculine sound. "So you don't have a high opinion of men."

He said it as a statement. I shook my head. "No, that's not true. I love men. I just think they only want one thing. On that subject, men and I agree."

"Sex," he answered bluntly. I appreciated a man who was direct.

I nodded and echoed, "Sex."

"When was your last relationship?" he asked.

I gave him a look that said, that's-not-really-your-business. "Heavy question for a first date."

He looked over at me, unapologetic. "You don't seem like the type who scares easily. I want to know you, Brynn."

His tone was deep and genuine as his hands shifted on the steering wheel. He seemed completely relaxed. I had no reason to question his motives, and I liked that he acted interested. Most men—and some women—lumped women who enjoyed sex into one of two categories: party girl, or slut. I *hated* both generalizations and wanted to ball or boob punch anyone who made it. I couldn't stand the double standard. Men were allowed to wet their dick with whoever they wanted, and no one batted an eye. In fact, they were often congratulated for it. Why were the rules any different for a woman?

"It was years ago," I answered in response to his relationship question.

"But you go out with a lot of guys?"

I nodded. "I like sex." We'd already established that, and I had no problem reiterating it. If he was going to have a problem with my sex life, he was going to have a problem with me and there was no point in continuing this conversation.

"What about you?" I asked. "When was your last relationship?"

"A year ago."

"College girlfriend?"

He nodded. "Some people grow together, others grow apart. We grew apart. It was amicable."

That was nice. The end of my last relationship sure as hell wasn't.

We came to a stoplight and Cade turned his head, meeting my eyes. He held my gaze and I did my best not to squirm under his stare. "I had something set up for tonight, but I think that will have to wait." He turned in a different direction at the next light.

"Where are we going?"

questions, however. He'd done it in the car and continued, "So you don't like romance?"

"That's not true, either," I said, shaking my head. "I love a good romance novel, and love the notion that the perfect guy exists and knows exactly how to make you happy in every way. The idea that someone is out there for everyone is appealing. But, I also don't like lying to myself, living in a fairy tale world, or setting up expectations that I know can never be met. Perfect relationships don't exist, and neither do perfect men."

He watched me from across the table, his brows pushing together in concentration. "I agree that perfect relationships don't exist. Every relationship takes work, and you have to constantly be willing to analyze, change, adapt, and grow or it won't be successful. But I do believe that there's someone out there for everyone. Someone who knows how to make a person happy—not only knows it—but tries hard every day to make it happen."

I considered his words. It was nice to know a guy like Cade existed, and believed in romantic daydreams. I hadn't seen it often in real life, though, and was suspicious of a relationship ever working for me.

Our server brought our drinks and food, and we both started to eat.

"Maybe relationships are successful for some people," I said, "they just haven't been for me."

He considered that. "Maybe you haven't found the right person."

I nodded in agreement as I ate. "A valid point. I'm not sure there is a person for me, though. I love who I am, but it took me a long time to get to this place. My history forced me to evolve. We all have a past, but mine made me intolerant of assholes, and helped me learn that I give zero fucks what people think about me. I speak my mind, and I'm difficult to deal with for people who can't handle the truth."

He shook his head. "I disagree. I know your type."

I narrowed my eyes. I hated being stuffed into any stereotype. "And what type is that?" I asked, ready for a fight.

"The kind of woman I've always respected and admired. You're strong, confident, opinionated, blunt, and when you want something, you make it happen. There's nothing I respect more."

I pursed my lips, shifting my eyes to my plate instead of him. "I wasn't always that way," I mumbled.

He looked like he wanted to ask another question, but held it back. I was fine with that since I didn't want to go into detail about my dating history. It would just make me stabby and ruin the rest of the night. "Did you grow up around here?" I asked, moving the topic away from relationships.

Cade nodded. "Not far. A town about an hour away. What about you?"

"I grew up in Texas."

"Texas?" he said, his eyebrows going up in surprise. "You don't have an accent."

"I've worked hard not to."

He took a drink of his soda. "You didn't like having one?"

"Not really. I don't like attention being drawn to me, and a southern accent in a city that's not in the south is a great way to stand out."

He chuckled.

"What?" I asked, my fork halfway to my lips.

"If your concern is attention, your accent is the least of your worries." His eyes dipped down slightly to my chest, and then moved back up. I blushed. I knew some people found me attractive. Occasionally I even looked in the mirror and thought it about myself. But that kind of self-praise was rare for me. The girl who'd been told she wasn't pretty for far too long was the one I always saw staring back at me.

"It's hard to believe," I said, shifting my food around on the plate with my fork.

He looked shocked. "That you're beautiful?"

I sputtered an agreement, not meeting his eyes. "Yeah…that."

Silence hung for a few seconds before I heard him say, "Look at me." His voice was a command. He sounded pissed, and my eyes snapped up to his. "When we walked in here, every person in the room turned their heads." He motioned to a table across from us. "The guy over there has been steadily ignoring his date since you sat down. I think his date probably hates you."

I made a face, dismissing his comments. "They probably think I look weird or something."

"No," he said. "They think you're hot. That's all. And you are. End of story."

My heart swelled up hearing Cade, a man I thought was

pretty damn hot himself, tell me in no uncertain terms that he thought I was attractive, and everyone else did too. It was a stark contrast to how I'd spent most of my life. When every time I'd walked in the room and noticed people noticing me, I'd wondered if it was because my clothes looked unflattering, or something was off with my makeup or hair. Not once did I ever consider it was because they thought I was pretty. Since coming to college, I'd been told I was attractive. But it was still inconceivable that people might actually find me beautiful.

"Thank you," I said, my voice soft. I met his eyes for a few seconds before looking back down at the table.

"You're welcome. It's the truth."

Nothing made me more uncomfortable than talking about my own body image issues, so I went back to answering Cade's accent question. "I didn't live in Texas my whole life, so the accent didn't catch on as much as it did with my friends who were born there. It was easy for me to shake once I moved to Colorado for college."

"That makes sense," he said. "Do you have siblings?"

I nodded. "A sister. She's quite a bit older than me. She's a doctor in Kentucky."

"A doctor?" He sounded surprised. "And you're going to be a therapist. I bet your parents are very proud of you both."

I lifted a shoulder. "They seem to be. She's so far away that I don't see her much."

"Is she married? Have kids?"

I shook my head. "No. She was really focused on school. Syd reminds me a lot of her, actually. It's why I was so vocal about Syd having a life outside of being a lawyer. Spending so much time on degrees, and so little time experiencing life is one of the things my sister says she regrets."

"Are you two close?" he asked as I took a drink of my water.

"No. She was leaving for college when I was just hitting my teen years. We talk every once in a while, but we don't have a lot in common. I think the older you get, the more your friends become like family. They know you better than anyone, and you choose them. You can be your true self with your friends, and not have to worry about judgment or backlash."

"You don't get that with your family?"

I paused, thinking about it before answering. "I think you can get it with family…to a degree. Your parents raised you to be a certain way, and will always have an idea of who they want you to be based on that. Your siblings will have similar opinions. They may accept the person you've become, but it will always be difficult for them to reconcile that with the person they hoped you'd be, and the choices they wished you'd made. I'm close with my family and I love them. I keep in touch, but they don't know me like they did when I was younger. And they're not with me every day to see the person I've become—I'm not certain they even care. But I love them. They've been really supportive of my dreams, and I appreciate them more than I can say. With friends though, you choose the people who accept you, challenge you, and want to be a part of your evolution. They're the people who you never have to censor yourself with. I was lucky to find Syd. She's pretty much my female soul mate, and I'm enormously fortunate to have her in my life. True, loyal, honest friends who would never say a bad word about you and defend you to the death…those are the relationships that matter most to me."

He was listening intently, and I was suddenly self-conscious. I'd gone into way more detail with that answer than I'd intended, and more detail than I usually would under any other circumstance. It was like he had a magic "Brynn info" wand, and was pointing it directly at me. I wanted to get the attention off of my life and personal philosophies. "Tell me about your family," I said, putting my fork down and pushing my dish away. I ate my usual half of a plate, and I'd have them box up the rest.

"I have one sister."

"Does she live near here?"

"An hour away, with my parents," Cade said, putting his own fork down. "She's younger than me."

"Are you close?" I asked, curious if his opinions on friends and family were similar to mine.

"Very. She's the best person I've ever known, and I'd do anything for her."

I tilted my head to the side. So…not the same philosophy I subscribed to. "You seem really protective of her."

He nodded. "I am."

"What about your parents? Are you close to them as well?"

He nodded again. "We have a different relationship

than most parents and kids, but I think that makes us stronger. They've always treated me like an adult, and encouraged me to be independent, speak my mind, and have opinions."

"That's definitely not the standard for parenting theories." I knew. I studied them in psych classes.

"They knew me well growing up, and have made an effort to continue knowing me as I've changed during adulthood. They're proud of the person I am, and support me. That means a lot." He paused, smiling as he thought. "Their parenting style is probably part of the reason I'm going into law. I like to argue, and I'm pretty vocal about my perspective."

I smiled at that. "No wonder we get along."

Cade was about to say something else when the server came over and offered us a dessert menu. Cade tilted his head toward the menu. "Choose something. They're known for their dessert. They serve gourmet s'mores."

"Ah," I said, nodding. "That's probably one of the reasons I haven't heard of this place before tonight."

He gave me a disbelieving look. "You don't like chocolate?"

I shook my head. "I love chocolate, but I don't do desserts."

He narrowed his eyes. "Why?"

I gave him a look that said he might be an idiot. "Because I'm a girl, and I'm supposed to look a certain way, and even talking about sugar makes me gain weight."

He leaned forward, putting his forearms on the table. "Does your appearance matter that much to you?"

I considered the question. It wasn't that my appearance mattered; it was that I used it as a tool. "No. I think everyone is beautiful, and would never judge someone on their appearance. But I've been judged for mine in a lot of different ways. This is the way I'm most comfortable. If it means I have to give up something I enjoy, then that's what I have to do."

Cade's gaze fell, his look disapproving. "You can't deprive yourself in one place, and not expect it to come out in another, Brynn."

I couldn't argue with that. I was a psych student. I knew all about deprivation, and that giving up one thing and trading it for a different obsession wasn't a healthy way to deal with issues. But I still tried my best to stay away from sugar and carbs. "Sugar is as addictive as cocaine. People even go through withdrawals when they give it up."

"I know about the studies," Cade said. "But having a dessert once a week isn't going to make you addicted, or change the size of your clothes."

"It might," I said, pushing the issue. It made me feel better to believe it, even if the logic wasn't exactly sound.

The server came back and Cade ordered a mint s'more. Then she brought the check and Cade paid it.

"Come on," Cade said.

I gave him a confused look. "Where are we going? Don't you want your dessert?"

"They'll bring it to me."

He stood and held out his hand. I took it, the spark between us still arcing when we touched. I was starting to wonder if it would ever go away. Maybe it would after we finally got naked, but for now, it was sticking around. We walked out the back of the cabin to a patio area. It was enclosed with glass from the floor to the ceiling, and overlooked a lake that shined like a mirror, the bright moon glinting off its surface.

Cade motioned to two chairs in a quiet corner that looked like they reclined. I followed him and sat in the chair beside him, still holding his hand. We leaned back, looking up at the sky. A shooting star flashed above us, streams of light trailing it. I gasped, pointing. "A shooting star!"

"Did you make a wish?" Cade asked.

"Always." Shooting stars were one of my favorite things. Anytime I saw one, I felt like they were a sign of good things to come. I hadn't seen one in a while, so seeing one tonight gave me a sense of validation and made me feel like I was on the right track.

The glass enclosed porch was surprisingly warm with the heaters around, and it was a perfect space to look at the stars and enjoy the peace of being away from the city, the noise, and the light pollution. The porch was also fairly deserted. Other than a couple on the other end of the patio, we were alone. It would be a perfect place for making-out.

"Do you know much about constellations?" Cade asked.

I tilted my head to the side to see him better. "Anytime I look at the sky, I always find the Big Dipper, Little Dipper, and Orion's Belt. But those are the only ones I know. I love looking at the stars though. Summer is my favorite because I can stretch out in the back yard and do nothing but stare at the sky. It's peaceful."

Cade met my gaze, his eyes dark in the night, the feeling of need between us seemed to be growing…at least for me.

We were interrupted by the server delivering Cade's dessert. It was a s'more, super-sized. The graham crackers were normal, but the marshmallow looked like half a bag of mini marshmallows had mated and formed one giant mallow. The marshmallow had been dipped in chocolate, and was sandwiched between chocolate mints. It looked amazing, and I really wished I had the metabolism to justify the treat. I kind of resented that Cade did. Syd told me he did some sort of weight lifting workout, and looked lovely without a shirt. I had no doubt. I was jealous I couldn't eat like him. Hormones made it so much easier for guys to maintain their weight.

"That looks mouthwatering," I said.

"Are you sure you don't want a bite?" Cade asked, holding it out to me.

My eyes shifted from the treat, to Cade. "Not of the s'more," I said, my tone suggestive.

His lips stretched slow and seductively. It was all I could do not to jump on him right there. His smile faded as he ate, and he seemed to be thinking.

"You have some marshmallow on your lip."

He ran his tongue over the silky skin like a caress, licking the spun sugar and chocolate off his mouth. I couldn't stop thinking about having that same tongue all over me instead.

"How about we get out of here and go somewhere more private?" I suggested. Getting naked and seeing Cade's gym results in person had been my original plan for the evening. Now I was even more interested in making it happen.

Cade finished off his dessert, and reached his hand out to me. I put my hand in his, thinking his thought process was running along the same sexy lines as mine. But instead he leaned back against the chair, tilting his head toward me. "Know what I think?"

I shifted my head in his direction, wondering what the hold-up was. This was not question asking time. This was take your clothes off time. "No…what?"

"I think you replaced sugar, with sex."

I stared at him, totally dumbfounded. That was exactly what I'd done, but no one other than Syd had ever called me on it before. I'd never let anyone else get that close. It irked me to no end that I'd given so much away, and this guy I barely knew had figured it out. It impressed me as well.

I'd been an emotional eater growing up, and had been overweight for most of my life. When I'd decided to get healthy, I'd cut out all the things I loved because I saw no other way to do it than going cold turkey. Food was tied to both emotions and sex in my brain. It had been easy to switch the two. Anytime I needed to deal with an emotional issue, instead of reaching for a treat, I now reached for an orgasm. Right or wrong, it was my way of coping, and I was fine with it. But I didn't like that Cade had so easily seen through me. I liked to think I was more complex than that. There was no point in denying his observation, so I said, "You're right. I switched one addiction for another."

He shifted his head back and looked at the stars, thinking. After a few minutes he said, "I'd like nothing more than to see you without those clothes, but it's not going to happen…tonight."

My eyes widened and I did my best not to sputter. "It's not?"

He pulled his bottom lip back with his teeth and shook his head.

"Why?" I asked, part pissed, part deflated. I'd been waiting months for this! Months!

"Because you're using sex as a way to deflect dealing with other issues, and I'm not going to enable that. I want you, Brynn. I think you want me too. And if we want each other as much as I think we both do, we're going to do this my way."

Anger and frustration roared inside me. "You're a lawyer, *Counselor*. Not a psych major."

His eyebrows went up. "But you're a psych major, and you know I'm right."

I did my best not to growl. It took a lot of restraint, and my question still came out snarly, "What exactly is *your* way?"

His lips curved. "Dating. We're actually going to date. Like two normal people getting to know each other with a natural progression of things that will eventually end in bed…or somewhere more interesting."

"Dating," I said the word, distaste lacing my tone.

He nodded.

"Without hooking up?"

He nodded again. "Not anytime soon."

"I told you, I don't do relationships."

"I'm not asking for a relationship. I'm asking for us to date. Repeatedly."

"Not exclusively?"

"Not yet."

I lifted a brow, disbelieving. "Unless I'm reading the two of us completely wrong, we have a shit-ton of chemistry. I'm pretty sure you feel it too."

"I do."

"And you think you can hold out and not have sex?"

He took a deep breath. "I'm going to try."

My lips curved slowly. "I'm going to take that as a challenge."

He nodded once in ascent. "Then we have a deal?"

I nodded back and held out my hand to shake on it. I let my hand linger in his, then trailed my fingers up his arm, to his chest. I moved closer and leaned down, our mouths within kissing distance. My own heart was racing, and I could see the veins in Cade's neck pulsing. I lifted my index finger, running it lightly over his lips before putting it in my own mouth and pulling it out slowly, sucking and licking it clean. "You had a little chocolate," I said by way of explanation. "And, Counselor," I whispered, my lips close to his ear, breath hot on his neck, "we have a deal."

## *Tips and Tits: The Word from Mistress A*

### Suicidal Sex Bees

*I read an article about bees that I initially thought was a joke. It took some research, but when I confirmed its accuracy, I thought: huh…based on my experience with men, that makes sense. Male honey bees basically commit suicide to have sex. I swear to the goddesses, it's true. When honey bees mate, the head of the dude bee's penis explodes inside the queen, and the horny little drones drop dead. The Queen takes a mating flight where male bees swarm her like she has some sort of magic vagina—she probably does, because aren't all vaginas magical? They fight for a chance to mount her (in the air! A commendable talent!), and eventually, one courageous little bee achieves success. Once inside, the drone's penis explodes, and the bee falls from the sky and drops dead. Dead. And penisless. The drones are fully aware of what they're in for. If I were a dude bee I'd say, screw it, I'll find another way to orgasm that doesn't involve weenie destruction and loss of life. But nope. The drones go into it knowing they'll die, and doing their duty. The queen has sex with several drones during her flight, and she saves the excess sperm up to use for later. From this little nature lesson, we learn that 1. Males of all species will do pretty much anything for an orgasm, and 2. Don't mess with a woman because your dick might explode.*

*Update: When I first learned about suicidal sex bees, I thought it was an appropriate comparison to the male species in general: that a man's driving force is sex. It's certainly one of the top forces on my own list, and I can't really fault the little honey makers. ...However, recent events have caused me to re-examine my thought process. I've discovered that not* all *men are suicidal sex bees.*

The evening had ended on a high note—at least from my perspective. I'd been horny as hell though, and had to spend a serious amount of time with my vibrator before I could finally fall asleep last night. I narrowed my eyes wickedly and hoped Cade had been in a similar predicament.

By the time I'd woken up this morning, I already had a text from him telling me he was looking forward to our next date. He was on top of this ridiculous dating game, but I wished he was on top of me.

I was drinking some coffee and getting ready for a girls' night with Syd and Courtney, but I couldn't stop thinking about how things had progressed since my first meeting with Cade. The one that I'd tried desperately not to think about, but kept popping up at the most inopportune times—namely in my dreams, and when he was standing right there in person—in easy clothes-ripping range. Those stupid dress shirts he wore and their stupid buttons were asking to be destroyed.

The first time I'd met Cade, before the coffee shop introduction, had happened two weeks before Halloween. I pulled out my journal. I didn't keep it regularly, but when something happened that I felt was important, I tried to write it down and re-examine it later. It was a trick I'd learned when I was younger, and one I still used when trying to work through problems and emotions. I opened the page to the date where I'd chronicled the entire meeting, and re-read the entry from October.

*Sex, scares, and hot guys. Great goddesses, I love Halloween! I found the perfect costumes. Sexy siren for me, and She-Ra for Syd. She'll hate the short skirt, but she needs to get out of her comfort zone.*

*I slipped into the dressing room to try mine on. Once all of the pieces were in place, I checked to make sure everything that should be in my costume, was. I wasn't planning on a nip slip, but with a corset this small, I could never tell when the girls might make an appearance.*

*I stepped out of the private dressing room into the larger dressing area with more mirrors so I could see myself from every angle. I noticed appreciative glances from a couple of guys behind me. The reaction both annoyed, and invigorated me. Men hadn't always looked at me that way, and I liked it.*

*The obsidian black and scarlet corset was almost completely see-through except for some strategically placed pieces of lace. It came with matching panties, the back of them covered in frills. Black fishnet stockings and studded six-inch high blood red stilettos completed the ensemble. The costume was hot, and judging by the reaction of the men around me, it was the perfect level of heat.*

*Pleased with my attire decision, I stepped down and walked over to a table full of products and a shelf above it, looking for accessories to add as the final touch to my sexy siren ensemble. A whip might be handy, though I wasn't sure if I wanted to carry it around all night. A masque wouldn't be a bad idea either.*

*As I examined my options, I had the unmistakable feeling of eyes watching my back. I put a box of body glitter down on the table and used the opportunity to glance up. A guy wearing dark slacks, a button-up white shirt open at the collar, and grey sports jacket was watching me steadily. He looked about my age, early to mid-twenties. His light blue eyes trailed slowly over my form, from my studded shoes to my fishnet covered legs, pausing to cast an appreciative glance at my chest before his gaze rested on my face. I didn't faze easily, but something about this guy, his commanding presence, had me holding my breath. His shoulders were wide, with hair the color of a wheat field mid-July. His square jawline was punctuated by a dimpled chin. He licked his lips, and I stumbled a bit.*

*I don't stumble.*

*Not even in six inch heels on ice during the middle of winter.*

*And he didn't back down. He held my gaze, unapologetic, and unwavering. I could feel the chemistry between us from across the room. I tried to move my eyes away, but they were frozen in place, held by his. It seemed like we were in some unspoken tug-of-war.*

*He came toward me, stopping less than three inches from my face. He had no problems with crowding my personal space. He was so big that it would have felt like an invasion from across the room—in fact, it had. With him this close, I got the impression he'd already fought the silent war between us, and conquered. He reached up like he was going to grab the back of my neck, and pull me to him for a heady kiss. My breath sawed out as my heart hammered in my chest. He watched me, his eyes assessing, and seeing something he liked. His lips lifted in the lazy, sexy smile of a man who knew he'd caught his prey. He was confident and absolutely sure of himself. His hand came down, and I was about to close my eyes when he picked up a box behind me.*

*"You don't want to forget these," he said, handing me the box. His hand brushed mine and my whole body tingled with pin pricks of heat.*

*He walked away.*

*I looked down at the box.*

*Handcuffs.*

I snapped the journal shut, not trusting myself to re-read it again without immediately calling Cade and begging him to get naked. He'd watched me, and I'd felt like he had wanted me, but then he'd turned and walked out without saying more than a sentence, not giving his name, and definitely not finding out mine. It had made me insanely curious about who he was, which was probably his goal. At first, the fact he hadn't asked for my information had been a hit to my ego…until I'd gathered my items and taken them to the register. Tango, the adult store goddess who'd been helping me find my costume had told me he'd stopped by the front to ask my name. A couple of weeks later, he'd walked into The Grind and Syd had formally introduced us. Brynn isn't a common name, and it probably wouldn't be hard to narrow down who I actually was. Especially since he was good friends with Syd, and Syd and I talked about each other frequently.

I'd taken Cade's ridiculous "no sex" idea as a challenge, but he had no idea how hard it was for me. It hit on every insecurity I had. Whether I believed it or not, for the past five years, men had told me I was attractive, and I'd never had a guy turn me down for sex. I hated admitting it, but I needed that validation. Cade was asking me to not get it. Repeatedly. Sure, he'd said he wanted me—more than once—but I firmly believe that actions matter more than words, and Cade was telling me there would be no action for a while. If he didn't desire me enough to want to rip my clothes off, it could very well send me into a downward spiral, and make me start believing the self-hate I'd spent so long trying to overcome. I'd have to make sure I kept that in check, and didn't let it happen. My self-esteem shouldn't be tied to whether a man wanted me or not. The psychologist in me was well aware of that. But I had relationship PTSD, and that validation was important to me, even if I didn't want it to be. It was something I struggled with daily.

I pulled some clothes out of my closet. We were going to dinner and a movie for girls' night. My hair and makeup were already done, I just needed to change. I pulled on some dark wash skinny jeans and a canary yellow scoop neck sweater, and went downstairs to wait for Syd. She was at Jax's, but she was picking up Courtney and me. I sat on the high back chair by the window so I could see when she arrived.

My phone buzzed on the table. I picked it up and saw a private message on one of Mistress A's social media accounts.

*Just so you know, I prefer commando as well.*

I read it and rolled my eyes, thinking it was another creeper messaging me—the internet was full of them, and it happened often. Especially with a job in the public eye that focused on sex. Though I imagined anyone who declared themselves a Mistress and had a sexy logo as a profile photo had a higher creeper hit rate than average. I was about to delete the message when I noticed the signature.

Master Z.

I narrowed my gaze at the screen. Was it really Master Z, or someone claiming to be him? I clicked over to his profile. The page referenced Master Z's website, and looked like his account. That didn't mean anything though. Anyone could create a fake account and pretend to be him. I went to his website and checked for social media links. I clicked on them to cross reference. It was the same page! So the message really was from Master Z! I narrowed my eyes, a low growl emitting from deep in my chest. Master Z had a serious set of balls.

I typed back a response.

*Congratulations. I'm glad my panty article was interesting. Thanks for not copying that one, asshole. Eat a bag of dicks.*

The man was infuriating. If he thought he was going to get in my pants after stealing my idea and then sending me stupid messages about the state of his underwear, he was seriously mistaken.

My phone buzzed again.

*I think we got off on the wrong foot. I'm sorry. I didn't mean to make you mad.*

I glared at the screen and typed back.

*Then you shouldn't have been a Grade-A douche pickle and stolen my idea.*

It buzzed again.

*You're right. I shouldn't have piggybacked on your success, and I apologize.*

My anger lost a little steam. I liked that he'd admitted what he'd done wrong, was direct, and apologized immediately when he realized I was upset, without trying to defend his actions. Those were hard character traits to find in a person. I knew the psychology behind a person admitting their culpableness and apologizing sincerely without defending their actions. It immediately makes the person who was wronged less upset, and they're more willing to forgive the one who hurt them. My heart rate started to calm a little, my reaction illustrating the psychology perfectly. I decided to engage him further.

*Why did you do it then?*

My phone buzzed.

*I liked what you were doing and admired you and your site. I thought it would be helpful to have a man's perspective as well. I never intended to steal your idea—I just wanted to complement it. And "douche pickle"...that's funny.*

I was slightly less huffy. I liked when someone had the balls to own what they'd done. A sincere apology mattered to me. Master Z had given me that, and only explained when I'd asked him to. That made it easier for me to hate him a little less.

I typed back.

*Thank you for the apology.*

He responded.

*You're welcome. I really would like to get to know you better.*

I shook my head, not comfortable with that in any way. I'd done my best to keep my identity a secret. I didn't want the news leaking now, and definitely not to someone who was essentially a competitor. I hadn't even told Syd, the one person I trusted more than any other person on the planet. I certainly wasn't telling this guy.

My fingers flew over the screen.

*No one knows me.*

He wrote back.

*By choice?*

*Yes.*

*We can keep it over messaging if that makes you more comfortable.*

I weighed the benefits of getting to know Master Z. He'd pissed me off to no end, but he'd apologized. And there were advantages to having someone else I could talk to about the situation we were both in. Someone who understood the need for secrecy, and someone I could brainstorm ideas with. We were essentially writing similar things, just from different perspectives. A collaboration at some point might not be a bad idea. I hated saying no to things, because you never knew what might come from an opportunity.

I typed out a response as I saw Syd's headlights pull in the driveway. I went out to meet my girls and sent the message as I got in the car.

*I'll think about it.*

# Nine

## *Tips and Tits: The Word from Mistress A*

### **Adult Toyland**

*Want to know what I love? Toy stores!!! The kinds that require proof of age to peruse. Contrary to popular belief, adult toys have been around for eons! If you doubt me, go take a gander at one of the many museums dedicated to the history of sex. Even the cavemen had dildos, and they're on display…though I question the person whose idea it was to make them out of wood. Splinters suck, and your nether regions are the last place you want them. In the early 20th century, women were often sent to mental hospitals, diagnosed with hysteria. In reality, they were just seriously sexually frustrated humans, and the men they were with had no clue how to navigate a woman's lady parts—or maybe just didn't care. The women patients were treated with vibrators and a doctor who knew how to work a clitoris. Thank the goddesses someone had been taught this essential information. If I'd been alive at the time, I would have faked hysteria to gain access to sex toys; I'm certain plenty of women had the same idea. The holy grail of battery assisted orgasms is a toy that moves, as well as provides clitoral stimulation. Personally, I have an entire collection. Depending on my mood, I like different vibrators for different things. If you're going for G-spot stimulation, that's a completely different toy than one for the clitoris, and there are hundreds of toy options within each stimulation category. Check out my list below, then go to your local adult toy store and ask the employees for advice. Don't be embarrassed—you'd be hard-pressed to come up with something they haven't heard before. If you're in a relationship, and your partner isn't a douche (and why would you be with someone who was?), go together. Browsing for sex toys can make for excellent foreplay, and I almost guarantee you won't be going home without naked on the agenda, and some new ideas. Also, I've said it before, but I'll say it again: if your partner's intimidated by toys, they're not good enough for you.*

We walked into the swanky restaurant and got a comfy circular booth before settling in and ordering drinks. The restaurant served small plates meant to be shared, so we ordered several items and waited for our drinks and food to come. The server had brought bread with various dipping sauces. Courtney and Syd both grabbed a piece. I did not. Carbs were not my friends.

"Are you still liking your new place?" I asked Courtney.

"I love it!" she said, dipping her bread in something that looked like olive oil and parmesan cheese. "Paige does too.

I'm happy we have a nice home and stability."

I nodded, glad they both had that as well. I got the feeling Courtney had been drifting for a while. It was good to see her in her element, doing a job she loved, and putting down roots for herself and her daughter.

"How's work?" Syd asked her, dipping her own bread into an olive oil and crunchy garlic mix.

"Good," Courtney said. "Some things are challenging, but overall I really enjoy it."

Our server brought our drinks. I loved fruity drinks because they made me think of stretching out on a beach in the sun, waves crashing in front of me. I wasn't sure why, but the beach grounded me. I loved standing in the sand, the grains cradling my toes. There was something about the rhythmic melody of water lapping against the shore that calmed me immediately and helped quiet my mind. I needed to move to a warmer location, and figure out how to get a beach house. Maybe if Mistress A kept going well, that dream wasn't out of reach.

"What's been difficult?" I asked Courtney.

Courtney took a sip of her drink, complete with a bubble gum pink umbrella, and answered, "We're working with several girls. Personalities are bound to be an issue when that many people are in one place. A lot of them have gone through trauma. Some have been the victims of abuse, some even rape. Others have given their kids up for adoption, or had abortions, and feel a tremendous amount of guilt, sadness, and anger. And a lot of women have no other support network. Family and friends are out of the picture for one reason or another, and many of them feel abandoned. It's a lot of emotions and baggage to work through, but we try to help with all of those things. We have a great team of counselors, and our staff work really well together."

"I can't imagine being a single mother," I said. "I think you're amazing for being able to do it."

She stirred her drink as she answered, "I had a lot of help."

"Still, being a parent is hard enough when there are two of you doing the work. You only have yourself and took it on without a second thought. I admire that."

A slight tinge of pink touched her cheeks. "Thanks, Brynn."

I narrowed the people in my life down from acquaintances to inner circle. There were several levels between. I'd decided long ago that life was far too short to waste time on people who had no interest in being real, loyal, and who didn't give a shit about me or my life. So while I shared a part of myself with everyone, only the people who truly cared about me would get to see me completely. My inner circle was my tribe. The people I could be one hundred percent myself with who supported me, cheered me on, and weren't afraid to call me on bullshit. It was a small group, full of the best people I'd ever met, and I was fine with the fact that not many individuals were included in that number. I was happy Syd, and now Courtney, were both part of my tribe.

Our appetizers arrived and we all grabbed a plate, trying different things.

"So..." Syd said, turning her shrewd gaze on me. I

immediately wanted to shrink back. I knew that look, and wasn't excited about her next statement. "Cade said you had a good time on your date."

I nodded and looked down, intently interested in the stuffed mushrooms on my plate. "We did."

"Are you seeing him again?"

I wrinkled my nose and sighed. "Unfortunately. Or fortunately. I haven't really decided which." Syd's eyes were the size of saucers, and Court's were almost as big. "Hey! It's not like I've never dated a guy more than once," I huffed.

"That's *exactly* what it's like," Syd said.

"I date guys repeatedly all the time," I defended. "I have a list."

"Of booty calls, and friends with benefits," Syd said, spearing a piece of pasta. "Not guys you actually date, date."

I frowned. "Cade was being difficult. I'll continue to date him until he's not."

"Difficult in what way?" Syd asked.

"In a way that involved him not removing his pants."

Syd's eyes sparked with amusement and she grinned. "He knew exactly what to do to keep your interest."

I glared and considered throwing my mushroom at her nose. "Probably with a lot of help from you." The irritation was evident in my tone.

Syd held up her hands. "I didn't say a thing about that. Cade's an intelligent, perceptive guy. He must have picked up on it."

"Clearly," I said.

"So what's the game plan going forward?" Court asked.

I pressed my lips into a line. "He made a proposal."

Syd and Court's eyebrows both rose with interest.

I poked at some sort of meat on my plate. "He thinks I use sex to deflect. I can't say he's wrong. He says he won't enable me, and we have to date before we get naked."

Syd's mouth dropped open. "You agreed to that?"

"For now," I said, biting the corner of my lip and narrowing my eyes. "You know I don't like to say no to things. I might end up surprised. I'll keep seeing him for now, and see what happens."

Syd's mouth slid up, amused. "I love Cade."

"I don't," I grumbled. "He thinks he can hold out and not have sex. I don't think that will last long. As soon as we have sex, he'll be off my to-do list, and I can move on."

"To-do list," Court said with a giggle. "I love Mistress A."

My heart instantly felt like it had stopped. Dammit! I'd said something Mistress A would say without even thinking about it! I gave myself a mental shake as a reminder to be more careful. I needed to compartmentalize my Brynn and Mistress A personas better in my mind so they didn't seep into each other and give me away.

Syd laughed, shaking her head. "I think you'll have a harder time getting rid of him than that. He knows what he wants and goes after it. He got you on the date in the first place, a pretty impressive feat if you ask me. Then he got you to agree to multiple dates. A cease-fire in a war zone would be no less impressive. I'm interested to see where this goes."

"Me too," I said on a frustrated sigh. I hoped wherever it was, we were getting there soon. "Me too."

We dropped Courtney off at her place, and then went back to the house. I expected Syd to leave me so she could spend the night with Jax, but instead she pulled into the driveway, cut the engine, and got out of the car.

"You're coming in?" I asked.

She nodded. "We need to talk."

I gave her a suspicious look as we walked into the house. Syd and I rarely declared that "we needed to talk," and if we did, it was because something was amiss.

"Okaaay," I said, lowering myself onto the soft couch and crossing my legs.

She sat next to me. "About Mistress A."

My breath caught in my throat and I did my best not to let my reaction show. Syd was excellent at reading body language in general, and even better at reading it with me because we'd known each other for so long.

She folded her hands in her lap and looked right at me. "I know it's you."

I gasped, my eyes bulging. My voice was stuck in my throat for several seconds as my mind tried to figure out the best course of action. Should I deny it? That would be a total lie and miscarriage of trust. I'd omitted things up to this point, but I hadn't told her an untruth. No, I wouldn't lie. Even if having someone else know would put me at risk, she'd confronted me point-blank, and I'd own it. I blew out a breath and closed my eyes. "How did you know?"

"A lot of things," she said, releasing a breath of her own. Her shoulders sank into the couch and her neck relaxed like a weight she'd been holding was gone. "Nothing that anyone else would notice. I don't think any other person knows you well enough, but there were things I saw. You and Mistress A are both similar in your opinions and attitudes, so I noticed that. Sometimes you'd repeat things that she'd said, like tonight when you mentioned your 'To-Do List'." Dammit! I was hoping Syd hadn't caught that.

"Or like the night I mentioned snow sex and temperature play, and you told me to use clean snow—that was the same line Mistress A had used in her post. Then you mentioned you were happy people were learning from Mistress A. The way you worded your answer made it seem like you were taking ownership of the posts. Also, in general, you're pretty vocal about all things sex-related, but anytime Mistress A was brought up, you often became more quiet than usual. Then there was you quitting your job. You've had that job for years and loved it. It was flexible and worked well with your school and volunteer schedule. You've always been concerned about money, so I couldn't figure out why you'd quit in your first year of grad school with so many bills to pay. You had to be getting money from somewhere else." She paused, looking at me from the side, "I briefly considered that you'd become an escort—"

I threw one of the couch pillows at her. "You did not!"

"You're right, I know you better than that. But an escort, or foray into the world of sugar babies, were two of the only explanations I could come up with for the money you seemed to have without working."

"I told you I'd saved money up." That wasn't a lie. I had saved some money before Mistress A started, and a lot more after.

She picked up the pillow I'd thrown, holding it on her lap as she shifted to lean back against the arm of the couch. "There's no way it would have covered everything, especially living expenses, or the new clothes and Coach bags you were buying."

I scrunched up my nose at that. I knew buying things could give me away, so I'd been careful, but I had rewarded myself with a Coach bag only because I was certain most people wouldn't even notice, and if anyone did—Syd included—they'd likely assume I got it on sale at a Coach outlet.

She kicked a leg out onto the coffee table. "So I started watching you and noticed you were spending a lot more time on your laptop, tablet, and phone than usual. Not only that, but you were writing a lot. Judging by how quickly you shut your devices off every time I walked in while you were working on something, I decided it was probably something you didn't want me to see, and not another paper for school."

She had me there. I had been pretty careful about what I wrote, and who saw me writing it, regardless of whether

I was at school, in a coffee shop, or at home. If I was writing in public, I usually only did it at a booth or a table that allowed me to shield my screen from anyone walking by. I wrote most of my posts in Google docs before pasting them into my site, and I rarely updated my site from anywhere but my house.

"But," she said, giving me a look, "the thing that made me certain of the connection between you and Mistress A was the Kitty Fisher story."

I looked at her with total disbelief. "*That's* what tipped you off?"

She grinned. "I've never heard another soul mention that story, but you've used it with me for years to justify the history of going commando. When it showed up in Mistress A's blog, that along with everything else I'd noticed, made me put two-and-two together. I made a guess, and guessed right."

I pursed my lips, annoyed that I'd dropped any hints, but especially one so glaring. It made me question everything I'd done…again. Aside from the initial slip-up that made people guess Mistress A was from the Winchester area, I thought I'd been diligent and taken all precautions possible. Apparently I hadn't. It's a good thing it was just Syd, and I was certain I'd never relayed the Kitty Fisher story to anyone else. "All of your evidence was completely circumstantial," I argued.

Her lips pulled up slightly. "But I was right."

I narrowed my eyes. "Good guess, Prosecutor."

She shrugged. "It's what I'm trained for—to find threads and make connections."

I scrunched up my nose, annoyed. "I kind of hate lawyers."

She flashed a too-sweet smile. "But not me."

"Not you," I agreed. "Dammit, though! I thought I'd been so vigilant!"

"You were!" she assured me. "There's no one else who knows you as well as I do. No one else will make the connections." She grabbed some candy from the dish on our coffee table and popped one in her mouth. "I'm amazed you were able to keep the secret!"

"Me too," I admitted, feeling relieved that I had someone I could discuss it with now. "It wasn't easy."

"I can't figure out how you're stopping people from finding out it's you, though. Everything is tracked nowadays." Syd said, genuinely confused. "You can't even buy groceries without the items being linked to your credit card."

I got up from the couch and went to the kitchen to grab a water bottle, and brought one back for Syd too. "I had some help from a friend who owed me a favor. He kept my name off things. I also have some advisors who told me the best way to handle the business side. I opened a company and everything runs through it."

She unscrewed her water bottle and took a drink. "But even companies have to be tied to an actual person."

I shook my head. "Not in Wyoming, they don't. You can set up an anonymous business with a point of contact, like an attorney, instead of having it tied to your own name."

Syd looked at me like I'd grown another head. "You did

a lot of research for this."

I nodded. "I didn't want to screw this up. It could affect my whole life."

Syd looked sightlessly at the wall, taking it all in. I couldn't tell exactly what she was thinking, and hoped she wasn't judging me. I didn't think she was, but people were weird when it came to sex and money. Finally her lips slid up and she looked back at me. "You're like a sex superhero!" she said. "Secret identity and everything!"

I laughed, thinking that was a superhero movie I'd like to see!

"Why didn't you tell me?" she asked, her face falling and her tone soft. I didn't want to hurt her, but knew keeping a secret like this would.

I gave her an apologetic look. "I know. I'm sorry. I couldn't. I wanted to. More times than I can even tell you. There's been so much going on that I could have used your advice for. I wanted to talk to you about it at least once a day. But the more people who know, the more the probability increases that someone will find out my identity. It could put me at risk everywhere. School…they could take away my scholarships, or maybe even kick me out," though the scholarship issue didn't really matter anymore considering the money I was making from my site. "It could affect my future job and whether I have clients."

"It might help you get clients," Syd pointed out.

I nodded in agreement. "But maybe not the ones I want."

She agreed.

"Part of it was also that I wanted to make sure I could keep some level of privacy in my personal life. When you put something out in public like that, it's no longer yours, and people are free to make assumptions at will. But all of those things aside, the biggest issue with revealing myself to anyone was CARE. What if the families we help were to find out, and then tell Charlie they don't want me working with them anymore? I've seen so many stories of people who have been involved in something sex-related and lost everything for it. Like the woman who wrote erotica novels under a secret pen name. Someone found out about it and the woman lost her job. It's horrible, and I completely disagree with the reaction. What someone does in the bedroom or in their free time isn't a reflection of who they are at work. I'm in the same position as that woman, though. I worry it could affect my volunteer position, and I wouldn't want to do anything that puts CARE, or Charlie, in a bad position."

Syd nodded sympathetically. "I understand that. I still wish you'd confided in me…we tell each other everything, but I see your point. I won't tell a soul. Not even Jax. This is between you and me, and that's it. It's like attorney/client privilege, only it's best friend/best friend privilege, which is decidedly more sacred."

I breathed out a long sigh, relieved to have the information off my chest, and grateful to have someone to share the burden of it with. I mean, I had Master Z to talk to about it, but I didn't even really know him, and definitely wouldn't be revealing my identity to him. Syd was my person, and I knew I could go to her to vent and get advice. There wasn't a more loyal person alive, and I trusted her implicitly.

"Thank you for being there, supporting me, and not judging me." I meant it sincerely. I didn't know what I'd do without her in my life.

"You know I'm the person who always will be. No more secrets. Ever."

I nodded my agreement and gave her a solid hug. I was lucky to have such a wonderful friend.

Before going to bed, I checked my phone, and saw a notification about a new post from Master Z. Curious, I scrolled down and clicked on it. The screen with the shadow-faced hot guy sporting an eight pack and tattoo popped up, followed by his latest post.

## Alpha Answers

*Everyone fights. If someone tells you they're in a relationship—any relationship, friendships included—and they don't fight, they're lying, or selling something. You can't agree all of the time, and you won't. The trick is learning to push through the conflict, truly listen and hear what the other person is saying, and work it out while making the relationship stronger in the process. Some people don't have this skill. They don't know how to deal with issues and instead shove them to the side and spend years holding grudges. It's not a healthy way to deal with problems. You need to work through the disagreement and move on. The difficulty is that different personalities deal with conflict in different ways; in no place is there a more stark delineation on this subject than between men and women. Most men are natural fixers. They hate drama, and want issues resolved immediately so they can move forward and not have to deal with the argument anymore. When women have a problem, they want someone to listen. They often need to vent, and want to know they've been heard. If men can learn to listen, understand, and be a partner instead of only trying to fix the problem, women will feel supported. Building trust is difficult, especially if you've done something to lose that trust. So, admit when you're wrong. Apologize. And remember that when you've hurt someone—and in life in general—listening is more important than being heard.*

I pressed the power button on my phone and settled into bed. As I stared at the ceiling before drifting off to sleep, I thought that maybe Master Z deserved a chance after all.

# Ten

## *Tips and Tits: The Word from Mistress A*

### Don't Dazzle Me

*One day, someone was crafting naked, accidently spilled some glitter and sequins on their who-ha, and said, "Holy vajayjay! That looks AH-mazing! I'm about to be a trendsetter!" Okay, I'm not sure if that's exactly how it happened, but I can't think of a more plausible explanation for Vajazzling and Dijazzling. This is the process in which first you have all the hair ripped from your happy places, and then sparkly little crystals are applied to your sensitive, now very* unhappy *places. I don't know who thought this was a good idea, but it has the potential to go south fast, and not in a good way. You don't want to end up as one of the unfortunate stories on* Sex Sent Me to the ER. *For the love of your naughty bits, if you're going to do this, DON'T make it a DIY project! Go to a professional! Aside from the initial pain, let's talk about the after effects. Great goddesses, the chaffing! The whole point of sex is friction and rubbing. You're going to end up with blisters at best, and there's a serious risk of losing some rhinestones in your lady bits. Don't even try to exercise. Those rhinestones will catch on your Lu-whatever leggings and trust me when I say trying to extract yourself from that sticky situation in the middle of the gym will be an embarrassing endeavor. I've dazzled some things in my life…mostly on paper or fabric. Those dazzles have the same amount of sticking force as envelope glue. Meaning they don't. So, aside from the painful wax, chaffing, and uncomfortable workouts you'll have to endure, you're also likely to find tiny little crystals all over your body for weeks. Like glitter herpes. Some women will tell you it's all about female empowerment. My hat is off to them. I'd do it for female empowerment too if I didn't have to wait until all the crystals were gone to have sex…I like sex way too much to go that long without it. Take my advice and just say vajazz-no.*

It was the weekend, but I was on campus picking up some notes my professor had left for me. I didn't mind, and I needed the information for the paper I was writing on sex and gender roles. I felt like it had the possibility to get published, which, as a first year grad student, would be *huge* for me. I picked the notes up and was headed back to the car when a felt someone slap my ass. I turned around, hand fisted and ready to swing. Collin jumped out of the way.

"Whoa!" he said, holding up his palms. "I didn't think you'd come out hitting."

I looked at him with total disbelief. "I'm in public and

someone just spanked my ass. What did you honestly think was going to happen?"

"I thought you'd realize it was me. How many other people walk around touching your ass?"

I scowled at him. "I deal with creepers on the daily. When someone touches my ass, I definitely don't assume it's a friendly fondle."

"Fair enough," he said. "I'll refrain from future ass grabs." He paused, then qualified, "In public."

I rolled my eyes.

"Where are you headed?" Collin asked.

"To my car, and then The Grind. I have so much work to do." For school, and my site.

"I'll walk to the car with you."

I nodded as he fell into step beside me. "How was your date with Alison?"

His eyes softened and his lips lifted. "Great, as usual."

I smiled at his enthusiasm. He really did enjoy spending time with her, and that made me love him even more. In a purely friends-with-benefits kind of way. "I can't get over how cool it is that you spend so much time with her." Some of the families I worked with at CARE were family members of kids with disabilities. I knew how much it meant to them—the families and the kids—when someone took a genuine interest in them. Collin was a good guy. "I know it means the world to her."

He tilted his head to one side while lifting his shoulder. "It's not a big deal, and it means as much to me as it does to her. If I can make her day a little brighter, I'll do it every chance I get."

I gave him an assessing look. I'd known Collin for a very long time, but I'd never seen him like this. Maybe it was just a maturity issue, and he was growing up. In any case, a girl would be lucky to have him. I knew why I avoided relationships, but we'd never really discussed why he did. I wondered why he hadn't pursued anyone. "Why don't you have a girlfriend, Collin?"

He gave me a look like he wondered where that had come from. "Because I'm the male version of you, and I don't like relationships."

I gave several frustrated nods. "Yes, but *why* don't you like relationships? You're attentive, compassionate, and kind. Girls would fall all over each other to be with you."

"I like the multiple girls falling all over me imagery," he said, back to his usual, cocky self.

"I'm serious."

"So am I. Which is why I don't do relationships. I like to party and be with different people. That doesn't work with monogamy."

"I guess it depends on the girl," I said, thinking through it as I spoke. "I mean, I don't know many who would be comfortable with an open relationship, but I'm certain you could find a girl who wanted the same lifestyle as you." I was definitely not the open relationship type—if I ever got in a relationship, I'd be all-in, with one guy.

He lifted a shoulder, clearly uninterested in the idea. "Someday I'll settle down and find that girl, but right now, I'm young and want to experience things."

I couldn't fault him. "I can respect that," I said. We came to my car and I unlocked it, then threw my bag in the passenger seat. "What are you doing for the rest of the day?" I asked, leaning against the side of the car.

"Meeting some friends at the gym," he said.

"Of course you are."

"Don't be a hater, B. Someday, you'll realize you want to look like an action figure too, and come lift weights with me."

"Mmmmm," I said, completely unconvinced. I did a lot of cardio. Occasionally I lifted weights, but only because muscle burned more calories than fat. And I didn't look like some of the amazing women out there. I'd love to have the courage to sport a lot of muscle and look like I could kick someone's ass, but I'd worked so hard to finally be lean that the idea of adding to my frame in any capacity freaked me out in every way.

"Someday," he said, pointing at me as he started to jog backwards in the direction of the Easton gym.

I laughed and shook my head as I got in the car and drove to The Grind. I was getting out of my car when my phone buzzed. It was a message from Master Z.

*Toys, huh? What's your personal favorite?*

I wrote back.

*Anything that moves and surprises me.*

Sex was the one area where I didn't mind surprises.

My phone buzzed.

*Is that the criteria you also use for men?*

I was having far too much fun flirting with a man who, until very recently, I'd loathed the existence of. I rarely flopped opinions, let alone changed them so quickly. But there was something about him that I liked. A lot. The banter between us was fun and easy. I had no doubt we'd have just as much fun in bed…which was an odd thing to think since lately, I'd only been thinking about sex with one person.

I was about to walk into the coffee shop, but shot off a quick reply.

*One of them.*

His response was lighting fast.

*I do surprises almost as well as I fuck.*

I read the text and felt the response right between my legs. I stood outside for a good sixty seconds trying to recover, and when I did, I grinned, thinking I was due for a good surprise.

"Know what's idiotic?" I asked, sliding into the booth and putting my wallet back in my handbag, and my fresh cup of coffee on the table. Syd and I were at The Grind. She'd texted earlier to tell me she needed caffeine, so I told her I'd meet her here. We'd been working for almost two hours on our own individual projects. She was doing something lawyer-y and I was working on my gender roles paper and research. I'd just finished reading an article about sex toys, which told me little I didn't already know, but it did send me off on a mental rant that was about to go verbal.

"I have a list." That wasn't surprising. Syd had lists for everything; including things she thought were dumb. I did as well, I just had fewer of them.

"Me too," I replied, "but this is seriously stupid. Vibrators that aren't waterproof. Even if you're not using them in the water, they still have to be cleaned!"

"Why are we talking about vibrators again?"

"Research. I was at the sex toy store—"

"You're always at the sex toy store."

"Not always."

Syd rolled her eyes. "I'm surprised they haven't named a section after you."

I grinned. "I'm not ashamed of that. I'm a girl who knows how to get her needs met."

"You have enough guys waiting to meet them for you that I don't know why you need toys."

"Not all the guys I sleep with have skills. And even if they do, they can still only last so long before needing to recharge. Plus, a man who knows how to get a woman off using a variety of methods is totally hot! You should know that; Jax isn't afraid of them."

She exhaled a long-suffering sigh. "Back to the vibrator."

"Oh, I found out some interesting information."

"Aside from the lack of waterproofing?"

"Yes!" I said, stirring my coffee to make sure the sweetener was dispersed. "I was researching the most popular sizes. I thought everyone would want the nine to twelve incher, but it turns out, some girls like average."

"But you're not one of them," a deep voice said behind me.

I turned around slowly, meeting Cade's sky blue eyes. He was standing under a light and so help me if he wasn't glowing. He didn't have the right to look so angelic when he was being more than a little evil with his date-before-sex plan.

My throat had dried as soon as I heard his voice. I took a sip of my coffee before speaking, "You know me so well." I tried to make it sound sarcastic since we'd only had one date and he really didn't know me at all.

"Good thing I'm not average either," he said.

I swallowed. Hard. "According to you."

His lips slid into a half-smile before he glanced over at Syd. I got the feeling he would have said a lot more if she hadn't been there.

"Did you come here to get coffee, or are you just stalking me?" I asked him, which was kind of funny since before I'd known who he was, I'd spent a good amount of time at The Grind stalking him.

"Both," he deadpanned. It would have been creepy if he hadn't grinned right after he said it.

Syd motioned to the seat next to me. "You can sit if you want. We've just been doing school stuff."

"What are you working on?" Cade asked me.

"A paper I'm trying to get published."

"What's the subject?"

"Sex and gender roles."

One of his thick eyebrows arched. "Are you taking a side, or exploring everything?"

"More of an exploration. How gender roles have changed in the last century, and how it's affected sex."

He nodded, looking off in the distance for a few seconds, lost in thought. "I think there are more factors at play than just gender roles," he said. "Birth control being more readily available, women getting more rights, health issues like AIDS and STDs, and a wider acceptance of sex in general."

I nodded in agreement. "All valid points, and things I talk about in the article. But what I'm specifically interested in is the perceived switch of sexual interest from male to female."

"I don't know that there's been a shift of interest," Cade pointed out. "Most men still love sex as much as they always have."

"Right, but women are being more vocal now than ever before. There's more acceptance, and the internet gives a large forum for researching information and finding people who have similar sexual appetites. So, is the shift a result of women finally owning their sexuality and speaking up about what they want and how they want it, no longer afraid of backlash and slut shaming? Or have they always had high libidos, but kept them contained in order to fit with the norms? How much effect does societal pressure have on women and their ability to express their sexuality?"

Cade tapped a finger against the table as he considered my points. "A great deal, I imagine," he said. "If someone says it's not okay to behave a certain way, most people will fall into line. It's the innovators who aren't afraid to step out. They're the people usually labeled as rebels. While there were probably always women who enjoyed sex and weren't afraid to talk about it before now, they were likely shunned for their opinions. Except Kitty Fisher," he said, lifting his coffee cup to his mouth before continuing, "she was praised for her lack of panties, I hear."

I raised a brow, and Syd matched it. "Reading Mistress A again?" Syd asked him.

His smile spread. "Every day."

Syd glanced at me, a fleeting look, and one no one else would notice. But I saw and understood her unspoken conversation without question. It reiterated what she'd said before: he reads your blog, and he doesn't have a problem with sex. In fact, he's sexually proficient.

I shot her one back that said: I know he doesn't have a problem with sex, he's just refusing to have it at the moment, and *that's* the problem.

I turned my attention back to Cade. "There were a lot of notorious women who weren't shunned for their interest in sex. Popular, wealthy, and even famous women. They had no problem pushing the envelope, and often pushed it as their own way to rebel. Some people just don't do well with authority."

Cade coughed to cover a laugh.

"What's so funny?" I asked.

"I think one of the reasons you might be connecting with the women in this paper is that you relate to them."

"Meaning I have no problem with sex? I completely agree."

"And that you don't do well with authority."

"She's guilty on that count too," Syd agreed.

I shook my head. "I'm fine with authority. What I'm not fine with is bullshit. If someone is acting in a way I don't agree with, I'll call them on it. I won't fall into line for the sake of keeping other people happy. It's not my job to control how someone reacts."

Cade's lips slid up, his eyes sparkling with intrigue. "Another reason why I like you so much," he said. "Give me a woman who's blunt and says what she thinks over someone who only says it behind another person's back any day."

I eyed him. "Then that's another reason I like you as well." And it was true. Maybe we'd stay friends even after we finally had sex. He was almost as outspoken as I was. I appreciated that.

Syd shut her book and put it in her bag. "I have to get to Red's to pick up She-Ra and Jax, but you two have a fun little coffee date."

"Hopefully it counts as a date," I said, my tone sarcastic.

Cade thought about it. "Maybe a little one."

I rolled my eyes. "Tell Blue Eyes 'hi' for me," I said to Syd.

"Me too," Cade said. "And be sure to tell him I did not call him Blue Eyes."

Syd laughed. "He'll appreciate that. See ya later."

She walked out the door and I had a feeling I wouldn't be seeing her until much later. She liked her alone time with Jax. I didn't blame her. They were best friends and loved spending every possible minute together. It wasn't an obligation, or something that was forced. They truly loved being around each other. If I ever decided to lose my mind and have a relationship, I'd want one modeled on Syd and Jax's. They were the perfect couple, and I had no doubt they'd end up married and live happily ever after.

"I can't believe how much Syd's changed," I said, turning back to Cade and resting my back against the chair. "She used to be so worried about getting into a relationship. I love that she's in it, finding her own way, and not fearing it anymore."

"I agree," he said. "She seems much happier now. Fear is nothing but deprivation that holds you paralyzed. No one should be chained there."

Those were strong words, and not something a person would likely say without experiencing that kind of emotion. I wondered where the words had come from. "What about you?" I asked, assessing him and his body language with a keen eye. "What do you fear?"

He met my eyes as he answered, "Not much."

I gave him a skeptical look. "Come on. Don't be the guy who shuts down and doesn't open up. You're not like that."

He raised a brow, indicating I didn't know what he was like. He was right to some extent. I didn't know him well, but I could read people and he was almost as direct as I was. I didn't see him backing down from the question.

"I'm not shutting down. It's the truth. I don't fear things."

"Why?" I asked, genuinely curious.

He shook his head. "You misunderstood me. Not why, but how."

I pushed my brows together, confused. "How do you not fear things?" I asked, trying to rephrase his statement and still not understanding.

He nodded. "Too many people live fear-based lives. Instead of enjoying the time they have and exploring as many experiences as possible, they worry about every possible thing that happens, or is about to happen. They look for the negative over the positive, and become experts at pointing out the bad over the good. Fear and negativity become an obsession that wastes a colossal amount of time. I won't do it. I want to live my life and enjoy it instead of picking it apart, and constantly worrying about what's going to happen next. The reality is that every day could be the end of your life, and it's a shame to live it cautiously. Fear is a liar."

I listened to him with interest. It was a fascinating perspective. What would you do if you had no fear? If you set your worries aside and instead of saying, "I'm not doing this because it scares me," said, "I'm doing this *because* it scares me." I could easily see that swinging in a dangerous direction, though. It's easy to make poor choices when you stop processing fear, or force yourself to push through it. Listening to gut instincts becomes more difficult. And professionally speaking, there was a subset of people who lived their lives with no fear—they were often classified as psychotic.

"There are people who have no fear, and lack emotion in general. They're called sociopaths, and truly believe all of their own bullshit. They think nothing can ever hurt them."

He kicked his leg out, shifting positions. "I'm not talking about people who are mentally ill. I'm talking about the people who get up every day and say: this shit scares the hell out of me, but I'm doing it anyway, because I can."

"Because they can?"

He nodded. "They're here, they're alive, and they're willing to take a risk or do something they didn't think they could because that is what truly living is. It takes courage to confront the things that haunt us; to step outside of the pain and listen to our own voice instead of the noise around us telling us who we should be, and what we can do. It's about finding the internal strength and confidence to overcome those demons holding us frozen. Being fearless is an emotional tool that can be used to help overcome. I have no respect for people who won't step out of their comfort zone…whether that's mental, physical, or emotional. Comfort is easy. Comfort offers no challenge and if there's no challenge, there's no growth. Comfort is not a life well-lived."

Cade's focus on living life made me think he'd lost someone. Grief was such a personal struggle and the process of dealing with it was different for every person who went through it. Some people took years to get over the loss of someone they cared about. Some never did. I couldn't imagine losing someone vital to my life and if I ever did, I was certain it would change me in every way. Probing about Cade's emotions felt like a personal invasion, especially when I wasn't sure if my loss theory was accurate. I didn't know him well enough to go into that kind of detail. If I ever did know him well enough, however, I'd be interested to hear more about his story and how it had affected his point of view. Instead of asking about loss, I continued on his current thought path, asking relevant questions. "So you're saying you're a risk taker?"

"I'd like to think so. Are you?"

I lifted a shoulder. "I think I am, but if you ask me to sit in a room full of snakes or spiders, I'll tell you every which way you can fuck off. There's a difference between fear and stupidity."

He laughed. "If you fear it, you can overcome it."

I tilted my head toward him in assent. "Of course I could. But it's a question of whether I want to. If it's a situation where I have a choice and overcoming that particular fear will do nothing for me in the future, I don't personally feel there's a point to putting effort toward it."

He looked at me and I could see the wheels turning in his head. Finally he said, "Sometimes you don't have a choice."

Ah, and there was the crux of the issue. Sometimes you really didn't have a choice, and what would happen in those situations? You'd either learn to deal with it and adapt, or you'd stay stuck making no progress. "It's true. Shitty things happen. Things we fear more than anything else. When one of those things does happen, you learn quickly that you can't control everything—which is an extremely difficult realization if you're a control freak like me," and, I imagined, Cade. "But when it happens, you really only have two choices. You have to decide whether to stay put, or move forward. You can't go back."

"Exactly," he said. "Which is why fear is idiotic. You can overcome anything, even things you didn't think you could live through. And you keep overcoming them until you don't keep living. That's the way it is."

It was a heavy conversation for only a cup of coffee, and I had to refrain from wanting to analyze him even more than I already was. I took a sip of my skinny latte and Cade mirrored the action before putting the cup down and shifting to rest his elbows on the table, leaning in closer to me. "Can I ask you a question?"

"Yeah."

"What's your favorite color?"

My brow furrowed in surprise. That's not the question I'd been expecting, especially after our previous topic of conversation. "My favorite color?"

Cade nodded.

"Blue."

"What shade? Cornflower blue? Sky blue? Royal blue? Cobalt?"

"Sapphire blue."

He pressed his lips together and looked up in a thoughtful way. "Slightly easier to get than the sky I suppose, probably less expensive too."

I frowned. "I hope you didn't ask me that question to get me a gift."

The corners of his lips slid up.

I shook my head. "Presents and things don't matter to me."

"What does?"

"Experiences. Things are just things. You can't take them with you, but memories make a difference. Memories are a lifeline."

He looked at me with renewed interest—like I was answering in ways he would have answered himself. "Good to know."

I played with the coffee sleeve on my cup. "Can I ask you a question now?"

"Of course."

"What was your initial blindfolding plan on our first date?"

He gave a slow, irritating, and positively seductive smile. "You'll find out…eventually. Like maybe on date number thirty."

I narrowed my eyes. "Well played, Counselor."

He pulled out his phone, flipping to the calendar screen. "Get your phone. We need to plan our next date."

"We've already had one real date, and now two coffee house dates."

He shook his head, pushing his lips out. "Coffee dates don't count."

My mouth fell open in protest. "You said they counted earlier! We're getting to know each other. They absolutely count."

"Changed my mind. They don't."

"The only way they don't count is if neither one of us speak."

"I'm spending more time with you, B. Soon. Deal with it."

I hated leaving things unsaid and undone. Cade was now one of those things. Even if I hadn't been interested in him, I would have gone out with him again just to find out about that blindfold.

# Eleven

## Tips and Tits: The Word from Mistress A

### The 'V' word, and We're Not Talking Virgins

*Ah, Valentine's Day. Some people love it, some people hate it. A person's preference usually depends on their relationship status at the time. I fall into the love category. Any day that celebrates romance and sex is a good day in my book. It's an excuse to get dressed up, put on some sexy new lingerie, and explore your wild side. I'm a proponent of that exploration happening daily, but some people need a special excuse. If you're one of them, this is it. Valentine's Day is also one of the few days of the year that you can almost always guarantee nookie. So, what should you do to spice things up and make it even better? First, I'll refer you back to my previous post on sex toys. Go to the store, find some new things you want to play with, and debut them on Valentine's Day. Maybe even give them to your partner as a gift. Or even better, go to the store together and pick something out— which I've already mentioned, is excellent foreplay. If there's something you've always wanted to try, whether it's a new position, role play, or even BDSM, now is the day to do it. I realize V-day is primarily a couples' holiday, but I don't want to leave the single people—like myself—out! Don't let the holiday depress you. Get out and do something. Have a girls' night, go to a party, or even better, go to a sexy party. They have them all over the country; look in your local paper, or visit your local sex toy store and there's a good chance they'll have a list of naughty get-togethers happening in your area. I know that's where I'll be this Valentine's Day. Maybe I'll run into you there.*

I had two problems: One named Cade, and one named Master Z. I couldn't stop thinking about Cade, or his promise that we'd be going out again, and soon. The fact he was withholding sex made him all the more appealing, and infuriating, to me. It made me want him more, which is a classic response. People always want what they can't have. Not for the first time, I silently wondered if Cade had taken some psych classes during undergrad. Sex wasn't the only thing about him that intrigued me though. I'd spent enough time with him now that I was getting to know him better. I liked the person he was, and wanted to know more about how he became that way. Like everyone, he had a past, and I got the feeling his might be more complicated than most. Every person is a combination of their life experiences. We all have reasons for doing what we do. I wanted to find out more about his history, and what made him tick.

As for Master Z, that situation was getting hotter on a daily basis. He was messaging me at least once a day now, and I was messaging him back. What had started as hatred for the guy who stole my idea had turned into a flirtation that was rapidly progressing to what seemed like an affair of sorts. A part of me felt guilty for it…like I was cheating on Cade. I wasn't. We'd established we weren't exclusive, but we kept going on dates and hanging out. It felt wrong to want to screw them both. It shouldn't, but it did.

"Hellooooo…earth to Brynn," Syd said, her voice pulling me out of my contemplation.

I shook it off, directing my attention toward her.

"Butter," she said slowly, her tone questioning my ability to comprehend words. "I need the butter."

I nodded, walking over to the fridge and grabbing a stick for her to make the frosting with. We were at CARE making Valentine's Day sugar cookies complete with heart and lip shapes. The cookies were cooling and the kids had gone to play until they were cold enough to decorate.

Syd microwaved the butter for a few seconds to soften it, then started mixing in the confectioner's sugar, vanilla, salt, and milk. I loved her frosting, and cookies. Valentine's Day was one of the only times I allowed myself to cheat and eat sugar, and it was all because of her sugar cookies. She glanced up at me while she added a little more milk, then turned the mixer back on. "What's going on with you? You've been acting preoccupied all day."

Because I *was* preoccupied. With Master Z. With Cade. With School. With blog stuff. Coming up with compelling content repeatedly was difficult. Marketing was such a big part of my job. I had to maintain and increase my audience in order to keep my advertisers. I needed to hire someone to help me with that. The business side was a full-time job by itself. Add that to writing content, and my school work, and I felt like I had three full-time jobs. I was doing well and making money now, but if I didn't keep interested eyes on my work and constantly grow my audience, I wouldn't stay that way. I had goals. I wanted to finish school, pay off my student loans, help my parents, and donate money to charities. It was a lot of pressure, and a lot of stress.

"Just a lot on my mind," I answered.

Syd watched me for a moment before separating the frosting into different bowls and putting drops of food coloring in each one. She did one red, one pink, one green, and left another bowl plain white. "Anything I can help with?"

I shook my head. I wished she could, but it was all stuff I needed to do on my own or hire someone to do for me. "Nah, it's just work stuff and school. The combination of it all is stressful. I'll figure it out."

Her brows came together in concern. There was nothing more frustrating than wanting to help someone and not knowing how. I understood that. But some things couldn't be helped. Sometimes you just needed someone there watching out for you, and knowing they had your back and supported you, even if they couldn't do anything to make it better. "Knowing you're there is help enough. I appreciate that more than I can say, Syd."

Syd put a knife in each bowl and motioned toward it. "Help me stir?"

"Sure." I picked up the green and started mixing. It was a light green that had been requested by the boys who didn't want only "girl" colors on their cookies.

"What are you and Jax doing for Valentine's Day?"

She stirred the red, her hand whipping around the bowl like she was a professional mixer. "I'm not sure. Jax planned it and is being super secretive, but I'm excited."

I smiled at that, happy she was so happy. This was her first Valentine's Day in a committed relationship. "I hope you've been shopping."

She gave me a wicked smile. "I took Mistress A's advice."

I arched a brow. "You did?"

She nodded. "It should be an eventful night."

I gave her a sidelong glance. "You need to wear the lipstick."

She shook her head adamantly. "I told you, I can't pull it off."

I rolled my eyes. "Don't be ridiculous. You can, and there's no better day for a sparkly bright red lipstick than Valentine's Day."

She finished stirring the last of the frosting colors. "Maybe you're right."

I looked at her, shocked. I'd been trying to get her to try it for years with no luck. "Seriously?"

"Yeah," she said with a smile. "I'm feeling feisty."

I laughed. "I like feisty Syd."

"What about you?" she asked, trying not to show her

level of inquisitiveness. "What are your plans? Something with Cade?"

Valentine's Day was the biggest relationship-related holiday of the year, and not a day to be gallivanting about on non-relationshipy dates. Being together on a day full of hearts, chocolates, and roses practically screamed, "Look at my loving and committed partnership!" I wanted nothing to do with that nonsense.

"I'm going to the Sin and Sass party," I said. Sin and Sass was held at a downtown club every year, and sponsored by my favorite adult toy store. There would be dancing, drinking, costume parties, and scantily clad men. I'd gone for the last couple of years and had enjoyed myself every time. I expected this year to be the same.

Syd wrinkled her nose.

"What's that face for?" I asked.

She gave a disappointed shrug. "That party is just an excuse to go out in public in your underwear," Syd said. "Just like Halloween."

I gave her a wicked look. "Who needs an excuse?"

She wiped her hands on a towel and met my eyes. "I was hoping you'd have a date with Cade."

I looked at her like she'd lost her damn mind. "A *date*? On *Valentine's* Day? Are you nuts? That's next-level relationship shit. We are *so* not there."

"But you could be."

I shook my head vehemently. "Nope. I'm not a relationship girl, Syd. You know that."

"But you're dating, Cade."

"Only because I want to have sex with him."

"If you were together, you could have sex all the time."

Point to Syd for that bit of logic. "I haven't had sex with him yet. Maybe I won't want to have sex with him more than once. Maybe he sucks at it."

She snorted a laugh. "I'm fairly certain that's not the case."

I gave her a look. "How do you know?"

She shook her head. "He got, and has held, your interest, B. That's not an easy feat. And he already told you he's not average."

I tilted my head to the side in concession. Another point to Syd. But still not a valid reason to change my plans. "I'm not in a relationship, and I go to the Sin and Sass Party every year. It's the perfect Valentine's Day activity for me."

Syd sighed and went to the doorway to call to the kids in the playroom. They all came running, taking spots around the table and island. Each of them picked out their cookies, and the frosting and decorations were shared between them. I watched as sprinkles were dropped everywhere and everything from the counter, to chairs and hardwood floor, was covered in sugar. I quickly decided I was glad this wasn't my own house because that spread of sugar and frosting would never come completely clean.

I was helping Maci place one of her big heart sprinkles when I heard a male voice drift in from the living room. I thought it was probably Charlie, or maybe even Jax. He came over a lot. I was wrong on both counts. I lifted my head as Cade walked into the room.

His eyes met mine and my breath caught in my throat. I

could look at him all day long.

The kids glanced up intermittently, staring with curiosity at the new person who'd walked into their space. "This is Cade," Syd said, introducing him. "He's a friend of mine and Brynn's."

Maci started to giggle uncontrollably. I looked at her wondering what was up. "Friend," she said, giggling some more.

"You mean *boy*friend," Todd said in a singsong voice.

Cade started to laugh.

I looked at Maci and Todd, trying to figure out what they were talking about, and where they'd gotten that idea. "No," I clarified, "Cade is just my friend."

"That you want to see naked!" Maci squeaked, her high-pitched little laugh sounding like a pixie.

My mouth fell open. I don't embarrass often, but one thing guaranteed to make me blush is a four-year-old talking about naked men. What the… I thought back to the previous conversation Syd and I had had about Cade after we made peanut butter cookies last month. How had the kids even heard that discussion? Let alone remembered it? They must have been listening from the other room and Syd and I hadn't been paying attention. Good grief. What other incriminating things had they heard?

"And Brynn doesn't wear pants at home!" Maci offered.

There you have it.

"Maci!" I said, my cheeks heating even more. "That was a secret!" That she wasn't even supposed to know, or hear! Holy warrior princesses, if she was offering this information freely now, what in the world had she told her parents? I was going to get fired from volunteering.

"She also likes your butt," Todd chimed in, pointing at Cade.

Good hell. Kids remember everything. And repeat it! I'd never wanted to muzzle a person before, but I was seriously considering it at the moment. How did parents have any secrets? I thought about it for a second…they didn't. The things kids at CARE had revealed to me about their parents would humiliate even the most stoic person. I'd just kept the information to myself, and hadn't even considered all the little ears that were as sharp as a bat's and hanging around listening for information from me to later impart. I'd be more careful in the future.

"I like her butt too," Cade said, trying to help me save face.

The kids all stared at Cade for a few seconds, and then broke into another round of giggles. Then they went back to decorating their cookies, and Todd declared he was frosting his lips like a submarine because a submarine would taste better than lips.

Cade caught my eye and shook his head in clear disagreement with Todd about the lip comment. I was already blushing so Cade's comment couldn't have made it worse, even though the heat that was flowing over my face made it seem like it had.

The kids were focused on decorating again, and seemed to have forgotten about Cade's butt and nakedness—at least for the time being.

I got up from the table and went to stand by Syd and

Cade for a little more privacy. Though I was now fully aware that the bat ears were in effect and I was on high alert. "I didn't expect to see you," I said to Cade.

"I told him to come get some cookies," Syd said.

I turned to her, my eyes narrowed. She'd done that on purpose, determined to get Cade and I to spend as much time together as possible. "She does make the best sugar cookies," I said.

"It's the secret ingredient in the frosting," Syd offered.

She'd never told me what it was, but it was delicious.

She went over to the fridge and grabbed some of the cookies she'd frosted earlier and put in the freezer so the frosting would set faster. "I think the frosting is hard enough now that they won't melt all over the place."

"Thanks, Syd," Cade said, holding the plate.

"Any time."

"What are you doing this weekend?" Cade asked, turning to me.

"Going to a party."

He nodded, and started to open his mouth to ask a question when a chorus of giggles and yells erupted from the table, frosting and sprinkles flying. A full on frosting fight was in effect, and I wondered how long the boys had been contemplating it. It seemed like a well-planned attack. Syd and I got between them before too much destruction took place, but I'd taken some collateral damage to my face and arm.

I walked back over to Cade, who looked enormously amused at my disheveled state. "Unfortunately, I have to go," he said, then leaned down his mouth right next to my ear, breath hot on my neck, "but I'd really like to lick that off of you."

Heat shot through me from my head to my feet. "I'll ask Syd to make us some frosting."

He grinned, and I watched him walk out the door.

After the cookie situation and subsequent frosting comment from Cade, I was ready to go home and relax. Syd was spending the night at Jax's—no surprise there, so I planned to make dinner and binge watch something on Netflix.

I got home and mixed a salad with spinach, walnuts, chicken, and a little feta for dinner. I topped it with strawberry flavored vinaigrette and some olive oil. I was an olive oil snob and only got it from a special store at the mall that imported it directly from Greece and Italy at certain times of the year to ensure proper freshness. The health benefits of olive oil were hard to pass up. I used it as a butter substitute in everything I cooked or baked, including treats. After eating Syd's sugar cookies, I had to be careful about my dinner.

I sat down at the table and started scrolling through my phone notifications dismissing the ones I didn't need to deal with, and saving the ones I did. One of the notifications was an update to Master Z's page. He had a new blog post. I clicked over to read it.

## Alpha Answers

*Valentine's Day can be the worst day of the year for a man, or the best. Not every woman wants flowers, jewelry and chocolates, though I have to admit I've never met a woman who wasn't a fan of roses. The next go-to on the gift list often includes something lacy, but buying lingerie is not for couple amateurs…women are picky about their panties. Or, as we've learned from some, don't wear them at all. This is a holiday where if you do things even minimally right, like making a dinner reservation and doing something to show you were thinking of her—be it flowers or even a card, you're almost guaranteed an orgasm. Really, the holiday should be named Orgasm Day. Don't risk getting this holiday wrong. Make sure you know your partner well enough to know what she likes. If you don't know the answer to a question, ask. It's far better to have a discussion about her expectations than to make her mad on the holiday that's supposed to be celebrating your love. Whatever you're doing this holiday, I hope you all get a happy ending.*

He'd messaged me earlier in the week to say he was going to write about Valentine's Day from a guy's perspective. So I didn't mind it as much as the previous times he'd flat out copied my blog post ideas and re-written them like a dude. I wondered what he was doing for the holiday, and if he was going to a party, too. I pressed my lips together, rifling through my mental calendar. There were a lot of Valentine's Day parties, private and public. But only a few public parties were well-known, and well-attended. I wondered if we'd end up at the same one. If so, there was a real possibility we'd bump into each other. And if we did, there was a real possibility we wouldn't even know it.

My phone buzzed.

*You're going to a Valentine's Day party.*

My stomach tightened at the communication from Master Z and my heart sped up as I replied.

*I am.*

*So am I.*

*I paused, staring at my phone. The biggest party happening in Winchester was Sin and Sass. Based on some of his posts, as well as the speculation from readers, I knew we were both in Colorado, and I'd guessed he was local as well. But even if we came face-to-face, there was no way we'd know each other. Neither of us had any idea of what the other one looked like. Before I could respond, he sent another message.*

I think we should meet.

*My heart started pounding and my mouth felt like I'd chewed on sand. Anxiety coursed through me. Meet? In person? No way. I was* not *ready for that, and it would put everything I'd built at risk.*

*My identity is a secret. Your identity is too. Meeting would void that.*

He wrote back.

*It's a masquerade. You can easily hide who you are with a wig and a mask.*

So he *was* going to Sin and Sass! That was the only masquerade I knew of that weekend. I couldn't argue with his logic either. Even before his suggestion, I'd planned on wearing a wig, and a mask that covered my entire face except my lips.

In all honestly, I was intensely curious about Master Z. A part of me wanted to meet him in person to see if he was everything he seemed to be on his blog, and everything I'd imagined. But another part of me worried that he was a fake—some idiot either super old or super young, using the blog and his correspondence with me as entertainment. I'd watched way too many episodes of *Catfish* to not suspect every single person I met online. I shook my head and typed back.

*Too risky.*

He responded immediately.

*The best rewards come with risk.*

That line of thinking sounded familiar. It was a common phrase, but still… I filed it away in my mind for further examination later. As for the meet-and-greet, I couldn't do it. I just couldn't.

*I already announced that I'm going to a public party. There's been a lot of speculation about whether we're both living in Winchester. People will be looking for me, and probably you, at the various parties, trying to figure out who Mistress A and Master Z are.*

*But they'll never know.*

*They might. We can't.*

*I disagree.*

*That's fine. But it still doesn't mean I'm going to meet up with you.*

I waited a full ten minutes. He didn't respond. The silence was ominous. What if Master Z *did* find me? What then? Would I recognize him? Would he recognize me? And if so, would I want to explore something with him? I hadn't had a male-assisted orgasm in a long time, and

Master Z clearly knew his way around a clitoris. Cade's promise to lick frosting off me flashed through my head and the guilt washed over me again. That bothered me. Guilt generally wasn't involved with lust, so the fact that I was feeling it in regard to both guys made me worried I was already in over my head. Meeting Master Z would definitely be a bad idea.

I chewed on my lip, thinking through all of my options and finally coming to the conclusion that I had no control over the situation. The only thing I could control was myself, and I wasn't going to miss out on the party because of guilt, or fear about possibly meeting Master Z. I already had my costume, and I was ready for a night of dancing, drinking and a little debauchery.

# Twelve

## *Tips and Tits: The Word from Mistress A*

### Smears and Tears

*We've all been there. Lipstick and sexy times. It can get everywhere. And I mean EVERYWHERE. Especially, if you're one of the people who enjoys giving or receiving a good blow job. If you're a girl wearing any bright, vibrant color—say a festive shade of pink or red for Valentine's Day—by the end of sexy times, you usually look like a sad little clown. Smears and tears. That's what you'll have. Lipstick is a messy business, but I'm here to make it slightly easier for you. I've discovered several brands of lipstick that I'm giving the Mistress A sex-proof guarantee. There are a few brands that work, none of which you can get at your local makeup store—they all require special ordering. Check my product page to see them. This stuff* does not *come off. You can do pretty much anything, and as long as you're not rolling around in heavy duty makeup remover and then vigorously rubbing your face on a towel during your sex-sesh, the lipstick will stay on. Trust me when I say it's been thoroughly tested. So before you go out to celebrate your night of romance, grab some lipstick that won't smear. Your face, and your partner's naughty bits, will thank you.*

"You know everyone is talking about Mistress A and Master Z possibly being at the same party, right?"

Syd and I were both home, getting ready for our big Valentine's Day dates. Her evening plans were with Jax; mine were with whoever I ran into at the Sin and Sass party and decided was hot. I'd locked my guilt away, and was totally fine with that—and a little curious about whether Master Z would show up. I wondered if I'd be able to figure out who he was.

I lifted a shoulder on a sigh. I did know people were talking, and there was nothing I could do about the speculation. "I've heard."

"Sooooo…" Syd said, dragging out the word, "do you think they're going to meet?"

I pursed my lips. "An offer was made."

I helped her apply the lipstick. It was tricky and had to be put on a certain way to guarantee it would stay properly. I'd been using it for years so it wasn't a problem for me, but it could be an issue for a novice, especially if they didn't get it in the proper lip line. Getting it off once it was on was a bitch.

"So…" she prompted again. "What's the story?"

I'd been sending Syd screen shots of some of my messages with Master Z, but hadn't mentioned the most recent one about him wanting to get together. Thank Thor she knew about my secret now. I didn't know how I'd functioned without having her as a sounding board. "He messaged me saying he thought we should meet at one of the parties in town tonight."

Her brow winged up. "What did you say?"

"Hold still," I said, trying to get the third coat on her lips. I finished applying it and stepped back, examining her from a few feet away. The color looked fantastic on her, like I knew it would. "I told him it was too risky and refused."

"What did he say?" Her mouth was parted and she looked like a ventriloquist as she tried to speak with as little lip movement as possible while the lipstick dried.

"Nothing." I put the cap back on the lipstick and stacked it next to the other makeup on the counter.

"Nothing?" she asked, her eyes getting bigger.

"Nope."

"That's ominous."

I scrunched up my nose, unhappy about his lack of reaction, and slightly worried as well. "That's what I thought."

"What will you do if you run into him?"

I lifted a shoulder, completely at a loss. "There's no way I can know if I do. There's no way he can know if he runs into me either."

Syd shook her head as I applied the sparkly gloss over the top of the bright red. "What if he's somehow figured out who you are?"

It was unlikely, but anything was possible. "My only option to ensure we don't accidentally meet is to not go. I'm not willing to live in fear like that. I still would have gone to the party if I hadn't started the blog. I'm not going to alter my decisions just because I have an alter-ego. I've been careful. I didn't tell readers what party I'd be at, and there are plenty around Winchester. I'm not worried." My answer reminded me of Cade's opinion on fear, and I realized we were similar that way. Yet another thing we had in common.

I put the finishing touches on Syd's lips and handed her the mirror. I hadn't let her see herself until now. Her blonde curls were tousled and sexy, perfect *Hustler* hair. Her eye makeup was light, but still highlighted her pretty lashes and big eyes. The contouring on her cheeks was perfect, and her lips looked glorious. If the lawyer thing didn't work out for her, she could definitely be a lip model. I couldn't believe she'd shied away from wearing bright colors before. She was more confident than that, and needed to take risks.

She looked in the mirror and her mouth formed a surprised 'O'. She moved her head from side-to-side, testing the different angles. She glanced up at me. "I really didn't think I could pull it off."

I rolled my eyes. "You don't just pull it off. You own it. And Jax is gonna freak!"

She grinned. "I hope so."

"He will."

She ran her hands through her hair, shaking out the

curls to give them more volume as she said, "Cade texted me earlier with a case question. It was just an excuse for him to ask what you were doing tonight."

My mouth fell open. "He gets information about me from you a lot."

"Because he sees me more, and he knows I want you two to get together, so I'm inclined to try and facilitate that."

I narrowed my eyes, annoyed. "There's no facilitating necessary. I also want us to hook up. He's the one cock-blocking himself."

"I want you to have more than just a hook up with him, and you know it. So does he."

"And you're well aware of my position on that."

She gave a long-suffering sigh. "Remember that verbal smack down you gave me about needing to stop worrying so much about school and that I'd regret not having meaningful romantic relationships at this age?"

I nodded, knowing where she was going with this.

She pointed at me. "You need to take your own advice."

"That advice was specific to you, because I know you. Personally, I feel like I'd only have regrets if I *did* have a relationship. "

Her expression was knowing as she said, "Someday you'll change your mind. And in case you were wondering, Cade is staying home tonight."

"Good to know." A feeling of relief flooding over me that he wasn't going to be out on a date screwing some girl who wasn't me. I immediately checked myself. We weren't in a relationship, and I was going out tonight with the express purpose of hanging out with hot guys and possibly hooking up. I had no right to feel relief over Cade's lack of romantic partner tonight. The fact I *had* felt it made me concerned all over again.

She closed her eyes and spritzed some rosewater over her face to set her foundation and give her a pretty glow. When she opened them, she met my reflection in the mirror. "So when you get bored of the asshat boys at the party who are drinking too much and looking for an excuse to get laid, you'll know where Cade is."

"Thanks for your concern."

She gave a wide smile as she stood. "You're welcome. I'm going to go change, but thanks for the lipstick."

"Jax is going to love it."

She grinned. "I know. Have fun tonight, and be careful."

"I will."

I put my dress on the bed, and got ready to be sinful and sassy.

The bass was pounding when I arrived, just like I liked it. I was wearing a two-piece scarlet dress that shimmered in the strobing pink, red, and white lights of the room. The top was a shirt made of almost sheer organza. It ended right about my belly button, showing about three inches of my stomach. The bottom skirt was crimson satin and flared out, stopping high on my thigh. I'd worn a lacy thong just in case, but I'd still have to be careful bending over or I'd flash everyone.

I'd put on a long, platinum blond, stick-straight wig to cover my own dark brown hair, and I was wearing a black mask covered in red and silver sequins and pearls. The mask covered my entire face except for my lips, lower cheeks, and chin.

The bar reeked of alcohol, drug store perfume, and sweat. The room was packed full of people who had used the event as an excuse to get dressed up in various costumes. Some were in sexy dresses. Some were in straight lingerie. I did lingerie a lot, and felt like I needed to be a little less noticeable tonight. Master Z's suggestion that we meet had me on edge. Every guy on the dance floor could potentially be him.

I scanned the floor and saw a plethora of couples gyrating…whether they'd come here as a couple, or had partnered up once they got here, I wasn't sure. I didn't think Sin and Sass was a place I'd choose to spend a romantic holiday with my partner, though. I'd probably opt for a candlelight dinner followed by hours of sex. I narrowed my eyes thinking that scenario wasn't much different from the one I hoped for tonight, only without the dinner and romance, and just the sex…provided I could put both Cade and Master Z out of my mind and simply enjoy myself. That was the challenge.

I walked onto the dance floor, and lost myself in the music, all other thoughts out of my head. Before long, a body was pressed against mine. I moved with him for a minute before I turned around. He was wearing black linen pants and a black dress shirt with the top four buttons open, probably to cool him off—and he definitely needed cooling. Good hell, he was probably Zeus's bad-boy prototype. He was tall, his shoulders broad, chest wide and all of that tapered down to a narrow waist. His hair was dark, almost black, and a flat black mask covered his entire face, except for his lips…which were full, and extraordinarily kissable.

We moved together to the beat, his hands going over my waist, and down my hips. There was an undeniable connection there and I wasn't opposed to seeing where it went—if he was interested as well. The song ended and I moved off the dance floor, deliberately not checking behind me to see if he'd followed.

I made my way to a couch near the bar and ordered my favorite sweet drink, liquid marijuana, and a glass of water.

The guy who'd been dancing with me sat beside me. "That sounds like a dangerous drink," he said. His voice was difficult to hear over the sound of the music, but I could tell it was deep, and I felt it straight in my core.

I crossed my legs and pressed them together before answering, "The sweet ones usually are."

His full lips curved roguishly. "So you like things sweet?"

I eyed him. "Depends on the situation."

The server brought my drink and water and I immediately took a sip, the fruity flavors making me want to be on a beach with sand between my toes and the sun blanketing my skin. I looked back at the masked stranger. His eyes were a deep forest green, and he hadn't taken them off of me.

I licked my lips, the sweetness of my drink still lingering, and his eyes darkened. "Have you been to the back room yet?" he asked.

I gave him a suspicious look. The back room? What was he talking about? I'd never seen anything but the dance floor and bathrooms. Furthermore, I'd been coming to the Sin and Sass party for years and I'd never heard about any special rooms. Was this a new thing? "I didn't know there was one."

He took my hand, his palm soft and grip firm, guiding me through the throngs of people. I hadn't had much to drink, and was fully aware this could be a bad situation. I didn't even know the guy. But I did know some jiu jitsu, so I decided I was safe enough for now, and could see where things went. I followed him, connected with one hand, my drink in the other. I was thoroughly enjoying the view of his ass.

We came to a black door that, despite having been to this club more times than I could count, was attached to a room I didn't even know existed. He knocked in a specific succession, two light taps, one harder, and a pause before a hard knock again.

Someone opened a slit in the door and I had to restrain myself from asking for the bootlegged liquor in my best 1920s gangster voice. The person behind the door said, "Password?"

I widened my eyes. I'd been joking with my initial comparison, but it really was like attempting to gain access to a speakeasy during prohibition!

Still holding my hand, my masked partner said, "Ménage."

I arched a brow. That didn't seem like a very secure password. It probably should have included random numbers and letters. "Ménage" was likely being thrown around all over Sin and Sass tonight.

A lock unlatched and the door opened. I followed my partner inside, trailing behind him.

The room was dark, decorated in deep merlot tones accented by black. It was crowded, everyone in masks. Some had full face masks, other's half. As we walked through the main room, I noticed a lot of skin—people were naked, or mostly naked. We wove our way through the throng of people; the common thread among Ménage attendees so far seemed to be sex—there was a lot of kissing and fondling going on. We passed a couple on a chair who were making out, the girl's shirt completely off. Others were walking around in lingerie that hid very little. Some were in lingerie that hid nothing. One guy was wearing tighty-whities with a werewolf breaking out of his crotch. I'm adventurous when it comes to sex, but if a dude dropped trou and was sporting a pair of those, it would give even me pause.

As I took in my surroundings, my heart rate increased more and more. I was a hard person to shock, but this came close. I'd heard of sex parties, but I'd never been invited to one, and certainly didn't think they existed in a place like Winchester. In fact, I hadn't been one-hundred percent sure they existed outside of *Eyes Wide Shut*. I felt like I'd just been thrown into central casting for the sequel.

I was fascinated, turned on, and trying to take it all in so I wouldn't miss a thing.

We paused on our way by the first room. My eyes were huge and I almost forgot to whisper as I hissed, "Oh my God! Are they about to have sex? Like, real, actual intercourse? In front of everyone?"

The girl was wearing a full face mask, and so was the guy. She was completely naked. He was naked except for a pair of leather pants that looked painted on. The pants were untied at the crotch, and he was hanging out and at full attention. It was obvious he hadn't been drinking any milk, and the hormone problems that had been plaguing all the cocktail weenies I'd run into recently weren't an issue for him. At all.

"They are," my partner whispered back.

As we stood there watching, the man bent her over a table, reached down, rubbed her clitoris, and then pushed into her. She moaned as he slowly started to pull his length back out, and then pushed in again.

I stared, and felt like I didn't blink once during the whole scene. The situation was so far out of my comfort zone, and I was having a hard time trying to reconcile that with the wetness between my legs. Giving up that much control in a public setting was something I'd never done, and not something I thought would turn me on at all, but apparently it did. We watched until the girl started moaning with her orgasm and the man followed soon after.

My partner still held my hand as we moved down a hall. We paused as we passed by a room where several people dressed as clowns, with full makeup and festive brightly colored wigs, were having sex, all in a group.

"What's the appeal here?" I whispered again.

"Anonymity," he answered. "The makeup helps people feel more freedom to let their wild side show."

I was Mistress A, and supposed to be all-knowing about all things sex, but some of these things I'd never even heard of. I needed to do more studying, and more research because it seemed there was a lot I still didn't know.

We came to another room where people were completely covered in latex suits, and fondling each other through strategically placed holes. I shuddered even watching them—I'd be way too claustrophobic for that. Plus, I'd lose so much sweat I'd probably end up dehydrated. But I'd studied a lot of fetishes for school and latex fetishes were surprisingly common. They acted as a second skin and in a lot of cases, made the wearer feel less vulnerable, and more confident. It wasn't for me, but I wasn't one to judge.

The man in black pulled me along until we came to the largest room, more people in full face masks and leather. The acts of debauchery occurring were many, and I had to take them in one at a time. One man was in the process of blindfolding a woman and looked like he was getting ready to tease her to orgasm. In another area, a woman was sitting on a chair with a hole in the center of it. A toy was attached, and being controlled with a remote by the people standing around her.

"How did you hear about this place?" I asked the man with his fingers still threaded through mine. I was Mistress

A for fucks sake, and didn't even know about it. How did he?

"I got an invitation."

"How?"

"I know people."

I narrowed my eyes. I hated when people weren't straight up. Why couldn't he just answer the dumb question? "What's with all the mystery?"

He nodded toward the other people in the room. "It's a masquerade. Mystery is the main event."

I snorted a laugh. "I would definitely not say mystery is the main event here."As I continued examining the room, a man sauntered up to us. He was totally naked, and once my eyes fell, I couldn't stop looking. He truly had the biggest dick I'd ever seen, and that included any I'd seen in porn.

"Hi," he said, his voice low and velvety.

"Hi," I breathed back, trying to sound nonchalant—like I wasn't staring at a dick that was longer than a sub sandwich.

I looked at his size, and wondered if a woman could really accommodate something of that length and girth. I was pretty sure they could. I mean, babies come out of vaginas and most babies were slightly bigger than his dick, but birth is painful, sex shouldn't be. A woman walked up to him and started rubbing her hands all over his body, both hands drifting down and gripping around his length. Two fists didn't come close to covering him. She called over another girl for an extra set of hands, and together, they went to work.

My gaze trailed from them to a group of people in a corner of the room spread out on pillows, all naked. With each new scene my eyes landed on, I was getting more and more turned on. Watching porn was one thing, but actually seeing it in person was a completely different sensation. I was shocked and excited, turned on and uncomfortable, but for the life of me, I couldn't *stop* looking.

I caught my partner's eye. A current bounced between us as he leaned over, his breath hot on my pulse point. He trailed a line of kisses up the side of my neck, over my jawline. "You're beautiful," he said, his voice husky.

I moaned something that I meant as a thank you, but his hand was currently moving around to my breast and I was having a hard time making words. His finger started tracing my nipple, the organza of my top brushing against the sensitive spot in a rough manner, making my skin pebble. He kissed my collarbone, the warm air hitting my skin as his hands continued their sensual perusal. If this persisted, it wouldn't be long before we were one of the acts on display.

My heart started to race and I panicked. Where was this going? Where did I even want it to go? Were we about to have sex in the middle of the room with anyone and everyone watching? Was I okay with that?

I needed to think.

I pulled out of the mystery dude's grasp. "I need to find a restroom."

He pointed toward a long hallway. I made my way down the corridor and found the door on the right. It was a private bathroom, and empty, thank Thor. I walked in and sat on a chair in the corner of the room. What had I been thinking? Yeah, I was a sexual creature, and yeah, I was adventurous, but I was having "more than friend" thoughts about two guys, one of which I'd never even met. I didn't need to add another to the list. I'd originally felt that hooking up with a random stranger might help me forget the situation with Cade and Master Z. I now realized that wasn't the case. Not only would I *not* be able to forget them, but I'd probably be thinking about them both during the deed, and that was just bad manners. If you're going to be thinking of someone else while you're having sex, you should be having sex with the person you're thinking of.

No, I thought with a decisive shake of my head. I wasn't okay with anything else happening tonight, even if the masked guy could seduce like it was his damn job. I might have been okay with it a few months ago, but now I had this weird hang up on Cade, and Master Z was throwing me for a loop, and I had no idea what I was doing, but I was pretty sure it shouldn't be a stranger in the secret sex room of a club until I figured my shit out. While I appreciated the secret sex room invitation because it was great research and gave me more topics for blog posts, I was ready to end my night and go home to relax in my living room in some comfy jammies and with HGTV.

I got up and opened the door, walking down the hallway. I looked around as I moved toward our original entry point so I could say good-bye to my potential hook up and thank him for getting me into the bang-bang room, but I didn't notice him as I made my hasty retreat. To be honest, I had no desire to go back in the rooms and possibly lose my willpower. I'd been in a long intercourse drought and doubted my self-control. The guy who had let us in the room was the same person who let me out.

I walked out the door, looking at my phone as I tapped on my ride app scheduling a pick-up. I wasn't really paying attention, so I didn't even see it coming.

"You're in so much trouble," a deep, familiar voice said.

I glanced up, my mouth dropping. What was *he* doing here?

As effortless as picking up a piece of candy, Cade threw me over his shoulder, and carried me out the door.

# Thirteen

## Tips and Tits: The Word from Mistress A

### Horny = Happy

*They seem as mythical as fairies, but there actually are things you can do to increase desire: Aphrodisiacs. Most of us have heard of things like oysters and chocolate, but I bet you didn't know that the smell of donuts and licorice can increase blood flow to a man's penis by thirty-two percent! In other weird smell news, the scent of licorice and cucumbers increased blood flow to a woman's vagina by thirteen percent! Scent plays a huge part in attraction. Your pheromones have got your back, and are looking for suitable mates for you—thanks, nostril matchmakers! And let's not forget about endorphins, the key that unlocks your orgasm-belt! Sweat and a high heart rate increase endorphins. So does working out, which, if your sex session is any good, should end in a puddle of perspiration anyway. But, if you're not interested in getting sweaty before getting naked, pop some chili peppers. They mimic the body's reaction to exercise by causing your heart rate to increase, and your body to perspire—you'll sweat, but it won't be deadlift-three-hundred-pounds-repeatedly sweat—and you'll release endorphins as well. If you're looking for something sweeter, and let's be honest, who isn't, chocolate has dopamine. The body's natural production of dopamine is highest during orgasm; if you're eating chocolate and coming, you're getting an exceptionally mood inducing double shot of dopa. So girls, next time you're looking for a perfume, try to find something donut scented. Dudes, my advice would be to start wearing cucumber.*

**Update: I didn't think I'd actually need to clarify this, but I meant the* scent *of cucumber, not an actual cucumber as an accessory…anywhere. If the girl you're with wanted to screw a cucumber, she could get it from the grocery store by herself, and there are much better toys than produce.*

"Hey!" I yelled, pounding my fists on his back. Five years ago, I would have been horrified at a man doing this. I would have spent the entire time on his shoulder thinking that he was about to fall over. No guy would have even attempted to pick me up. I wasn't throw-her-over-your-shoulder-worthy then, at least, not according to the asshats I'd dated—the douchebags I had once thought cared about me, and wanted me. Now, though, I kind of regretted not being heavy enough to make the thought of picking me up obsolete. I had no idea why Cade was doing this at all. "What do you think you're doing?"

"Taking you home," he said, making his way through

the club. A few people noticed us and gave Cade fist bumps like he'd won a prize. It pissed me off.

Despite the fact that I'd been in the process of scheduling a ride, there was nothing I despised more than being told what to do. I'd do the exact opposite of what I was told just to spite the person. It was my own special way of telling them to go to hell. "I don't want to go home," I hissed, pounding some more. Abruptly, I became excruciatingly aware of exactly how solid his back was. Involuntarily, my hands unclenched from their fists and my palms splayed out, running over his back and the soft, cotton, white t-shirt he was wearing, feeling every bit of hard, bunched up muscle. If he was this big and hard on his back, he had to be the same in other places. I looked down noticing that I was in a prime location for viewing his jeans-covered ass, and it was even better from this angle. I was now a lot more interested in him than I had been thirty seconds ago when he'd potato-sacked me and dragged me out of the party. Still, I didn't like being hauled anywhere, and I wasn't pleased about being thrown over his shoulder like future French fries. "Put me down," I said in my angriest voice.

He laughed. At my angry voice. Now I was really pissed.

"So you can go back inside and have someone take advantage of you?" His voice was incredulous. "No. Not happening."

What. The. Fuck? "Who the hell do you think you are?"

We made it outside the club. Outdoor heaters were blazing by the front benches where people waited for rides. The place was deserted though, because everyone was still inside having a good time. He put me on the ground and held me in front of him, his hands on my waist. I looked down, rearranging my top so my boobs gave me the advantage, and lifted my eyes to his, blazing. "It's not your job to decide what I do, or who I do it with."

He reached up and moved his hand over my forehead, brushing back the hair that had come loose from under my wig. "You're better than that, Brynn. Just because you don't think you're worth someone treating you well doesn't mean I have to agree."

I blinked, totally stunned. When I got my wits back, it was enough to utter, "What the hell, you tickle-dick? I know I'm worth it! I'm worth not getting sucked in by men who just want to use me. I know a lot more about that than you think I do, asshole. I spent the majority of high school with dipshits who thought they had the right to use me because I didn't fit the same pretty mold that the other girls did. Well, I fit it now. And I'm not the one being used anymore."

The words came out in a rush—things I hadn't intended to admit out loud. Few people knew about my past, fewer still would even believe it. I was a completely different person now than I had been then.

Cade's jaw was held tight. "That's what happened to you?" he asked through his teeth. "Boys manipulated and used you because they thought they could."

I did not want to have this conversation. "It doesn't matter," I said, waving him off. "It's in the past."

His shoulders had a firm set to them that said he was ready to argue, and in it for the long haul. Fucking lawyers. Always ready to argue. "It matters because it hurt you, and the result of that hurt is affecting your actions now."

I rolled my eyes. "My actions are fine. They're exactly what I want them to be."

Anger flashed over his face. "I know what's happened at some of your other parties. You were damn lucky Syd was there to take care of you. I'm not letting that happen again."

I couldn't argue that I'd made some poor choices in the past, but I'd been smarter about it since, and wouldn't put myself in dangerous positions. I'd taken self-defense courses and did jiu-jitsu three times a week. I watched my alcohol intake, and didn't drink anything that I hadn't been holding and watching the entire night. I'd learned from my mistakes and he had no right to use them against me.

I crossed my arms over my chest, glaring at him with every ounce of anger I contained. "I don't regret my past. It made me who I am." I wasn't just talking about the parties in college and the guys I'd met. I was talking about high school and every man who had mistreated me then, too. It had hurt at the time. It still hurt when I thought about it. But it had made me into the person I was, and I cherished every cruel comment, every stab of pain I felt, because it meant I was alive, I was strong, and I was better than I had been before. It took courage to overcome and evolve, just like Cade had said during our discussion about fear. I was proud of who I'd become.

A vein on his neck pulsed with frustration. "And led

you to situations where you could have been hurt."

"They were mistakes. Everyone makes them. And you, of all people, have no right to judge me."

His eyes narrowed. "What's that supposed to mean?"

"Your theories about fear," I said, poking him in the chest. "Something traumatic happened to you, and it has informed the adult you've become and the decisions you've made. Just like me. It's not a bad thing. Every person on the planet has their own issues; few are brave enough to examine them, analyze them, and make the changes they want to make in their lives. You have. I respect you for that. So have I, and I deserve your respect back. I'm the sum of my experiences combined with my choices. I've overcome and grown, and I'm better for it. I'm happy with how far I've come, and where I'm going. Everyone has secrets. That includes you, Cade. Don't probe for mine if you're not willing to share yours."

He stared at me for what felt like more than a minute without saying a word. Then he sighed. "Something traumatic did happen."

I gave him a surprised look. I hadn't thought he'd go into details, and especially not outside a club in freezing weather. Most men were not great at communication, and I wasn't expecting him to elaborate or share.

He rubbed the bridge of his nose with his thumb and forefinger. "Someday, when you haven't been drinking and aren't more obstinate than usual, I'll tell you what it was."

He pulled out his phone and called a cab, which was ridiculous since I'd started the ride process fifteen minutes ago before he'd gone caveman. "It should be here in the next ten minutes," he said, after he got off the phone.

I sat on a bench by the heaters. He sat next to me, his thigh brushing mine. A jolt rushed through me and I trembled at the connection from such an innocent touch.

"What are you even doing here?" I asked. I'd never seen him at a party like this before. He didn't seem like the party type. At all. And he definitely didn't seem like the "Masquerade party on Valentine's Day where debauchery was guaranteed" type.

"Rescuing you, apparently," he said dryly.

I ground my teeth. "I didn't need rescuing. We've already established that."

The corner of his lips lifted in a sexy half-smile, and I had to refrain from punching him in the shoulder…mostly because I was worried about what the shoulder punch would do to my hand. He had muscle. A lot of it.

"Seriously. I wouldn't have guessed this was your scene."

He shrugged. "I like all different scenes. Experiences, remember? I like to have them."

I did remember, and was now intensely curious about his past, and what had happened to make him embrace being fearless.

"How did you know it was me?" I asked. "I had on the mask and the wig."

"Your lips gave you away," Cade said, his gaze falling to my mouth. "That red. I don't think I've ever seen it on anyone else."

I stared at him, stunned and a little turned on that he'd

noticed my lips. I mean, that's one of the reasons I painted them bright red and covered them in glitter, but still…it was nice to know they'd caught the attention of the person I intended them to.

"I don't believe that," I said softly. "You just guessed, which was a little dangerous. You could have hauled any girl out of there, and another girl might have been significantly less understanding than me."

He sliced his head once to the left. "Wouldn't have happened. I know exactly who you are."

My stomach twisted. He'd said it in a way that indicated he really did know who I was. I was about to press further, but he continued talking. "Your lips are the kind of lips that sear into a man's brain and make him think of every mouth-related fantasy that's ever existed. They are, without a doubt, completely unforgettable."

Part of me thought he was exceptionally sentimental and over-the-top, and the other, normal, girly part of me, was preparing to swoon. Because how many men in the world actually take the time to really see a woman, and articulate their feelings like that? Not many. The emotional self-analysis a man would need to work at in order to express himself that way would make most men's heads explode.

"It's nice to know I made an impression," I said, my voice breathy.

"From the very first day I met you."

"You made quite an impression yourself."

He kicked his feet out in front of him and leaned back as he grinned. "I'm glad you thought so."

"Why didn't you tell me your name?"

He lifted a shoulder. "Seemed more fun not to."

"But you got my name from the store owner."

"I did."

"And didn't try to contact me for weeks."

He looked at me from the side, his face a study in amusement. "Because you were expecting me to. You're used to men falling dick over feet to get your attention. I wanted to be the one who stood out because I *didn't* act like a hormone crazed thirteen-year old."

"It gave me a complex."

He winced. "That's not what I intended. I apologize."

"I thought you were going to kiss me."

"I thought I was too. It took a colossal amount of restraint."

A smile played at my lips. "That makes me feel better."

"That I was in pain?"

"That you wanted me."

His eyes darkened as they met my gaze and held it, the electricity flowing right between my legs. "Desire has never been a question when it comes to my feelings for you."

My eyes widened as he scrubbed a hand over his chin. He looked like he was having a serious mental struggle. His lips pursed and finally he said, "I didn't want this to happen here, but fuck it. I can't wait."

His lips met mine in a desperate merging, like I'd been drowning and his essence was giving me the air I needed to survive. A shiver ran from the top of my head to the tips of my toes as his tongue pushed into my mouth and tangled with my own. His arms, corded with muscle, wrapped around my waist, pulling me closer to him as my hands moved over his back. Maybe it was my current sexual drought, maybe it was his stupid plan not to have sex until we dated, but I'd never felt a connection like I felt with Cade Brett. I wanted him inside of me more than I'd wanted any other man in my entire life.

"Come home with me," I begged, my breath coming fast and hard, like I'd forgotten to breathe for the duration of our kiss.

He groaned into my ear, one hand moving around the front to caress my breast. He started playing with my nipple and I moaned. He groaned again. I reached down, touching him through his pants. He was hard as a rock, and he was huge. "Come home with me," I said again. "It will be a night you never forget."

His hand started to inch up my back as I heard a car pull up. Cade pushed into my mouth hard, then pulled away. "Not yet, B."

I pushed him off me, my expression angry. I was horny, annoyed, and swiftly realizing that I wasn't going to get the release I wanted tonight because I was dating a guy who apparently possessed superhero willpower and was an asshole of steel.

"You need to be taught the art of wanting, Brynn."

"Don't try to analyze me, Counselor. I understand want more than you know. And disappointment. Wanting is all I dealt with for years. I won't go through it again."

He pressed one hand against the door of the car and leaned into me. "I'm not asking you to. I'm asking you to give us a chance. That means a relationship, *and* sex. Lots of sex. More than once, and more than you just getting a fix."

"I can't promise you that," I said, angry.

"I'm not asking you to. I'm simply asking for you to try. I want you. For more than one night."

I tried to stay angry. Part of me still was, but he was blowing everything I'd believed about men out of the water, and I wasn't sure how to proceed. "I'll think about it," I said, getting into the car.

On my way home—my tongue gently tracing my lips—I realized that for the first time in my life, a kiss had left me breathless.

# Fourteen

## Tips and Tits: The Word from Mistress A

### Kiss me

*Ah, the elusive kiss. It can be rip-your-clothes-off awesome, or it can suck monkey balls. There's rarely an in-between. You either have the technique and chemistry with your partner, or you don't. I've dated guys who kiss with all the precision and liquid force of a fire hose. It doesn't matter how enthusiastic you are if you have no form. If you don't know what you're doing in the kissing phase, chances are high you have no clue when it comes to the rest of your partner's body. No one wants that, and regardless of your gender, your kisses are being judged. Every dreamy-eyed romantic has* that *kiss. They're probably thinking about it right now. Maybe it's from a book, a movie, a scene they watched play out in real life and wished they were participating in. Mine is from* The Return of the King. *Then I watched the extended edition with the background info about the kiss and it almost ruined it for me. Almost. I try not to think about that truth bomb. Let's get down to why this kiss just does it for me…and pretty much every other woman on the planet. Aside from the fact that dirty-haired Aragorn is gone in the scene and they've cleaned him up horribly—bring back the dirty!—the scene is practically doctorate-level kissing. Aragorn hasn't seen his soul mate for months. Last he checked, she was an elf on death's door. Yeah,* way *not cool he hasn't checked on her in a while, that bit does not a romance hero make, but he gets a pass for being busy helping to save the world. When Arwen shows up at Aragorn's coronation, moves that flag and he sees her, every woman I've ever watched the scene with gives a collective gasp. I still gasp. Every. Single. Time. Here's the thing about girls. We all want to be desired. We want to be the object of your fantasies, and we want you to want to fulfill all of ours. We want you to let us know that, with words and more importantly, actions. Actions, like a bomb-ass kiss! We all want a guy who looks at us the way Aragorn looked at Arwen. Like he'd only been taking shallow breaths since the last time he saw her, barely alive, but now she's there and he's about to be resuscitated with her lips. Dudes…strive to kiss a girl like Aragorn—doing it with dirty hair gets bonus points. If you do, there's no telling what you might get in return. Ladies, find a man who makes you feel like a goddamn elf queen.*

I wasn't sure how I was feeling about Cade at the moment, but it included some weird butterflies in my stomach that had been in hibernation for years. I wasn't pleased they were suddenly bursting from their cocoon, and that it happened around the same time

Cade and I kissed.

He'd put me in the cab the night before. I'd begged him to come home with me again, but he had refused, though the regret on his face was obvious. I sighed, thinking about it. It was by far, the best kiss I'd ever experienced. *Return of the King* level skill, and I didn't think many men possessed that kind of lip magic. Even thinking of it made my heart, solidly protected in a wall that let no man pass, feel like it was ready to burst. All of my organs were betraying me.

He'd texted to make sure I got home okay, and to tell me he looked forward to our next date. He didn't mention when that would be, or if he'd be throwing me over his shoulder and abducting me for it as well. I'd decided to wait and see what Cade's next move was. Normally, I would have been the one making said move, but he'd been calling the shots from day one at the sex toy store with the handcuffs. He clearly had more willpower than I did, and could abstain far longer than me. He had an agenda, and I'd bide my time and follow along until I thought he was ready to make a move, or I got sick of trying to figure out his plans. Gaining the upper hand was not something I wanted to waste energy on at the moment, however.

I'd slept like a passed out drunk girl, and then I'd woken up to this message from Master Z:

*If I'd made you feel like an elf queen, you wouldn't have left without a trace.*

I'd stared at that message for longer than I cared to admit, then reread it.

Stared some more, reread it again.

That went on for a good ten minutes.

At some point, I'd had the sense to sit down. The guy I'd danced with, drank with, followed upstairs to the sex room, was Master Z. I had so many questions running through my head I couldn't even unscramble them all, or begin to answer them. How had he known it was me? He'd never seen me before. I hadn't even given clues about what I would be wearing. The only explanation I could come up with was that he knew me. Somehow, he knew me, and knew I was Mistress A. Who could he possibly be? I was at a serious disadvantage if he knew my real name, not to mention that it put everything I'd built—personally and professionally—at risk. I hadn't spent much time trying to figure out his identity, but maybe that needed to change.

Aside from the logistics and questions, there was a niggling stream of thought running through all of my doubts. Master Z was even hotter in person. Way hotter than I'd imagined, and the moments we'd shared during the sex party were pretty damn epic as well. I'd wanted to see the guy without his clothes. If I'd known it was Master Z, I wouldn't have freaked and run out of the orgy faster than rabbits screwing. I would have stayed there and considered doing some screwing of my own. Why hadn't I suspected him? I remembered a fleeting thought had flashed through my mind, like 'what if this is Master Z', and then I'd quickly pushed it out so I wouldn't be saddled with the guilt I was feeling over my conflicting emotions for Cade and Master Z. The brain is excellent at helping with denial when you don't want to look at things too closely.

Once I regained my composure after reading Master Z's text, I went downstairs, opened Syd's leftover stash of sugar cookies, and started to inhale. I'd steadily been eating myself into a daze ever since. It wasn't like me at all. Not in any way, shape, or form. At least, not in the past five years. I was an emotional eater. For a long time, I hadn't been aware of that fact. But when I'd finally realized it, I'd shut that shit down. Now my life consisted of non-fat, no sugar, and extremely limited carbs. I basically lived on rabbit food and protein. I wasn't saying it was healthy. I'd gone from one extreme to another, and like Cade had accurately and infuriatingly pinpointed, I'd switched sugar for sex. But sex at least burned calories. I'd accepted deprivation and unhappiness as part of my diet.

I was on the couch, the Tupperware container of cookies on my lap, with HGTV on when Syd came home. I barely registered her presence as I stared blankly at the screen.

"Hey!" Syd said, dropping her stuff on the table by the door.

I mumbled a noise that was meant to come out as "hi" but through the cookie crumbs in my mouth, came out sounding like a disgruntled Ewok instead.

I saw Syd move slowly into my line of sight until she was standing right in front of me, blocking my view. I didn't care. It's not like I was actually watching TV. And I'd seen this one anyway. They totally picked the wrong house and were going to go over budget on renovations. Syd was holding a coffee. I eyed it, envying her morning beverage and wishing I had my own. Syd's own eyes were huge with shock, then immediately softened to concern. "You're eating cookies."

I nodded, grabbing another one from the container and taking a bite. It tasted like heaven and bliss. I had no idea what number this cookie was, but I guessed I was getting close to the double digits of eating my feelings.

"Sugar cookies, Brynn," she said slowly. "With frosting."

She was saying these things like she thought I wasn't aware of the sugar, butter, and carb content. I knew what they contained. "Yep."

"You're holding the entire box."

I nodded, agreeing again. "It's an eat-your-feelings kind of day."

"I never see you eat *anything* like this."

"Nope. And I'd never eat it in front of anyone else. That's why I'm home. On the couch. You won't judge me, though, so it's okay."

Syd pursed her lips, and I could tell she was working up to a rant. "I hate that. You'd never see a guy forgo dessert in public, or not finish it for fear of judgment. Why do we do that as women? If you want a cookie, pie, or a piece of cake, you can eat it! Eat the whole damn cake if you want! And you don't have to feel bad about it!"

I sliced my head up and down once. "Thanks for the permission."

I heard her growl. Syd had strong opinions, and wasn't afraid to share them. If there was any injustice in the world, she'd comment on it. I was the same way, I just had issues with food.

She sat next to me on the couch, attempting to move my cookie box and get my attention. I had a death grip on the sucker. She finally gave up. "Do you want to tell me what's going on?"

"I'm having guy issues."

"With Cade?" she asked.

"He's one of them."

She blinked. "Who's the other?" She sounded offended that she didn't already know.

I wrinkled my nose. "Master Z."

Her jaw dropped. "Master Z, as in *the* Master Z?" Her tone increased in pitch with each word.

"Same one."

"You *met* him?"

I nodded.

"Last night?"

I nodded again.

Her eyes were huge. "How was it?"

"Memorable, to say the least." I finished my cookie, and thought I should really stop eating them, but they were delightful, and each bite helped me repress my feelings.

Syd blew out a sigh and took a sip of her coffee.

"Kissed Cade, too," I said.

"What?" she yelled, spitting her coffee all over her clothes and the floor.

"He was there. Recognized me. Hauled me out of the club when he thought I was drunk. I wasn't. I'd only had a couple of drinks, and I'd been chasing each one with water, but he's bossy and paranoid."

She went into the kitchen and grabbed a towel, then came back to clean up the coffee mess. "I'm glad he decided to go. Someone needs to be at parties with you and have your back."

Her words registered. "Wait, did you say you're glad Cade decided to go? Did you tell him I'd be there?"

"I did," she said without apology. "I worry about you in those situations alone."

I rolled my eyes. "I was fine, Syd. And I would have been just fine if Cade hadn't shown up. I've been in scary positions before, and now I know how to avoid them."

"There's always a risk, Brynn. I worry about you and when I told Cade you'd be at the party alone, he was worried too. You can be mad if you want, but it just shows you have people who care about you."

I glared at her, trying to stay annoyed even though I knew she was looking out for me. "I wasn't happy about it."

She shrugged. "Sorry, not sorry." She finished cleaning the coffee off the floor and got as much out of her clothes as she could. "So how did that lead to a kiss?"

I lifted a shoulder. "Fighting's good foreplay."

Her brows went up. "How was the kiss?"

I sighed, remembering his lips and the ache that had pulsed in my chest for the rest of the night after I'd gone home alone. "Even more memorable than I thought it would be."

"That's basically the same answer you gave for how you felt about Master Z."

I winced. "I know. It's a problem."

She eyed me closely, her face changing from confusion, to realization, to shock. "Oh my hell! Do you like them both?"

I took another cookie.

"You do!" she said, pointing at me. "Oh my God, oh my God, oh my God!"

"Yes," I agreed with an abundance of reticence. "It appears I've caught feelings."

She rolled her eyes. "It's not a disease."

"Speak for yourself."

She took a breath deep from her chest, sat up straight, and put her palms on her thighs before looking straight at me. "I'm going to give you the same speech you gave me not too long ago about not wanting to end up alone. You want a relationship, B. You're just afraid, and up until now, you haven't found the right guy."

"I'm not sure I have now, either," I said, waving a cookie. But as I thought about her words, I realized she was right. I was afraid, and I hated letting fear rule my life. But look at what had already happened? I'd consumed almost all of Syd's container of sugar cookies. If I kept up this relationship shit, it wouldn't be long before I was bathing in a tub of uncooked brownie batter.

"Do you know much about Cade's past?" I asked, curious whether he'd shared the information with Syd.

She pressed her lips together like she was trying to keep the words from coming out. "I know some."

She stopped talking, like she didn't plan to continue. I was not on board with that. "And…" I prompted, looking at her and really seeing her for the first time since she arrived. I noticed her face looked like she was trying a new shade of makeup called road rash. She must not have listened to my advice about how to take the lipstick off.

"And that's not my story to tell."

My mouth dropped. Syd was my best friend, my person—yet she was keeping the secrets of a random guy she'd known for a year over telling me, her bestie. "What the hell?"

She shook her head. "You value loyalty above all else, B. Don't ask me to break the trust I have with another friend because you're curious."

Dammit. She was using my own arguments against me. Damn lawyers again! I was surrounded by them and their excellent arguments.

"He said he'd tell me eventually," I pointed out.

"Then ask him."

I could tell I wasn't going to get any other information out of her, so I turned my attention to the mess on her face instead.

"Judging by your face, you had a fantastic night. Did Jax like your lips?"

She blushed. "Yes. Until I couldn't get it off."

"What's happening with that?" I gestured in a circle like I was trying to outline her lips, which would have been impossible because everything around them was red, as if she'd tried to scrape the stuff off with sandpaper. "It looks like a situation."

"You happened!" she said, frustrated.

I recognized the look. I'd had a similar problem the first time I'd tried to get the lipstick off, but I'd had the sense to use some coconut and lemon oil, which was much less harsh than whatever removal method Syd had attempted.

"It won't come off," Syd said. "Seriously. Did you test this stuff before you recommended it?"

"Of course I did! That's why I recommended it. And I wear it often!"

She ran her fingers lightly over her lips like they were tender. I had no doubt. She didn't look like she'd been kind. "Nothing makes it move. Not makeup remover, scrubbing, or prayers to multiple deities."

"That's kind of the point. It stays on through *everything.* Sexy times included."

"Right, but I'd like to go to bed and not wake up looking like I bit Jax in his sleep and accidentally got an artery. What's it made of? Turpentine?"

I rolled my eyes. "I don't care what it's made of as long as it stays on." I got up, went to the bathroom and put some lemon and coconut oil on a makeup remover pad, then brought it back to her with a hand mirror. She rubbed it on her face, taking the lipstick right off.

"Works like a charm," I said.

"I can't believe it came off. You have no idea what I went through."

"I told you how to get it off before you left. You were just preoccupied."

She lifted a shoulder in concession. "I was about to spend all night having sex with Jax. Can you blame me?"

"Nope, I really can't. But next time you have a problem, text or something. I could have helped."

She leaned back against the couch cushion letting her

shoulders, neck and head rest on the pillow behind her. She moved her neck so she could see me. "I'm guessing you haven't seen the speculation about Mistress A and Master Z yet today?"

I furrowed my brow. "Nope. I saw the message from Master Z this morning and didn't check anything else before going straight to the cookies."

She glanced down at the cookie container that pretty much only held crumbs. Another friend would have been judgy. Syd was not that friend. "Everyone is trying to guess who they both are. Pics have been posted of people at parties all over Winchester last night. People are tagging anyone they think might have been Mistress A and Master Z."

"Great." That was all I needed.

"You were in some of the photos."

I blew out a long breath. "Even better."

"I mean, you had that wig and mask on, so I don't think anyone knew it was you,"

"—Master Z did. Cade apparently did too. I might as well have been wearing a damn name tag."

Syd shook her head. "The people on social media were just speculating that the hot blond in red seemed like a good Mistress A candidate."

"I shouldn't have mentioned anything about where I was going, or what I was doing. I'll have to stay quiet about events in the future."

"You're rarely quiet."

"It will be a learning experience."

We sat in silence for a few minutes, the voices on

HGTV narrating my thoughts as I considered Cade, Master Z, the speculation about Mistress A, and all of my other predicaments. I'd gotten myself into some doozies, but this was far more than I'd bargained for.

"They just put wallpaper in their kitchen and you didn't say a word," Syd said. "You hate wallpaper almost as much as small dicks. I'm worried, B. I'm really worried. Tell me you're okay."

I shook myself out of my thoughts and stood. "I'll be fine," I said, walking up the stairs. "I just need to figure things out."

Syd's eyes were full of concern. "You know I'm here for you."

I nodded, appreciating the support. This was something I needed to figure out on my own. I had things to do, and sitting around in my jammies, eating cookies wasn't helping me to do them. I could wallow in self-pity and indecisiveness, or get something done. I decided to get shit done. I got to my bedroom, pulled out my phone, and messaged Master Z.

*If I'd known it was you, I might have stayed.*

# Fifteen

## *Tips and Tits: The Word from Mistress A*

### Shock and Awe

*The first time I saw* Eyes Wide Shut, *I watched it with a combination of shock and scandal. It felt like something I shouldn't be seeing, but at the same time, I didn't want to turn away. In the world of sex, few things are more hush, hush, than sex parties. Even in today's hyper-connected society, it's difficult to find them, and even more difficult to secure an invitation. But if you do, a world of knowledge will—sometimes quite literally—be at your feet. Every party is different. Some have a theme: ie. leather, costume, BDSM, orgy. Others have a large area for socializing and various rooms with different sex acts taking place. It's like watching porn, except the people in the rooms are right in front of you. It's the height of exhibitionism—if that's what gets you off—and can pique all of your senses. It's basically a sexy shock and awe for your naughty bits. I'm a firm believer in being open to all possibilities and trying anything once. If you ever get the chance to attend an event, I'd say give it a chance. Just know that most parties are a judgment free zone, with people who are completely comfortable in their own skin. If you don't fit that profile, sex parties definitely aren't for you.*

I blew out a long breath as my shoulders sank into the back of my chair in the library. I'd started trying to divide my schedule between school and Mistress A. Mistress A was taking a lot more of my time than classes and homework. I'd decided to only reply to comments and messages at night, and go to classes and work on papers and research during the day.

I'd finished my homework and closed my eyes, trying to be in the moment for a minute, and in that time, heard my stomach rumble. The meditation would have to wait. I grabbed my bag and walked over to the commons area. It was only three o'clock, and a couple of the food trucks that usually loitered around campus at lunch would still be there. As I was walking, I felt hands go around my waist and almost jumped sky-high. I pushed away as I turned, trying to get a look at the person invading my space. I shook my head when I saw him. "Collin. I should have known."

"I didn't grab your ass this time."

"Thanks for the consideration."

He grinned, and it was hard not to grin back. Collin was charming that way.

"Where are you off to?" he asked.

"Getting some lunch from one of the food trucks."

"Good idea. Can I join you?"

I lifted a shoulder. "Sure."

We both got our food. Collin ordered a sandwich, and I grabbed a chicken wrap. We took it inside the student center and found a table in the corner overlooking the campus outside. The snow covered everything in a blanket of white, most of which had been trampled by students. It was still beautiful, though.

I took a drink of lemon water from the container I always carried with me. Lemon water was cleansing, and tasted better than regular water, so I always had some on hand. Collin unzipped his coat, and I stopped with my wrap halfway to my mouth, my jaw hanging open as I stared at his shirt. "Does your shirt really say 'I enjoy vagina'?" I was stunned speechless.

His lips formed a mischievous grin. "Hilarious, right? I got it as a joke, but I've been wearing it everywhere."

I shook my head. "I don't know if people will think it's funny, or be offended."

He shrugged as he took a bite. "Probably both."

"You really don't care about what people think." I said it as a statement, not a question.

"Neither do you. It's one of the reasons we get along."

I gave him a dubious look. "I think I care a little more than you. I don't think I'd ever wear a shirt that said 'I enjoy penis'."

"But you do enjoy it," he said, pointing his sandwich at me. "And there's nothing wrong with that."

"I don't need to announce it to everyone."

He looked at me for a minute, like he wanted to say something, and then stopped. That was weird.

"What did you do for Valentine's Day?" I asked him.

He finished his bite before answering, "Went to a party." He took a sip of his drink. "How was Sin and Sass?"

I stared at him, wondering how he'd known I was there. "How did you know that's where I was?"

He shrugged. "That's where you always go for Valentine's Day."

True…but still. I hadn't questioned the guy I'd been dancing with at the party enough and he turned out to Master Z. Now I was extra suspicious of everyone. "It was good. I didn't stay too long."

"Why not?"

Because I'd been overwhelmed at the sex room experience with one guy I was having feelings for, and then been physically removed from the location by another. "I just wasn't feeling it."

He was about to take another bite of his food, but stopped and held his sandwich in front of him, considering me. "That's not like you. No hot guys at the party?"

"Too many," I said. "That was the problem."

He balled up his wrapper, leaned in closer, and held my eyes, his gaze intense. "Maybe you need to pick one."

I held back a gasp. Pick one? Did he mean I should pick between the two guys I was currently lusting after? Or that I should pick a guy in general? I felt a knot form in my stomach, and sensed an undercurrent of mystery in his tone. Like there was something I should be figuring out, but wasn't. I tried to shake it off. "Maybe we both do."

He nodded. "I'm thinking about it."

I couldn't stop thinking about Collin and our lunch. Could he really be Master Z? He was the same height and build as the guy at Sin and Sass. His hair color was lighter, but Collin easily could have colored it for the party. Surely, I would have recognized his voice? But everywhere we'd been that night, it was either loud, or we were whispering. Beyond that, voices were easy to disguise. The more I thought about it, the more I realized I had no freaking idea, and my mind was all over the place. I decided that I needed to get away and get out of my head. I went to the gym, doing a combination of cardio and light weights, and lost myself in the workout. I didn't love working out—for some people, it was practically a religion—but it helped to clear my head and after all the sugar cookies I'd destroyed, I definitely needed it. I spent a couple of hours there before showering and heading home. I stopped at my post office box on the way, and grabbed some letters and a package, then took them all into the house.

I often got things from companies wanting me to review their products. Usually things like role playing costumes, sex manuals, and erotica books. I'd use those for sure. But of all the packages that had started coming since I'd become Mistress A, the ones I liked the most were the toy boxes. They were usually things that were newer to market, and stuff I hadn't tried before. I certainly wasn't going to turn down a hundred-dollar vibrator when they sent it for free, and I was happy to test it out, and offer a review.

I ripped the name tag off the top of the box and shredded it—it was habit, and the first thing I did when I got a package addressed to Mistress A's company. Forgetting to do that could lead someone directly to me. The post office workers saw it, but the post office box was in my company's name—which was different than Mistress A's name. Neither the company, nor Mistress A was tied to my own legal name. If anyone ever put all of the information together, I'd just say I'd been contracted to pick up the packages from that box. Plausible deniability was the key to managing a secret identity. I opened the box, hoping it had some naughty battery-power inside. I squealed when I saw the various items. It did! A few vibrators, dildos with suction cups, and some leather restraints…

I heard a knock on the front door and stopped sifting through the box to answer it. Jax was on the other side. "Hey, B."

I smiled and put a hand against the door jam. "Hi, Blue Eyes."

"Syd asked me to meet her. She was studying, but should be here soon."

I nodded, opening the door wider and stepping out of the way.

Jax walked in and sat on the couch, noticing the box of sex toys sitting on our coffee table. "Uh…looks like you're a little busy," he said, motioning to the box. "I can wait outside and give you some privacy if you want?"

I rolled my eyes. "I wasn't using them." Yet. "Plus it's like, ten degrees out there. That's not very friendly."

"Well, this," he said, motioning to the array of climax helpers, "might be a little *too* friendly." Jax looked over the collection and picked up one that promised an orgasmic rotation.

I shrugged. "Research."

His brow lifted. "Uh huh."

"This one looks promising," he said, picking up one that had multi-speed and thrusting capabilities.

I looked it over. "You should take it…see what Syd thinks."

He grinned at that. "You think I won't take you up on that offer, but I will."

"No, I knew you would take me up on it, which was why I suggested it. You're a good man, Blue Eyes."

He smiled and put it back on the coffee table. If he didn't take it with him, I'd leave it in Syd's room and tell her it was a gift from Jax. She'd turn red, and then take it anyway. I giggled at the thought.

I heard voices on the porch right before Syd walked in, Cade trailing behind her. My stomach immediately started doing somersaults. I hadn't seen him since the Sin and Sass party. Her smile grew when she saw Jax, and she came over, pressing her lips to his in a long kiss before noticing me. "Hey," she said, then she glanced at the toys on the table. "Niiiice." She picked up one that looked like it could find a G-spot better than ninety percent of men.

"Did you raid the sex toy store?" She raised one brow. "Because I think you'd make an excellent naughty toy bandit. In fact, I think that should be your new nickname, sex toy bandit…STB."

I screwed my nose up in distaste. "That sounds like a venereal disease."

She waved a hand in front of her face. "We can tweak it."

My gaze moved to Cade. Cade's eyes went from the box, to me, and back to the box. He didn't look horrified, so that was a plus. Most guys were intimidated by toys. His eyes held mine, heat flashing behind them, and I immediately felt like an entire tiny army had started to cha-cha in my stomach.

My cheeks heated. I'd never been embarrassed about sex before. Ever. I was unashamed of my sexual experience and history. But with Cade standing there, I couldn't be redder. "It's just some research," I mumbled.

Cade raised his eyes to mine, one corner of his lips lifting. "Need some help?"

My breath caught in my throat and my mouth fell open.

Counselor Cade totally just said that!

Out loud!

In front of my friends!

My defense has always been sarcasm, so I snorted before saying, "I could give you a tutorial if you need it."

His brows shot up, his lips quirking like I'd issued a challenge. He glanced down, picking up a pretty ribbon that looked like it was supposed to be some sort of restraint, and took my hand, wrapping the ribbon around it. "So you're skilled in Japanese knot tying?"

I caught Syd's wide-eyed stare from across the couch. "Uh…I…uh, forgot my pen at school," Syd stammered, getting up off the couch, pulling Jax with her as they awkwardly stumbled together, "and I really like it. Great pen. Pink. Sparkly ink. We'll be back. Later." She looked from Cade to me. "*Lots* later." They shut the door in their hasty escape.

Cade picked up one of the toys from the box. "Do you know what this is?"

I looked at it and wondered if he thought I was some sort of virginal idiot. "Of course I do. It's a flogger."

"Do you like to be spanked, B?"

I eyed him, my interest piquing. A lot of men weren't into sexual experimentation, and I was intrigued that he was one of them.

"I like all kinds of things," I said, my voice soft and sultry.

He came toward me, his hands running up my arms, gaze hot as it went over me. "That's good, because I do, too." His lips trailed a line up my neck and over my jaw. I fumbled with the buttons on his shirt, trying to get them all undone and get his stupid shirt off. I'd been waiting to see him naked for what felt like an eternity. As his shirt opened, I inhaled a sharp breath, looking at the perfection of his chest and abs. My eyes trailed over his body, catching a bit of a design on the side of his ribs, but before I could investigate it further, Cade covered my mouth with his, and I was lost to the sensation of his body against mine, his tongue exploring my mouth. I was so distracted that it took me several minutes to realize the ribbon was wrapped around my wrists, and he had me backed against the wall. He stepped back, looking at me in my shorts and flimsy tank top. My nipples pushing against the thin fabric. He took the pearl of skin into his mouth through my shirt and I writhed against him.

His lips pressed against mine again, his tongue tracing my lips as we kissed, then he moved back, took my tank top in both of his hands, and ripped. I gasped. "I'll buy you another one," he said. He leaned into me, his length hard against my stomach, and I wanted him with every part of my soul. "Take off your clothes," I said.

His lips lifted, slow and deliberately. "You're not in charge today, B."

I narrowed my eyes and managed to grind out, "Wait until I am."

"We'll see," he said, his voice rough. His hand inched down, past the waistband of my shorts. He grinned again. "You weren't kidding when you said you don't wear panties."

I shook my head.

His hand met my core and he teased the ball of nerves at my center. I was writhing, wanting more, the restraint binding my hands and making everything even hotter. His hand slipped down and he pressed one finger into me. "So wet." His voice was husky, his breath hot against me.

He slipped in a second finger, and it took me less than thirty seconds for my muscles to start clenching around him. He slowed down, giving me a few seconds of a break before he started thrusting his fingers faster. Within a minute, I'd come again. He did that two more times before my legs gave out and I sagged against the wall.

"It's my turn," I said, my gaze going hungrily to his pants and his cock pressing against them.

His smile was slow as he took my hands and undid the ribbon wrapped around my wrists. "Not this time."

I blinked, dumbfounded. "What do you mean?" Not this time? He was turned on, I'd felt it. He was ready for me and I was more than ready for him. I'd been waiting far too long already. Since when did a man turn down sex with a half-naked girl he seemed pretty damn into?

"I told you, we're taking this slow," he answered, handing me the ribbon. "That was just for you."

"You don't want to have sex?"

He took my face in his hands, his eyes twin, dark pools of desire. "I want to push my dick inside you and make you scream louder than you ever have before. But first, you need to know I want you for far more than what you look like, or your legendary sex skills. I don't think you believe that yet."

It was all I could do to keep my jaw off the floor.

He ran his hand down my chest, my tank top hanging off of me in tatters. He pinched one of my nipples, then bent down and sucked them both, adding teeth. He stood, his expression a wicked promise. "Next time, I'll make you really come."

Cade left, blue balled. I felt bad about that, but it was

his own damn fault. I offered to help rectify the situation. He'd just grinned and said he'd be thinking of me while he took care of it when he got home.

My phone buzzed. A message from Master Z.

*I want to take you out.*

I sighed. We'd already been over this.

*I told you, I don't want to reveal my identity.*

There was a long pause in the conversation.

*I have a way to fix that problem*

I gave the screen a funny look.

*How?*

*Just trust me.*

Another funny look.

*Trust you? I don't even know you.*

*But we've already met. You just didn't know it. What does your gut say?*

I paused this time, trying to gauge my own reaction. He'd been a gentleman at the orgy—which is not a place one would usually expect gentlemanly behavior. I considered it a few minutes longer before deciding nothing ventured, nothing gained, and typed back my reply.

*Okay.*

*Meet me this Saturday at seven-thirty. I'll text you the address.*

I tapped my phone against my thigh, my eyes narrowed in thought. I'd meet him, but clearly Master Z knew who I was. Even if he didn't know my real name—and I couldn't be certain he didn't—he had a good idea of what I looked like. I had a hard time believing he'd found me at the Sin and Sass party if he didn't know my real identity. I didn't like being at a disadvantage. It was past time to remedy that situation. I picked up my phone and texted my computer genius friend who'd helped me keep my secret a secret. As far as I knew, Mistress A was at master level encryption. I wasn't sure how Master Z had figured out as much information as he had, but I wanted to know if my friend had any ideas. And aside from that, I wanted him to track down some things for me, too. I wanted to know Master Z's identity.

# Sixteen

## Tips and Tits: The Word from Mistress A

### Sugar Tits

*You read that right. Nipples, penises, boobs, vaginas, balls, and even entire people if you'd like, can be made from cakes. Erotica bakeries used to be few and far between, catering only to specific needs like bachelor and bachelorette parties. Now the bakeries have gone mainstream, and you can get yourself a penis éclair or boob cupcake any old time you please. The real thing is only slightly better than delicious mounds of cake, and there's something naughty about licking a donut shaped penis. If you don't want to try a threesome but want to watch your partner lick a boob, or cock, or clit, nothing is sweeter than doing it with frosting. Like all bakeries, the quality of food depends on the business making them, so do your research first, but if you're in the mood for some sugar tits, or some sugar for your partner to lick off your tits, try an erotic bakery.*

"What color do you want?" I asked Kelly, the little girl with white-blond hair sitting across from me.

"Pink!" she yelled. "With sparkles!"

I laughed. "Pink with sparkles it is."

"Mine are lots of colors!" Maci said, wiggling her fingers. "Like the rainbow!"

"Rainbows are my favorite," Syd said, rummaging through the nail supplies for the stickers.

"I want a star on mine," Maci said. "On this finger." She pointed to her index finger.

"Okay." Syd grabbed some of the nail art pieces and prepped them for Maci's hands.

We'd been doing manicures at CARE all afternoon. Each girl had chosen different color combinations, and Maci and Kelly were our last two nail makeovers. Kelly was new to CARE. Her family had been staying here since her sister was in a car accident. Something about distracted driving. Her sister was expected to make a full recovery, but she'd be in physical therapy for several months.

Syd and I finished the girls' nails. "Wave your hands in the air or blow on them to help them dry," I cautioned as the girls ran off.

"Okay," their voices echoed in harmony as they went out the door and into the backyard.

I started picking up the fingernail polish and manicure tools. We made sure our mess was tidied up around the house before finishing our shifts at CARE, then walked to our cars together.

Syd looked around the parking area to make sure it was empty, and no little bat-ears were present. They'd been playing in the snow earlier, and now were all inside where it was warm. When we'd left, the girls were engrossed in a movie, and the boys were playing some video game. "Holy shit, B!" Syd hissed. "Watching you and Cade last night at the house was like watching fireworks up close!"

It was the first time we'd had any privacy to talk today and I was dying to give her the play-by-play. I leaned against my car and grinned. "I know, right?"

"What happened after we left?"

I gave her a whispered summary of Cade's seduction, including the ripping of my shirt. Syd gasped and practically started applauding.

"Also," she said, "you should know that if I didn't know you were Mistress A before, the dildos on the table would have given it away."

I gave her a glare. "I could have passed them off as research for my thesis. That's what I told Jax."

"Jax doesn't know you as well as I do. I'm not stupid."

"It's hard to hide when I live with you." Even though that was a descriptor I used loosely lately since she was rarely home.

She nodded. "And we're best friends. You can't really keep things from me, either."

"I tried to, but it's far easier to have a co-conspirator," I said with a wink.

Syd laughed and we gave each other a hug before we got in our cars. Syd left to meet Jax, and I went back home. I sang along with my favorite old Pearl Jam song and was belting out the chorus as I pulled into the driveway. I saw a familiar face sitting in one of our patio chairs on the back deck, probably freezing his balls off.

Usually I didn't see him this quickly after a "date." He must have been more excited about the previous night than I'd thought.

He held out a box as I walked up the stairs.

"What's this?" I asked, taking the box and unwrapping it. I pulled out a tank top almost identical to the one I'd been wearing the night before, and a few additional tanks as well.

"Don't worry, I bought you more than one. I plan to rip those off, too."

My mouth dried at the thought and I had to swallow before I looked up at him. "You're the most direct man I know."

He tilted his head in agreement. "I'm straight-forward, and go after what I want," Cade said. "I see no reason to waste time or mince words."

I gave him a considering look. "Yet, I still haven't seen you naked."

"That's not time wasted. That's seduction. All part of the plan."

"If you say so." I unlocked the door and Cade followed me inside. "Have you eaten yet?"

"Nope, but I ordered us pizza. Syd said you like it with lots of veggies on a thin crust."

I was surprised that he'd gone to the trouble to ask Syd about what I liked to eat, *and* ordered us dinner. Pizza wasn't exactly my first choice after the cookie monster fiasco, but I could eat a slice.

"I got salad, too."

I blinked, wrapping my head around the fact that he'd just read my mind. "Thanks for doing that. It was nice of you to think of getting us dinner."

"I should have checked to see if you had plans first, but Syd said you're usually home at night."

True. Night was when I worked on Mistress A. "I'm going to go change, but I'll be back in a minute."

"I could help," he offered.

"You could," I agreed, "but it would probably come with stipulations." Like a commitment, or something equally absurd.

He laughed. "You might like them."

If the stipulations involved more Japanese knot tying and tattered clothes, he was probably right.

I changed into some comfortable shorts and a zippered hoodie, and checked my makeup and hair. Everything looked fine. I was hoping tonight would be the night I really did get to see all of Cade.

I heard a knock on the door and saw Cade opening it as I came down the stairs. "Let me get you some cash," I said, going to my wallet.

He looked at me like I'd lost my mind. "No."

I arched a brow. "No?"

He nodded. "You're not paying. Not with me. Not ever."

I gave him a look back. "That's ridiculous."

"It's the way I was taught, and the way I'd want my

sister treated."

I wasn't in the mood to argue with him, but it was probably something we'd have to discuss again at some point because I liked paying my own way. I got some plates, cups, and silverware out of the kitchen cabinets and put them on the table, then sat across from Cade so I could see him better. "What's your sister like?" He'd mentioned her before, and they seemed close.

"She's funny, kind, and amazing. I love her."

My heart warmed at his protectiveness of her. "How old is she?"

"Nineteen."

Nineteen? And still living at home? That seemed odd, but maybe she was taking a break from school or something. "Do you see her often?"

"Not as much as I'd like."

I picked at my salad, wanting to ask him a question but unsure how. I decided to just go for it. "At the Sin and Sass party, you said you'd tell me more about your past sometime."

He nodded. "I will." He picked up a piece of pizza and took a bite. "But first, I want to talk more about you and your past."

That was random, and he was avoiding the topic of himself again. What was he hiding? "That's more than a twenty-minute conversation."

"I'm fine with that. I want to know what it is about having a relationship that scares you?"

I shook my head, and finished my bite of food before I answered, "They don't scare me, I just don't want one."

"That sounds like fear to me."

I shook my head. "Not fear. Experience."

He stopped with his slice of pizza halfway to his mouth, then put it down and looked straight at me. "Who hurt you, Brynn? You mentioned a little about it previously, but I want to know more."

It wasn't a topic I talked about frequently. In fact, only Syd knew the real story because Syd was one of the few people I trusted. But for some reason, I felt comfortable with Cade. I trusted him. He wanted insight into my past because he wanted to get to know me and be someone important in my life. He wasn't like the other men who had hurt me. I saw that now, and it made me less hesitant to open up. He'd put the time in so far, and it seemed like he planned to keep putting it in, even if I wasn't totally on board. But right now, I was, and I decided I wanted to share.

"High school was hard for me," I said.

"Hard like you didn't fit in?" Cade asked.

I shook my head. "No. It's not like I was unpopular. I had a lot of friends. I went out a lot. But guys weren't really interested in me…at least, not for dating."

Cade's eyes narrowed. "What were they interested in you for, Brynn?"

"Everything *but* dating. Everything but commitment."

"Why?"

I sat forward in my chair, my back rigid as I took a sip of my water. I didn't like talking about it, and I knew the reticence was coming through in my body language. "Because I didn't fit the mold. I was overweight. Pretty, funny, and popular with a great personality that everyone loved. Student Council president, and track team member, but overweight. My size mattered more to guys than all of the other things about me."

Cade was listening intently, in a way most guys don't. Most men tune women out, but Cade wanted to really hear what I had to say, and was interested in it all. It was another way he was breaking the mold of my previous experiences. "That would be frustrating."

"It was. I had a horribly low self-esteem and I was weak and easy to take advantage of." I took a deep breath, hating that I had to relive the memories to tell the story. Really, it wasn't just one memory. It was a culmination of mistreatment that had sent me over the edge, and turned me into the person I was today. It wasn't something I regretted, because I liked who I'd become, but remembering the process of getting there wasn't any less agonizing. "I had a crush on a guy and finally, after a year of trying to get him to notice me, he did. We'd been seeing each other for a while—a few months. And by seeing, I mean he'd take me somewhere super unclassy for our "dates" which were really just excuses to fool around. We'd end up in a dark park, in another town, at night, where no one would see us…or know us if they did happen upon the car."

A line formed between Cade's brows. "He didn't want anyone to see you together?"

"Exactly," I answered. "He always came up with some excuse for it. Like, he wanted to keep our connection a secret, or he wasn't sure he was ready for a relationship yet. All a load of bullshit. I knew it deep down, but didn't want to believe it. I liked him so much, and wanted to be with him more than I wanted to listen to the voice in my head that was trying to convince me to have some common sense. I was willing to do anything for him. Our first date was to a movie at a drive-in theater, in a town an hour away. He parked as far from the other cars as possible. We stayed in the car the entire time, and it was dark, obviously. We went to the drive-in a lot after that. He said he thought the movies were romantic because they reminded him of our first date. I now know it was because it was the perfect place to take someone he was ashamed of."

Cade's jaw tightened and I saw a vein in the side of his neck pulsing. It wasn't a story I liked telling, but Cade needed to understand where I was coming from. Why I'd done the things I had, how my past affected me and the future he seemed to want between us, and why I felt like it couldn't happen. "It was also the perfect place to fool around in semi-privacy. We started off the normal way. Exploring, touching. I was so self-conscious that I didn't want him to see me at all. But he always said I was beautiful, even though he encouraged me to keep my clothes on. Eventually it moved on to other things: blow jobs, and actual sex. He wasn't the first guy I'd fooled around with, but the others had treated me similarly—as someone they could use. I thought he was different, though. He was an excellent tutor for a high school kid, instructing me on what guys liked, but I always came away wanting. He couldn't care less about whether I got off. He only cared about himself. He never wanted to see me naked, and wasn't interested in having sex in normal places…like a bed. He made sure we were never in a place where we could be caught by people we knew."

Cade's lips were pursed and he looked like he was on the edge of violence. For someone who was normally so restrained, I was surprised he'd taken umbrage in my defense. "How long did this go on?" he ground out.

"About five months. Most of my senior year of high school. Like I said before, he wasn't the only guy I'd fooled around with. Guys don't care what you look like if your tongue is on their dick. But, he was the asshole I let take my virginity. He'd promised me a future to get what he wanted," I looked down at my hands, the memory more painful than I anticipated it being, "and then pulled it out from under me."

Cade's eyes were flashing with anger. "What did he do?" Something in my heart swelled to see Cade reacting this way, with as much fury as I'd felt at the time. I'd lumped all men into one category that day, and I shouldn't have. Cade didn't fit in that douchebag box, and there were a lot of great guys who didn't fit in there either.

"He asked me to the senior prom. I was overjoyed, and so excited. I'd never been to a dance with a guy who actually liked me, and no one knew we were dating. We were both still keeping it a secret, so the dance was supposed to be our announcement that we were a couple. I went shopping for the perfect dress with my friends, got my hair and makeup done, and waited for him to show up. He was supposed to pick me up at seven. He didn't. Seven passed, then seven-fifteen, seven-thirty…" I waved my hand in front of me, "you get the idea. He wasn't returning any of my calls or texts.

"Finally, at nine o'clock, I'd had enough. I decided I wasn't going to sit at home waiting for a man to make me happy. I didn't know what had kept him. Part of me was still convinced he was a good guy and something had happened that made it so he couldn't reach me. I had some girlfriends who didn't have dates, and they had decided to go to the dance as a group, so I went to the dance to meet up with them. When I got there, I saw my boyfriend. He was dancing with one of the prettiest and skinniest girls in school." I took a deep breath, seeing the whole scene play out again in my mind, feeling the pang of pain in my chest like it had just happened. "He asked her to be his girlfriend that night."

Cade's anger had been building progressively as my story went on, but now he looked ready to punch something. My heart felt like it was going to burst and my throat constricted. Having someone else support me like that, even when I was simply telling the story, meant the world to me.

My gaze drifted down as I picked at a string on my hoodie. It was easier to keep going if I wasn't looking at him. "I was devastated. I'd been so excited at the prospect of my first real relationship, and I'd stupidly told some people I thought were my friends about my secret boyfriend. Then I hadn't been able to produce one. The gossip was horrible, and the guy I'd been dating was one of the ringleaders of the tormenting, trying to draw attention away from himself. I should have called him out, but I had no proof we'd actually been together, and I wasn't as strong then as I am now."

I took a deep breath before telling the rest. "I ended up spiraling into depression, and there were times I didn't think I mattered enough to be alive. I didn't believe I was worth anything, and based on how I was being treated, it was clear other people thought I was as worthless as I did. I shouldn't have put so much stock into other people's opinions. I learned from that. At my lowest point, I realized I had a choice: I could take the bottle of pills I was holding and end the pain, or I could push through it, and *become*. I had a moment of clarity where I realized I was letting the person I didn't believe I was hold me back and control my destiny. That made me angry, and the anger helped me welcome the pain and what it would take to push through it. I decided I was going to figure out who I wanted to be, become that person, and live life unapologetically."

I shrugged my shoulders. "It's not like the relationship and my past with guys was something horrible, or seriously traumatic, thank God. I wasn't raped, or abused by a boyfriend, or anything like that. I have friends who did go through those things, so it feels wrong even talking about this like it had a serious effect on me. But it did. We all have a past that influences who we are today, and that's a huge part of mine. You needed to know about it."

He shook his head repeatedly. "It *was* traumatic, Brynn. It altered you, and how you thought about the world, men, and relationships. It changed your direction, and made you actually question your life. For that reason alone, I want to hunt this guy down and beat the shit out of him. Don't you dare try and diminish your emotions, or how you reacted to being treated like you weren't wanted and didn't matter. That asshole, and any man who has ever treated you poorly, deserves to be put through hell."

I shrugged, still feeling bad about feeling bad, but I was glad he listened and understood that it had affected me. "It was the impetus for my personal revolution," I continued. "Over the next six months, I lost eighty pounds, changed my hair, took professional makeup courses, and moved away to go to college. Suddenly, every man I ran into wanted to date me. In public. In the daylight. They were proud to have me on their arm, and wanted to show me off. It infuriated me. I changed because I wanted to, not because I wanted a man to want me. For a long time, I wished I hadn't lost the weight because then I'd at least know that if I ever found the right guy, he would want me for me, not what I looked like.

"I hadn't changed a damn thing about myself except my clothes size. But now I was visually desirable, and that's all the guys who wanted to date me seemed to care about. I already had a healthy distrust for men because of how I'd been treated before, but the change in attitude toward me simply because I altered my physical appearance solidified my opinion that I should never trust another man. If I couldn't trust them, I certainly couldn't have long-term romantic relationships with them. But I wasn't going to deny myself sex. I liked that. A lot. However, from that point on, I was going to be the one doing the choosing. I would be in control through the whole process, and that way, I'd never be hurt again."

Cade reached across the table, took my hand, and looked into my eyes. "I'm sorry they did that to you, Brynn."

I looked away, a lump forming in my throat as tears pricked my eyes. I was deeply touched by his support, but uncomfortable with showing my emotions in front of him. It made me feel even more vulnerable when I was already emotionally naked.

"Look at me," he said.

I raised my eyes slowly, meeting his as tears threatened.

"I wouldn't have cared about your weight."

I shook my head slightly. I'd been with a lot of men; they all cared. Maybe he'd changed as he got older, but I felt confident that if he'd known me in high school, he wouldn't have given me a second glance. The hot guy didn't date the overweight girl. It just didn't happen. "That's because you only see me now. You wouldn't have even noticed me then."

"How do you know?"

"Because I know your type."

He held my stare. "And what, exactly, do you think that is?"

I lifted a shoulder, trying to convey that I didn't care, even though it was exactly opposite of how I really felt. "Man."

The remark was cutting, but it was true and had been my experience for my entire life. I was nothing if not honest.

He shook his head as he leaned in closer. His shoulders were back, the movements strong and confident. "Don't lump me in with your past experiences. You'll only be disappointed. And you'll miss out on the best experience you could ever have."

I pressed my lips together, my heart pounding even harder. "I'm fine on my own."

"You're letting a number on a clothing tag regulate your self-worth."

My expression turned to outrage. "No, I'm not!"

Cade's expression changed to disappointment. "You're not a bullshitter, B. Don't bullshit yourself."

My mouth fell open, shock evident on my face. "What the hell are you talking about?"

"You say you're not letting your weight dictate your confidence, but that's exactly what you're doing. If you gained fifty pounds, you wouldn't go after men like you do now. You wouldn't believe in yourself enough to do it. You were the same person five years ago that you are now. How you look shouldn't determine that. Don't let bitterness rob you of what you could have."

I stared at him, completely stunned. I'd never looked at it that way before. I'd let my appearance determine my actions when I was younger, and I was still allowing it to happen, just in a different way. Cade pointing it out pissed me the hell off.

Instead of focusing on everything he'd said, because I knew he was right, I chose the one thing in his monologue I could attack. "Of course I'm bitter. I'm bitter about every dance I wasn't asked to, every flower I wasn't given, every longing look I didn't receive. I'm bitter that instead of love, I got pity. Pity, and a bunch of guys with assholitis who used emotion and my low self-esteem to get what they wanted from me. I'm furious with the people who told me I'd have a date every night if I only lost fifty pounds. Like my worth should be dependent on an arbitrary number on a scale. And to every one of those shit-eating douchebags, I lost *more* than fifty pounds. I'm everything they all wanted, and now I'm the one calling the shots. I'll never trust a man again. Relationships are bullshit. They're for women who don't care about being walked on. I've driven that road—lived on it. And I won't do it again."

Cade watched me for a few minutes, his face hard as granite. Then he stood, and walked out of the house, the door slamming shut behind him.

## *Tips and Tits: The Word from Mistress A*

### Kink for Newbies

*Maybe you like to be tied up? Maybe you like to be spanked? This is a discrimination-free zone, and no one's going to give you judgy eyes for your preferences. We all have kinks. Things that turn us on and make us fantasize about what we'd like to experiment with sexually. A lot of people are uneasy about exploring those fantasies with their partners. I'm going to implore you right now to finish reading this post, then put your phone down, turn off the TV, get comfortable with your partner, and have a frank discussion about what turns you on. Make sure you're alone and have plenty of time, because this chat is likely going to end with you both naked. Things are often labeled "kinky" if they fall into the realm of BDSM. That's fine, but kink is really about anything that's considered out of the "norm." Norm is anything beyond missionary position… so we're all a little weird. Own that shit, and do what makes you feel good! If you want to try a whip, go for it! Maybe you've always wanted to have sex outside. Find a place and make that fantasy happen! You don't have to feel bad about things that turn you on. Our sexual appetites can come from many places, including our pasts, or it might just be something you've always wanted to try. Don't feel bad about that. Talk to your partner, experiment, have a good time, and own your kinks!*

It was the night of the big date with Master Z. I was hesitant about going out with him, and still not sure I trusted him. But he'd promised that we wouldn't see each other, so I chose to believe him. I was about to walk out the door to meet Master Z when I got a text from Cade.

*Do you have plans next Friday? I'd like to take you somewhere.*

After the way our last conversation ended, I wasn't sure I'd be seeing Cade again for a while. He seemed *really* pissed, and I hadn't heard from him since. But he was also relentless about the two of us dating, so I wasn't completely surprised.

I texted back.

*Next Friday is good.*

*Great. I'll pick you up at four o'clock.*

Four? That was early for a date that didn't involve a senior's menu, but it would work.

I got in my car and drove to the address Master Z had given me. He said he'd be there earlier than me, but not to worry, we absolutely wouldn't see each other. The address was a house, with a sign out front that said, *See* in fancy letters. The outside was well-lit, and the parking lot had several cars. I walked up the recently shoveled and salted path, and knocked. A man in a white dress shirt with a black napkin over his shoulder opened the door and invited me in. I told him I was meeting someone and he seemed to know exactly who that someone was. Several shelves stood next to the hostess stand. He asked me to remove my shoes—thank the goddesses I'd worn socks…Z should have told me about wardrobe requirements—and put them on one of the shelves. So far, this was the strangest date I'd ever been on. The host then blindfolded me, and asked me to place my hand on his arm.

Although hesitant, I did as he asked, and slowly followed him into a room taking small, tentative steps. I wondered what I was walking into. Was everyone blindfolded? Were they all staring at me and silently laughing? Maybe there was another sex party happening and everyone would be naked when I took the blindfold off? We moved straight down what seemed like a hallway or aisle, then turned right. My arm brushed something that felt like cloth, and I smelled a wonderful aroma coming from somewhere in the house.

The host stopped, and helped me into a chair, explaining where the table was, where the corners were, and telling me if I needed to get up for any reason, to let my server know. Then he told me where my dinner date was seated—straight across from me—and took off my blindfold. The room was completely dark. In fact, "dark" didn't even cover it. It was pitch black. It was so void of light that my eyes weren't adjusting at all. I couldn't even make out shapes.

"It will take a minute for your eyes to adjust."

The voice was low and sounded familiar…probably from us talking a little bit at the Sin and Sass party when he'd been explaining the various sex acts and positions.

"Can you see anything?" I asked.

"Not really," he said. "They keep it this dark for a reason. Even after your eyes adjust, you're still essentially blind."

"Why am I not wearing shoes?"

"When you lose one of your senses, using your other senses—like touch—is important. You take your shoes off to give you more information about the texture you're walking on. It's easier to know if you're stepping into water if your feet are bare."

I nodded, thinking he had a point. "Are we going to be stepping into water?"

I couldn't see him, but I could hear the lightness in his voice as he answered, "Not yet."

We ordered our drinks, and were told the menu. I picked chicken and steamed vegetables for the main entrée. Master Z picked steak. I should have guessed he'd be a slab of protein eater.

The server left, leaving us in total silence. It would have been an uncomfortable position in the light, but even more isolating in darkness. I decided small talk was better than nothing, and as far as dates went, this was one of the most unique ones I'd ever been on. "I have to say, this is a pretty incredible first date."

"I'm glad you like it," he said. "I once went to an event raising awareness for blindness. The dinner was completely held in the dark. The servers were all blind as well. It was an enlightening experience."

"I bet," I said, considering that. A life without sight was one I couldn't begin to comprehend. Not being able to do things we take for granted: like watching a beautiful sunset, going mountain biking, or even looking deep into someone's eyes…it would be difficult to get used to. "I can't imagine not being able to see."

I heard a shift of a chair and realized he, or someone else in the room must have moved. It was amazing how quickly I'd started relying on my other senses.

"It would definitely be difficult," he said. "Babies born blind have to go through a completely different learning process than those who aren't."

"Really?" I asked, sincerely interested. "I've never thought of that before."

"When a child learns, a lot of the process is visual. If the child is blind, they're literally in the dark, and have no idea how to navigate this new place, or what the terrain is. Even walking is hard. They have to go through physical therapy to learn to put their feet out flat. They don't understand what they're stepping on, so they constantly curl their toes and feet up. They can hear, but without a visual reference to figure out where the noise is coming from, they can't pinpoint location. Hand-eye coordination doesn't work, so they have to learn to coordinate by hand-ear, and that takes longer. Until they do that, they typically won't move around to explore the area they're in. As they get older, even speaking is a challenge because they can't see lips to mimic others, and learn how to form words."

I was captivated by his explanations. "That's fascinating! I had no idea."

"I'm your go-to source for strange trivia."

"It's not strange, it's really interesting. Where did you learn all of that?"

"I read a lot."

I heard a creaking across the floorboards, which had felt solid under my feet on the way in. I assumed the floors were wood. The servers put our drinks down and moved our hands to show us the location of the glasses before stepping away again.

"So, A," Master Z said, "should I call you A?"

"Sure, why not, Z."

I swore I could feel his smile from across the table.

"Are you wearing the red lipstick?"

My lips curved up as I lifted my drink to my mouth, trying not to spill it all over me. Before the night was through, I was going to end up wearing my whole dinner. I didn't even want to see myself when we walked out of here. "I am."

"It looked good on you at the party."

"Thank you."

Two servers came to the table and placed our salads in front of us. They explained where the bowls were, and used our hands to show us the location. Then they placed our hands on the silverware, indicating where our knives and forks were. I lifted my fork, gingerly stabbing at my lettuce, hoping I'd get something on the tines. I brought it to my lips, completely miscalculating the location of my mouth, and then started laughing.

"Miss your mouth?" Z asked, his tone amused.

"So hard."

He started to laugh too, a deep, throaty sound that seemed vaguely familiar, as I cleaned up the mess on my face—at least, I hoped I had.

"I thought it would be a good way to get to know each other," he said. "Heighten the senses."

As if my senses needed any more heightening. They were primed, and ready for release. They just didn't know which guy they wanted giving the release to them.

"What did you think of the back room at the Sin and Sass party?"

I had a lot of thoughts about it, none of which I wanted to be reminded of unless Master Z had plans for getting naked in the dark as well. "It was a learning experience," I said, images from the night flashing through my head even now. "What did you think?"

"I enjoyed it…until my partner left."

I shrugged, even though he couldn't see me. "Sorry about that." My tone was apologetic. "I didn't know it was you, and I had some things I needed to figure out. Being there wasn't helping."

I took another bite of food, this one more successful. "How did you know it was me?"

"I wasn't sure, but your lipstick was a hint. You've mentioned it on your blog a few times."

That didn't seem like a legit explanation. There were a

lot of girls wearing red lipstick. I mean, none of their lips sparkled like mine, but still. "Almost everyone there was wearing red or pink lipstick. It was a Valentine's Day party."

"I took a chance."

I wasn't buying it. My lipstick couldn't have been his only hint. I worried my hands in my lap. I had a niggling feeling Master Z knew who I really was, and I wished I could figure out how. "Kind of a big risk to take. I could have been someone else entirely, and then you could have been punched. You almost were anyway."

He laughed again, a rich, full tone, and again, I got the feeling I'd heard it before. "No risk, no reward."

I recognized the line. He'd said it before. So had Cade. I sat there in the dark analyzing my competitor. It didn't escape my notice that the conversation I was now having with Master Z was incredibly similar to the one I'd had with Cade. I narrowed my eyes, wondering if maybe the two of them knew each other. I'd considered that Cade might be Master Z on more than one occasion, but the Sin and Sass party had cemented them as two separate people in my mind. I'd left Z at the party only to walk outside and run straight into Cade, who looked nothing like Z had, and was wearing completely different clothes than Z had been when I'd escaped the sex room. Maybe there was another connection between them though.

The servers brought out our entrées next, going through the same routine, showing us where the food was located on the plate. One of these times, I'd get the food to actually make it into my mouth without any collateral damage. "I do not excel at this." I wiped my face for the fiftieth time. "I'm going to have to practice eating with a blindfold at home."

"I'd be happy to help."

I smiled, wishing I could see his face. I liked him, and liked flirting with him in person even more than over text. "I might be willing to let you."

"I could lay you across this table right now and give you the best orgasm of your life."

I almost choked on the water I'd been attempting to drink. Luckily I hadn't gotten much in my mouth before he decided to put orgasms on the menu.

"The other people eating might not enjoy that."

"Not my problem."

I gave a soft laugh. "I guess we could use the excuse that we're doing research."

"Or tell them the truth: that I've been thinking about fucking you for months."

I almost choked again. "Jesus, Z! You have to warn me before you say stuff like that."

He laughed and changed the subject, "What do you like most about your job?"

I thought about it before answering, "It's fun; I like that aspect. And I love sex, so it doesn't feel like a job. I get to do something I'm passionate about. I enjoy talking about sex and giving advice, but most of all, I like that it's helping people. Those are my favorite emails to get; the ones where people say they've learned something, or that because of something I posted, they sought help from a doctor or therapist for an issue they were having. Helping people is rewarding."

"I like that too," he said. "Helping people."

We were silent for a few minutes as we ate, then I said, "As much as I hated you for copying me at first, I do think it's smart for people to have a male perspective. I can talk for days about what women want; but I can only guess, or use my own knowledge base, to figure out what men need."

"I'm glad," he said. "After your first blog post addressing me, I didn't think we'd ever be able to have a dialogue."

I snorted a laugh. "Oh, getting me to respond will *never* be a problem."

I didn't mean it to sound sexual, but it did. He chuckled softly. "That's something I've never questioned. I'm certain you're a girl who knows exactly how to get off, and can instruct any guy who can't figure it out."

My traitor cheeks heated, and I was overwhelmingly glad for the darkness. "I am," I said, owning it. I knew what I liked and had no qualms with getting it. "But what I meant was that I have no problem speaking my mind, especially when I'm pissed. If you can't handle honesty, you shouldn't have any sort of relationship with me because I'm all about truth and calling people on bullshit."

He laughed. "I figured that out from your writing."

"And you still asked me on a date. Brave man."

"Like I said, no risk, no reward. And to tell you the truth, I have a thing for strong, outspoken women."

Again, an opinion he shared with Cade—and Collin, for that matter.

They brought out dessert—a chocolate cake with chocolate ganache frosting, drowning in a heavenly sauce. I took one bite to be nice since he'd ordered it, and then another because it was so damn delightful. Then I had two more just to spite Cade for saying I was letting my clothing size dictate my self-worth.

"Chocolate," he said, his tone playful. "We're increasing your dopamine levels as we speak."

I grinned at that. "I'm glad you've been reading my posts."

"Always. And I've been meaning to ask you a question."

Something started rubbing up against my leg. For a minute, I wondered if a stray cat had wandered into the house, but then I realized it felt like a foot, covered in a sock, and it was moving up my leg…slowly. I ran my tongue over my lips and decided that I liked experiencing Master Z's naughty side in person.

"What turns you on?" he asked, his voice low.

I moved my other foot, rubbing his leg in return.

"A lot of things," I said, thinking about it and getting distracted by his touch. "Mystery, adventure, men willing to try new things. What turns you on, Z?"

He moved his foot a little higher, caressing my leg as he went. "Girls with glittery red lips."

I could feel the heat rising in my cheeks, and was again grateful for the lack of light.

"What," he said, his foot now between my legs, "do you think the chances are of me getting to see you naked? In person? In the light?"

At the moment, with his foot doing lovely things between my thighs, the chances were high. But I didn't want to get ahead of myself and agree to something I wasn't ready for. Naked, in person, was a guarantee he'd see me. All of me. And would know who I was.

"I think…" I said, moving my own foot between his thighs, "that it's becoming more of a possibility."

His toes wiggled and the seam of my jeans pressed in. "How much of a possibility…do you think? Percentage wise."

"Hmmm," I said, rubbing my foot over the bulge in his jeans. It was large. As large as I remembered it being at Sin and Sass and I was impressed all over again. My cocktail weenie streak seemed to be over. "I'd say at least fifty percent."

"What would I have to do to get that number higher?"

I bit my lip and answered, "Surprise me."

His chair scraped across the wood floor, and somehow, summoning superhero sight, he managed to make it over to my side of the table without knocking or tipping anything over. His hands cupped my face, his thumb stroking my cheek. His breath scorched me as he moved closer, and his lips pressed into mine in a passionate kiss, our tongues twisting as heat seared my body. I rose off the chair toward him, wanting more of him. My hands ran over a hard chest, down a stomach that rippled with muscle. He was strong, and I wanted to see him, touch him, without the barrier of clothes. I was totally on board with the orgasm on the table plan if he was. He pulled back, his breath hot on my neck and I could hear the smile in his voice as he answered my challenge, "I can do that."

The date with Master Z hadn't ended with sex. I still wasn't ready to reveal myself to anyone other than Syd. Master Z had taken it well, better than I would have. Better than I did, in fact. I felt like I had blue ovaries, instead of balls, for the rest of the night, and I'd had to spend a significant amount of time with one of my vibrators. It got the job done, but it still hadn't compared to the sexual fireworks I knew I would have gotten if I'd ended up in a bed—or on a table—with Z.

I'd replayed the night in my head several times, and had come to the conclusion that something was off. In the back of my mind, something about the kiss with Master Z seemed incredibly familiar. I'd paid attention to the feeling, and his technique. Between the kiss, and the voice I thought I'd recognized, Master Z *had* to be someone I knew. I was even more curious about it now, and couldn't wait for my genius IT friend to get back to me with his investigation results.

The rest of the week flew by. It was Friday morning, and almost time for my date with Cade. I hadn't seen him since last weekend, and he hadn't made much of an effort to get in touch with me. I thought it was strange, but I didn't understand his ways. If I'd been in charge, we would have had sex months ago, and this whole situation would be over and done with.

I had, however, heard from Master Z. Several times. My

lips curved up just thinking about it. The fact we still hadn't visually seen each other was kind of hot. It lent an air of mystery to the relationship that made it feel dangerous and exciting. I'd really enjoyed our date, and thought he'd done an excellent job planning it. Our messages throughout the week had been flirty, and we were going out again on Sunday. Maybe it made me a bad person for dating two different guys in the same weekend—both of which I wanted to screw. But I wasn't exclusive with either one of them, and I wasn't going to feel bad about that. My new mantra was "no guilt."

I'd just finished writing a Mistress A post and was about to shut down my laptop when an email popped up from my IT friend.

It was short. Two sentences to be exact. Two sentences that would be engraved on my brain for the rest of my life.

*Took some time to trace things, but I found Master Z.*

*His name is Cade Brett.*

## *Tips and Tits: The Word from Mistress A*

### Tassels and G-strings

*One weekend in Vegas—full of alcohol and poor decisions—I saw a male review show. The strippers were definitely* not *a part of those poor decisions, however, and I will always fondly remember the three minutes, thirty-seven seconds when I was tied up and manhandled by a rather large man pretending to be a vampire.*

**Pause**

*See, I even took a break from writing this post to think about it again.*

*I'm not going to name the particular show we saw, but there were bowties involved. And abs. Good lord, the abs. I don't think any man on stage (or the ones jumping off to dance with the audience) had more than three percent body fat. I wanted to feel bad for their lack of carb intake, but all I could do was stare and whisper thank you to their trainers. These guys did things with chairs, beds, and even motorcycles that should truly be included as Olympic sports. I'm fairly confident in my abundance of sexual knowledge, but I witnessed positions I didn't even know bodies were capable of contorting into. There are still songs I can't hear without my mind immediately being taken back to that stage and those buck naked, perfect asses, nothing but a flimsy piece of cotton or hat covering them. For women, the show is all about the story. The fantasy and the feeling the men on stage create, as well as the ability to lose yourself in a visual orgasm that promises nothing but pleasure later. Men are different. They're visual and could generally care less about whether there's a story, or if it makes sense, as long as someone's naked and they get to see some boobs (or ass, depending on their sexual preference). If you're not comfortable with a strip club (though I recommend trying it at least once if you and your partner are both willing), grab some tickets to a burlesque show instead. Burlesque shows are just as titillating—pun intended—with enough story for women to be engaged, and enough boobs and ass for men to enjoy themselves. Go if you're single, and definitely go if you're in a relationship. Trying new things is the key to building your bond, and staying happy long-term.*

My mouth fell open and didn't go back into normal resting position for a good ten minutes. The rest of the day, I wandered around with the email on repeat in my head. "I found Master Z. His name is Cade Brett."

Like every other man I knew, Cade's name had crossed my mind as a Master Z candidate, but I'd quickly pushed him down on the list. Number one, he was a law school student. He was busy. He didn't have time to be running a sex advice blog—which I knew first hand. That fact probably explained why his posts weren't as frequent as mine. Number two, he just didn't seem like the type. I knew another side of him now, but the buttoned-up counselor was the image I'd always have as a go-to in my mind.

But thinking back on it, there had been clues all along. The similar voices—though Master Z's was deeper, something I was sure Cade did on purpose—and they both had the same tall, muscular body type. I'd spent enough time ogling Cade that his body alone should have given him away. There was also the way Cade had responded to things Mistress A had posted. He always knew about my most recent posts and had opinions, and was well-versed in everything sex-related himself. I would have paid more attention, and probably figured it out on my own if it hadn't been for the Sin and Sass party. His hair had been black, his eye color was changed, and he'd been wearing a mask. When I left for the rest room, he must have ditched the wig, mask, contacts, and clothes, and switched to his alter ego, Counselor Cade. Tricky, tricky.

I'd told Master Z he needed to surprise me. He definitely had. Now the question was: what was I going to do about it? I'd been working on my poker face, but felt like it wasn't going to be helpful in this situation. When my emotions are strong, they're always etched across my expression. I'm the type of person who can't stand holding feelings in, and would rather get it all out in the open and deal with issues. I couldn't decide how to bring it up, though…a punch to the stomach as soon as I saw him? I was pissed he hadn't just told me, but then, I hadn't told him my secret either so I couldn't be too upset. I was almost positive that he knew Mistress A was me, however. I was annoyed he hadn't approached me about it, or come clean about his Alpha activities. We had plans today…he'd be picking me up soon. I sunk into the couch, staring blankly out the front window and blew out a long breath. I had about six hours to decide what to do.

Cade picked me up at exactly four o'clock. A late snow storm was forecast for tonight, and snow was starting to fall lightly, like cotton from the sky. I tried to hide my annoyance about Cade's secret keeping as I got in the car, buckled my seatbelt and settled in, but my expression must have come off as suspicious because he looked right at me and asked, "Is something wrong?"

Oh yes, many things. And they all started with his alter ego. "I'm fine. Where are we off to?"

He put his hand behind my head rest as he turned his head to back into the street. "A little drive."

"A drive? In a snowstorm?"

One corner of his lips kicked up. "My SUV has four-wheel drive, and I've been driving in the snow for years."

Neither of those things made me feel much better, but it wasn't because I questioned his ability to handle the roads, it was because I'd really rather not be stuck in an enclosed space with him right now. Six hours wasn't enough time for me to figure out how to merge Cade and Master Z in my head, and decide how to deal with them both. I needed to get my mind off of it. "How was your week?" I asked. "I haven't really heard from you." Which technically, was true, but I'd heard from Master Z repeatedly, with an abundance of flirty naughtiness and references to sex on tables in dark rooms. My personality and Mistress A's were fairly similar. I felt like our two identities fused well together. But Cade and Master Z seemed like they were on completely opposite ends of the spectrum. They were both alphas, which was a parallel, but Master Z seemed more uninhibited than Cade—or maybe he was just more vocal about it. Maybe he'd done that by design so it wouldn't tip me off, but it made me wonder who the real person was—Cade, or his guise?

"Good," he answered. "School was busy, but I'm excited it's Friday. How was your week?"

"Good," I echoed back. "Busy with school. Went on a date." Normally I wouldn't have mentioned something like that. I wasn't the type who liked jealous partners, and we weren't even in a relationship. But I wanted to see how he'd react to the news since he'd been my freaking date!

His eyebrow arched. "Did you?"

I ran my tongue over the inside of my cheek. "Uh huh. Super-hot guy. He *really* wanted to have sex. I could barely keep my hands off him."

Cade's lips started to quirk up, but he schooled his features immediately. "Some men don't know how to be seductive."

I narrowed my eyes. "Some men like to give a girl what she wants."

He gave me a sidelong glance. "Some girls don't know what that is."

I took offense to that. If there was one thing about me that had been consistent for the last five years, it's that I knew exactly who I was and what I wanted.

"Some men," I said, my gaze like a laser on him, "are actually two people." I was done with the charade and wanted answers.

He kept his eyes on the road and didn't respond.

I tried to keep my voice level, but really I wanted to scream. "At what point, do you think, you were going to tell me that you're actually Master Z?"

His expression didn't change, like he'd been expecting the question to come up at any moment. I was frustrated he'd waited for me to piece it all together, and that I'd had to bring in a third party when he could have asked me about it as soon as he realized Mistress A and I were the same person…which he had to have realized long ago since he'd been flirting with both me and Mistress A ever since. Cade wasn't the type to date more than one girl at a time.

"I'm not sure," he answered, totally calm and like he wasn't worried that he was sitting next to someone who was on verge of becoming stabby at any moment, "but it would have been soon."

"Mmmm," I said, an irritated note to my tone. "And how long have you known I'm Mistress A?"

He exhaled a long breath and bit his lip before glancing over at me. "I started to suspect it at Courtney's house warming party."

My mouth fell open and I couldn't form words for several seconds. "Courtney's *party*?" Including the party, he'd seen me a total of three times at that point, and had only had two actual conversations with me. "You didn't even know me then!"

He lifted a shoulder, unapologetic about his mystery solving talents. He should be a damn detective instead of a lawyer moonlighting as a sex advice blogger. I realized the blog had made me busy and self-involved, but damn. My observational skills needed some work. "Syd talked about you all the time. I hadn't met you, but I knew a lot about you based on what she'd said. Like the fact you dated a lot, you liked sex, and you weren't ashamed of it. I completely respected those things. Then at the party, Mistress A was brought up and your body language changed. You shrank back a bit like you didn't want to be noticed, and you were less outspoken in the rest of the conversation. I thought it was interesting, so I started noticing. Every time I was around and Mistress A was discussed, you did the same thing, folding in on yourself and becoming quieter. Then there was the news about you quitting your job, as well as the posts that seemed to mirror things I knew were happening in your own life. Not to mention the box of sex toys on the table. Some of those instances, like hiding what you were working on and being constantly aware of your word choices, were actions I identified with from being Master Z. But one of the biggest tip-offs was the fact that you brought up not wearing panties repeatedly—both as Brynn and Mistress A—and then included the no panty preference in your response post to Master Z. Still, I wasn't absolutely sure until we were at the Sin and Sass party."

Dammit, dammit, dammit! I thought I'd been so careful, but Cade had singled me out as easily as Syd. Maybe I wouldn't be able to keep this a secret like I thought I would. The realization put me in a foul mood. I folded my arms across my chest and glared out the window at the falling snow.

"You did a good job hiding it, B. I only knew because I'm good at observation."

"That really doesn't make me feel any better."

He glanced over at me, a smile playing at his lips. "Don't be upset. It's not like I told anyone. I knew how important your secrecy was to you. I still do. Your identity is safe with me…and I hope mine is safe with you."

I mumbled an agreement, and sat in silence, thinking about the situation I'd managed to get myself into and mad at myself for allowing it to happen. "If you suspected it was me that early on, what made you decide to start the Master Z blog?"

He took a deep breath. "Syd and I had talked about Mistress A when the blog first became popular. She made a comment that she wanted to know who the mystery blogger was. The more I read Mistress A's posts, the more I respected her—" he paused and glanced over at me, "—you. And I also wanted to know who she was. Mistress A was passionate, smart, and funny. I opened the blog right before I began to suspect it was you. I didn't start Master Z to combine forces with Mistress A, but I'd be lying if I said I didn't hope it would happen. Men and women have a completely different thought process about things. If you can get in each other's heads and try to understand where the other person is coming from, it can make or break a relationship. I thought having a male and female perspective on the same subject would be helpful."

I couldn't deny his points, and after my initial anger at Master Z's blog had died down, I'd thought similarly. There were always articles in women's magazines with men giving women advice, and articles with women giving men advice in men's magazines. At some point, collaborating wouldn't be a bad idea…I just needed to wrap my head around everything else first.

"I should be a lot madder at you than I am," I finally said.

"Frankly, I'm surprised you're not. I thought I'd need riot gear when you found out." I punched him in the shoulder for that and he grinned. "Why aren't you more mad?"

I lifted a shoulder. "I'm not sure. Maybe because we've already had the fight about you stealing my blog posts and ideas. We just did it as Mistress A and Master Z."

"But I kept the truth from you."

I raised a brow. "You're a brave man to remind me of that." I shook my head, thinking about it. "I kept the truth from you, too—though I didn't know you were Master Z. Still, I'd be a hypocrite if I got mad at you for protecting yourself when I've been doing the same thing."

We kept driving, me still staring out the front window, and noticing Cade look over at me periodically. We'd been riding in silence for so long that his voice startled me when he said, "One thing I can't figure out."

I gave him a look. "There are so many things you have no clue about, it's not even funny."

He tilted his head toward me in concession. "That's fair."

The silence filled the car once again until I said, "What can't you figure out?"

"Why the 'A' in Mistress A?"

I'd chosen the A after one of my favorite goddesses. "Aphrodite. Goddess of pleasure."

"And love."

"I cared more about the pleasure part."

He smiled and shook his head. "I knew there would be meaning to it; I just didn't know what it was."

"I initially chose Scarlet, but it was taken."

"Why Scarlet?"

The real reason was that my favorite Scarlet was ruthless, used men to get what she wanted, and was a force of nature. She embodied everything I wanted to be—or everything I'd thought I wanted before I met Cade. I amended the full reason and said, "It's based on my favorite Scarlet in literature. I like women who go after what they want, and aren't afraid to speak their mind, regardless of consequences."

He nodded. "That makes sense. It's one of the reasons I like you, too."

I looked over at him, seeing him through a different

lens now that I knew both of his sides. I liked what I saw, and wanted to learn more. "What about Master Z? What's the reasoning there?"

"Master because I'm an alpha and like being the dom in relationships. Z because it's the last letter of the alphabet. I like the finality of it, and that it's an uncommonly used letter."

"It's not uncommon in porn," I pointed out.

He grinned. "We should watch some of that. Together."

Heat immediately coiled between my legs at the thought of watching people have sex, and viewing it with the two personalities I'd been wanting to get naked with for months. "Now sex is on the table?"

He gave me a look. "You had that option at dinner the other night."

I rolled my eyes. "You wouldn't have followed through."

"You're wrong."

I blinked, totally taken off guard. "You've been dragging this out and not letting us have sex for months, but you would have been fine with a diddle in the dark on a restaurant table? What the hell, Cade?"

"Cade's been dragging it out to get you more invested and build a relationship. Master Z had no qualms. I was trying to get you to meet up with Master Z from the beginning. If you'd agreed to it earlier, we could have had sex a long time ago."

I just stared at him. I had no words. Until I did. "But I wouldn't have even known it was you!"

"Probably not at first."

I shot him a lethal glare. "Oh, I would have been so fucking pissed."

"You're pissed anyway. I was willing to take the risk."

I shook my head, running all this new information through my mind again. I felt like I was on information overload. "I still can't believe it was you all along! You were at the party as both Cade *and* Master Z! When you threw me over your shoulder and dragged me out of the party, you were wearing something completely different than Master Z had been!"

"I changed clothes."

"Master Z's hair was black!"

"You're not the only one who can put on a wig."

"Master Z's eyes were green!"

"Contacts."

"Master Z's voice was different."

"I disguised it."

I shook my head, thinking back to all of the times I should have figured out it was Cade, but didn't. "You, the buttoned-up lawyer who seemed almost as anal about following rules as Syd, weren't anywhere near the top of my list of guys who could be Master Z."

His brows shot up. "Who was?"

"I seriously considered Collin."

He laughed a lot. "I don't know him well, but I wouldn't have placed bets on people thinking it was him."

Suddenly a thought struck me. "Your tattoo!" I gasped, everything clicking into place in my head. I'd only seen it for a few seconds while his shirt was undone the day he'd ripped my tank top to shreds, but it was in the exact same place as the shadow-faced guy in the photos on Master Z's site. "Oh my God! That's really you in the photos on the Master Z website!"

He shifted, leaning his leg against the door and shook his head. "I'm not that dumb. It's a model. I wouldn't have risked using my own pics on the site. Even cutting my face out, it still would have been too easy to identify me."

"But you have a tattoo in the same spot."

He winced, like he was remembering something unpleasant. "Kind of. It's a scar that I later had incorporated into a tattoo."

I looked down at his side, like I'd be able to decipher the tattoo/scar through his shirt. "That's a strange place for a scar."

He pressed his lips together, a vein near his temple starting to twitch. "I got it in a car accident when I was sixteen."

I caught my breath and had to exhale before saying, "You were okay though, obviously."

He grimaced again. "I was. But my passenger wasn't."

I inhaled a rattled breath, pieces of the Cade puzzle falling into place. That explained so much. His commitment to live life without fear, and his feelings about making the most out of life because it's short. Going through a trauma like that changes you, especially if you feel like you hurt someone else too. Guilt is an incredibly toxic emotion. "I'm so sorry, Cade. I can't imagine what that must have been like for you, but I'm sorry you had to go through it."

"It's okay. I've come to terms with it. I had a lot of counseling."

That made sense as well. He seemed to know a lot about therapists, and had analyzed me on his own. If he'd spent time in his own sessions, he'd have a better understanding of that than someone who had never participated in therapy.

The car slowed as we turned a corner, and then pulled into the driveway of a modest-sized rambler. The home was gray brick with black shutters and a large garage. It looked like it sat on at least an acre of land. "It's actually part of the reason we're here."

I pushed my brows together, confused. "Your accident is?"

He nodded, looking sightlessly off into the distance. "The person in the car with me was my sister."

# Nineteen

## Tips and Tits: The Word from Mistress A

### Sex with Strangers

*I've written about fantasies before, but have recently been introduced to the popularity of anonymous sex. There are entire websites and apps dedicated to people finding other people who want to meet up to get hot and dirty…and no, I'm not just talking about Tinder and Grinder. The entire point of these encounters is sex. Only sex. Nothing else. With a complete stranger. If names are used at all, they're usually fake. I've talked to a number of people who have tried this. Most say the appeal is that it makes the sex seem exciting and dangerous. The majority of participants never have sex with the same person more than once. Mistress A is a judgment free zone, but I do have concerns. Number one being that we're pro safe sex at Mistress A, and partakers in anonymous sex aren't likely to go over their sexual histories before humping-up. I also can't help wondering what happens if your anonymous sex partner suddenly becomes your restaurant server, neighbor, or boss? That's next-level awkward. I'll try almost anything once, but I might be careful about this one.*

"I was driving to get ice cream with my sister, Ivy, on a Friday afternoon. She was in the passenger seat. We were at a stoplight and the light turned green. I started to go through the intersection when another car came through going about fifty miles per hour. The car hit the passenger side." I gasped, immediately putting myself in Cade's place. If I'd been driving with a passenger and then been in a horrible accident, I would have never forgiven myself. The fact that it was his sister, who he cared for deeply, must make that guilt even worse. I would have felt responsible for the rest of my life. I reached over, placing my hand on his leg, a tiny gesture of support as he continued, "The car was unrecognizable. It looked like a pile of metal. Ivy was covered in blood, glass, and shards of metal. I reached over for her, trying to make sure she was okay. I kept yelling at her to wake up, but she was unresponsive. They said I was going into shock. I don't remember much except me yelling and crying. I truly thought I'd killed her. They kept telling me they had to take me to the hospital and I was screaming for them to let me stay. I felt like it was all my fault, and I needed to stay there to help her—like being there would be able to ensure she came back to life."

I squeezed his leg, my heart breaking for the teenager who had gone through something so traumatic. "You didn't do anything wrong, Cade. Your light was green. The other car hit you."

He took a few deep breaths as he stared out the window. I felt like he was watching the scene replay in his mind, and hoping he could change the outcome. "I know. And that's easy to see now, but at the time, I just felt helpless. I had a broken arm, two broken ribs, and some of the metal had punctured my side, causing internal bleeding. They took me into surgery and I had no idea if my sister would be alive when I came out."

I felt awful for Cade, and what he'd gone through. It would be hard at any age, but especially at sixteen. The fact he was still driving a car and didn't have PTSD was a miracle. I reached over to give him a hug and try to comfort him. Reliving such a difficult moment was not easy.

He hugged me back in a way that made me feel like I was holding him up, steadying him. "She lived," he said. "Barely. It took the emergency responders over ninety minutes to cut her out of the car. She had internal bleeding they almost weren't able to stop, a broken leg, broken arm, and three broken ribs." His voice caught before he said, "And she was paralyzed from the waist down."

"Oh my God," I breathed, shaking my head and hugging him tighter. My heart already felt broken for him, but it kept fracturing more with each new detail. "I can't even imagine what that was like for you to go through, but I'm so sorry, Cade. It wasn't your fault. But I'm sorry."

He took a ragged breath. "I kept thinking, what if. What

if I'd taken a different route, what if we'd left five minutes later, or five minutes earlier? What if we hadn't even gone?" His head dropped to his chest. "Her life would be completely different."

I shook my head fervently. "You can't think like that. The 'what if' questions will eat at your spirit and sanity until neither exists anymore. There's nothing you can do about what happened, Cade. One of my favorite quotes is, "Don't look behind you; you're not going that way." "

He tilted his head to the side in agreement. "I know that now, but like I said, it took a lot of therapy for me to get to a place where I wasn't blaming myself every time I saw Ivy. She never held me responsible, and took the change in stride. I envy people who can do that—see a new circumstance as a challenge they want to face head-on and overcome. It takes me time before I can adjust."

"But you did," I rationalized. "You faced the trauma of what happened and figured out how to move forward. It's courageous and commendable. You used your fear to overcome the things that were haunting you, and help make you into the person you are now. You should be proud of that."

He looked over at me, emotion flashing through his eyes, and I felt a connection like I'd never felt with another human. We were sharing a real, intimate moment that had nothing to do with sex, but made me feel more vulnerable than I ever had. "We were hit by a mom of two girls: Grace, a five-year old, and Quinn, a three-year old. The kids were in the backseat. Their mom was texting."

My sharp intake of breath punctuated his statement.

Loss is always difficult, but the loss of someone so young from something that could have been easily prevented felt even more tragic.

"Her kids were fine, saved by their airbags and car seats, but she died from the impact. Grace and Quinn were left without a mom, all because she wouldn't put her phone down and watch the road. A stupid text, and driving distracted took her life, and completely changed my sister's."

I felt tears prick my eyes for Cade, for Ivy, for the two little girls who were left to grow up without the most important woman in their life. "Oh my God, Cade. I'm sorry. I'm sorry this happened to you, I'm sorry it was senseless. I feel horrible for your sister, for the woman's family, and especially for you, for carrying the guilt."

He looked over at me, his features seeming lighter, like telling me had lifted a weight. "Thank you," he said, squeezing my hand. "I'm okay now. It's something I'll always deal with, but I've been able to move forward, and part of that is because of what an incredible person Ivy is." He unbuckled his seatbelt. "I want you to meet her. That's why we're here."

The snow was falling more heavily now as Cade opened the car door and took my hand, leading me inside his family's house. Christmas lights still hung from the eaves, camouflaged by snow.

Cade didn't bother to knock; his family must have been expecting him. I noticed the neutral ocean-like grey, blue, and cream tones as we walked into the kitchen. I approved of the wall color choices, and white kitchen cabinets with a large grey and white marble slab island; I was certain the *Property Brothers* would approve also. A woman with honey blond hair and soft lines around her eyes and mouth, indicating she'd lived a happy life, sat at the table working on her computer. "Hi Mom," Cade said, walking over and giving her a kiss on the cheek.

Her smile lit up the room. "Hi, sweetie. Nice to see you." Her gaze turned to me. "This must be Brynn." She looked at me, warmth radiating from her. "She's as beautiful as you said she was." She got up and came over, giving me a welcoming hug. I glanced at Cade over my shoulder, eyes wide. I was shocked she knew my name and he'd told her about me. "I'm Sue. It's nice to finally meet you."

I smiled back at her, trying not to be awkward. I'd never really done the meet the parents thing before…in fact, I'd actively avoided it. "It's nice to meet you too, Sue."

"Is Ivy in her room?" Cade asked, looking toward the hallway.

Sue nodded. "She's waiting for you. I know you need to get back before the weather gets worse, and don't have a lot of time, so go spend as much of it with her as you can."

I followed Cade down the hall to a door. He knocked and I heard a high-pitched shriek of happiness, and then a lyrical voice answer, "Get in here, Cade!"

We walked into the room and Ivy was sitting in the coolest wheelchair I'd ever seen. Hundreds of ribbons were threaded through the spokes, and her chair was covered in art work.

"Your chair is incredible!" I said, looking at the colors and designs more closely. It looked like a collage of things. Faces, flowers—I recognized hydrangeas and lilies, music notes, the Eiffel Tower and the London Bridge…the list went on. I assumed the items she'd chosen were chosen for a reason, and I wondered what they were.

Her lips tilted up. "Thanks! It took me a few months to come up with the design and then draw them on." She said it without a hint of boasting, just stating fact.

"*You* drew these?" I asked, stunned. The work was detailed, the bright, pop-art colors blended impeccably, and it looked like it had been professionally done.

"Ivy's an excellent artist," Cade said. "She's the one who designed my tattoo."

I looked at her with even more awe. "That's amazing! I love Cade's tattoo!" What I'd seen of it, at least.

She grinned. "So you've seen him naked."

It was a statement, not a question, and my cheeks immediately flamed. Apparently being able to make me blush was something they both had in common.

Cade laughed at Ivy. "You're going to scare her off."

I switched back to our previous conversation. "Your artwork is amazing, Ivy. You're really talented! I love that you decorated your chair this way. How did you choose what to draw?"

She shrugged. "They're mostly my favorite things, or things that matter to me—like places I want to travel." She looked down, playing with the wheels, like she was used to them being an extension of herself. "The chair has a motor option, but I don't need it, and like pushing myself.

Keeps my arms buff, and makes me super-hot. One day I'll be rolling around Paris and London." She grinned, and her eyes sparkled with the movement. She had an incredible attitude, and an infectious smile.

"So…," Ivy said, eyeing Cade, "are you going to introduce me?"

His eyes softened and his lips went up, his love for his sister obvious even from where I stood. "Brynn, I'd like you to meet Ivy. Ivy, Brynn."

"I've heard a lot about you," I said.

"Me too," Ivy said. "Are you his freaking girlfriend, yet? Because he *really* wants you to be his girlfriend."

"I…uh," I stuttered, dumbly.

She paused, her eyes going over me before coming back to rest on my face. "I can't blame him. I like guys, but damn, I kind of want you to be my girlfriend, too."

Cade reached down and ruffled her hair. "Seriously, Ives, you're terrifying her. You're going to make her run out of here and start walking home in the snow."

Ivy pushed her lips out and narrowed her eyes like she was trying to be menacing. "I *am* pretty terrifying in my chair and all," she said with a hefty dose of sarcasm.

I laughed at her ability to joke about the situation, and immediately liked her sarcastic nature. I took some time to look around the room. One wall was all black, and had chalk drawings in every color on it. "Is that a chalkboard on your wall?" I asked, walking over to inspect it more.

"Yep," she said. "It's a paint that turns any wall into a chalkboard. It's my new favorite thing. Cade painted it for me."

My eyes found his and he looked down like he was embarrassed at the praise. "Cade's a good brother."

"An *excellent* brother," she said with emphasis.

My gaze trailed over the rest of the room: a bedspread in light blue with a gold, puckered headboard sat against one wall. A white chair with a matching square table next to it was placed by a large window overlooking Cade's backyard. My perusal stopped at her book shelf where I found myself looking at a photo of Cade, Ivy, and two little girls, one in Cade's arm and one on Ivy's lap.

"That's Grace," Cade said, pointing to the girl he was holding in the picture, "and that's Quinn."

"They were over here earlier this week," Ivy said, braiding some purple and blue ribbons that dangled from the arms of her chair. "Grace is on the middle school girls' basketball team, now."

My brows shot up. "You keep in contact with their family?" That was an extraordinary thing to do. Most people would have been furious about an accident like that. Cade's family had done the opposite. Forgiven them, and embraced them.

Cade's shoulder went up. "Too much time is wasted carrying grudges," he said. "Think of how much energy goes into that. There's no point. It's like you've said before, you can't change the past."

Ivy came over and took the photo off the shelf. "I lost the use of my legs," she said. "They lost their mom. Their loss seems much greater than mine."

My mouth gaped and I stared at them both, stunned. Their ability to move forward was almost unbelievable;

their ability to forgive and put others before themselves bordered on divine. "You're both incredible. Seriously."

To prove it further, they both brushed the compliment off like they didn't deserve some sort of humble, noble human award.

We spent the next few hours talking and laughing, Ivy telling me stories about Cade—many of them embarrassing, like the time he ripped his football pants right down the back during the middle of a game—and Cade returning the favor. They asked a lot of questions about me, and for one of the first times I could remember, I wasn't afraid to open up. Maybe it was my comfort with Cade, or maybe it was just because I really liked him and his family, I wasn't sure.

Sue came in with dinner, and we all sat around Ivy's room, eating and talking about everything going on in our lives. I couldn't remember the last time I'd enjoyed a family get together this much. I didn't get to see my own family much, and loved that Cade was still connected to his. I'd been so caught up in our time together that I didn't realize how much time had passed. We still had an hour drive to get home.

"You need to leave before the weather gets worse," Ivy said. "The roads are gonna be wetter and scarier than an airplane bathroom."

Cade gave her a look. "Meet Ivy, our resident meteorologist."

She glared and threw a pillow at him. "When have I ever been wrong?"

He held up his hands in defense. "It was a compliment,

I swear!"

We grabbed our things and said our goodbyes. Sue was lovely, and apologized for Cade's dad being out of town on a business trip. I told Ivy I'd come see her again soon. And I meant it. Regardless of what ended up happening with Cade, Ivy's positive attitude and feisty personality were things I absolutely wanted in my life.

Cade opened the car door for me and we started our drive home.

"Thanks for coming," he said. "I'm sorry we stayed so long."

"Don't be. I enjoyed it." And I truly had. I loved Cade's family, and Ivy was now one of my heroes. She had the best attitude and as our conversation had continued, before long, I realized I didn't even notice the chair. She was an extraordinary person who had been through an immense tragedy, but she hadn't let it define her. Instead, she'd used that to build herself into the person she wanted to be. I respected her a great deal.

"I have a confession." He bit the corner of his lip before glancing over at me. "I've never brought a girl home before."

I froze, totally shocked. "Not even your college girlfriend?"

Cade shook his head. "Ivy was part of the reason Cami and I broke up. Cami thought I spent too much time with Ivy, and couldn't wrap her head around the fact that I considered Ivy my responsibility. She didn't like the idea of Ivy becoming my dependent someday when my parents couldn't take care of her anymore."

I blew out a whoosh of a breath. "That's a lot to take on. But if she loved you, it shouldn't have mattered. Ivy should have been as important to her as she was to you."

Cade eyed me closely. "Those were my thoughts exactly."

"I really, really like her, Cade. I'm truly so impressed by her and what she's been through, and overcome. She's smart, funny, and seems pretty resourceful. Has she ever expressed interest in leaving home and going out on her own?"

Cade laughed at that. "Repeatedly. I think it's hard for my parents to deal with that thought. They want to protect her."

"She doesn't seem like she needs protecting."

He tilted his head in agreement. "She doesn't. I'm sure she'll push back against them soon and do her own thing."

I'd been watching the roads and weather as we drove, and noticed the snow had stopped wafting to the ground in light, soft flakes. It was now falling at a rapid rate, and the area illuminated by Cade's headlights looked like a wall of snow. White-outs were scary, and definitely not a time you wanted to be on the road. The temperature had dropped rapidly after twilight, the pavement slick and getting worse. The fog wasn't helping the situation. We drove in silence for the next few minutes, Cade concentrating on the road. I was about to ask if we should turn around and go back to Cade's parents' house when without warning, something was abruptly in front of us blocking the road, the snow and fog obscuring our vision. Cade hit his brakes hard so he wouldn't run into whatever it was, and we went sliding off into oblivion.

# Twenty

## *Tips and Tits: The Word from Mistress A*

### Omelets and Orgasms

*I don't know about you, but I loathe the alarm clock. Nothing is worse than waking up before your body is ready. What if, instead of a blaring alarm clock, you were woken up to the pleasant buzzing of a vibrator? A vagina virtuoso—I'm not gonna lie, I wish the genius was me—came up with the glorious idea that waking to an orgasm was far better than being jolted out of a sexy dream by some horrible song, DJ, or beeping that makes you wonder if it's time to get out of bed, or run for your life because surely, the only thing making such a horrible noise would signal the beginning of the zombie apocalypse. The orgasm alarm is a vibrator that you attach to your panties—yep, even I'd put on some undies for this magnificent toy. It has thirty freaking levels! Let that sink in for a second.*

*THIRTY!*

*You set the time you want to get off, and it goes off…starting slow, and building to a crescendo over five glorious minutes. Trust me when I tell you that it will wake you much more effectively than a cup of coffee. And this handy little vibrating egg timer is also great for foreplay. Set it to go off anytime, anywhere. Everyone will wonder why you're smiling so much! There isn't currently an option for men, but I'm told they're working on one right now, so sign up for the newsletter and check back! When it's in stock, it sells out fast, so get your orgasm alarm ASAP!*

We came to a stop in a flurry of snow. We hadn't hit anything, just slid—but it had felt like we were skidding down some kind of hill. My heart was a hammer against the inside of my chest, my lungs burning because I'd forgotten to breathe. I took a few deep inhales to invoke calm, and remind myself it was over and we were fine. Thank Thor for seatbelts and a safe car. I looked over to check on Cade. His face was pale and he seemed a little stunned. He shook himself out of it.

"Are you okay?" Cade asked immediately, his eyes assessing me from head to toe. He reached over, his hands on me like he was checking to make sure nothing was broken. He closed his eyes for a moment, his chest moving up and down with effort. Considering he'd been through a horrific car accident once already in his life, and had just relived what could have been another one, I was surprised he was holding it together. I wouldn't have been. His eyes came up to mine and he let out a rattled breath.

"I'm fine," I said, trying to reassure him. I was far more worried about *his* mental state than I was about my own. "It was just a little ice." I wasn't too shaken; things like this happened all the time during winter. I'd slid off the road a few times myself—but it was a completely different experience for Cade given what he'd been through with Ivy. "Are you okay?"

He nodded, pressing his lips into a line like he was convincing himself to push past the emotions he was feeling. He opened his door. "I need to see what we landed in."

We both got out to evaluate the damage. The SUV had slid into a ditch. The ditch didn't have water in it, just snow, so that was a bonus. The SUV wouldn't be washed away. And it was still sitting on all four tires. But the sides of the ditch were covered with slick, wet snow. Cade stood back, putting one hand up to his chin, then bent down gauging the depth of the ditch and the terrain. "I'm going to try and get it out with the low-wheel drive," he said as he stood. "Make sure you stand over on the other bank, far from me so if I slide again, I don't hit you." I nodded as he got back inside. He tried to give the SUV some gas, then a little more, but the tires bit at the snow, spitting it in every direction. They couldn't gain any ground in the deep, wet fluff, let alone get up over the bank. He got out of the car again, cupping his hands in front of his mouth and blowing on them to take away the chill. I had a coat, but my arms were wrapped around myself trying to preserve every ounce of heat.

"Do you have anything we can use for traction?" I

asked.

"Not on snow this deep."

He stepped back, looking at the snow, the ditch, and the embankment we'd have to climb to get back up onto the road. He turned back to me, a dismal look on his face. "There's no way we're getting out of here without help." He pulled out his phone and thumbed through his contacts. He hit send, and heard several beeps. "No service. Damn it."

Of course there was no service. Just like in every horror movie, they're miraculously in a no-phone zone. I didn't think those still existed. Apparently they do. In Colorado. During blizzards. I checked my phone, too. No service. It was either weather-related, or our phone companies needed to improve their reception. "This stretch of road is pretty deserted at night, especially in a storm. There aren't any houses around for miles." He shut off the engine. "I think our best bet is to wait until morning. We'll be able to be seen from the road by then, or we can at least get out and wave someone down for help as cars start to pass by."

I nodded and followed him to the SUV. He opened the back doors one at a time, and folded the back seats down. Then he pulled out a heat-retaining blanket that looked so much like a foil anti-alien hat that I questioned whether it was really capable of containing any heat at all.

He opened the back lift gate and unfolded another blanket—this one with some actual batting inside—and spread it out on the floor of the car. Then he put the foil blanket on top of that. "Climb in," he said, pulling the foil back.

"Climb in? What are you going to do, tuck me in?"

"I'm going to tuck us both in."

Cuddle time with Cade/Master Z? I certainly wasn't going to turn that opportunity down. I crawled under the blanket and Cade followed, pulling the lift gate down once he was inside. We both had our coats on, and the car was still fairly warm from the heat that had been running when we slid, but I knew it was only a matter of time before it cooled down. Staying warm was key. Cuddling and conserving body heat would help that.

"I have a winter emergency kit. It has water and some snacks, so we should be fine. We just have to keep warm until someone finds us." I turned, pressing my back to Cade's front, his arms wrapped around me protectively. He made me feel safe and calm, two emotions I wouldn't normally have under these circumstances—the difference was Cade. I realized I trusted him, and for the first time in my life, I was comfortable with having that feeling about a man.

I felt his breath on the back of my neck, warming other parts of me as well. I knew about survival basics. I also knew the best way to stay warm was to cuddle with someone while you were both naked. I grinned at that. I wasn't sure I could handle naked Cade. That would surely lead to other things—which might not be a bad idea since we were trying to keep the heat level high. Apparently Cade was thinking the same thing, because I felt something long and hard pressing against my ass. I blew out a breath. It was going to be a long night. I decided to try and get both of our minds on something other than each other's naughty bits. "Are you sure you're okay?" He'd been quiet since we cuddled up.

"Yeah," he said.

The one word answer followed by silence didn't convey reassurance. "That had to be scary," I said. "Considering what happened with Ivy and the accident."

I felt his chest press against me as I heard him take a deep breath, and then felt him release it. "The fear comes up every once in a while. Specifically in circumstances that remind me of the accident, like this."

"That's totally normal," I said, trying to soothe him. "Past trauma can be triggered by something similar happening in the present."

"That's what my therapist said when I was going through counseling after the accident, too."

I ran my hand over his in gentle circles, hoping the touch and movement would help him relax. "I'm glad you got help and talked through it. Too many people don't, and then the mental trauma can affect them for years to come."

"It wasn't really my choice. My parents were insistent."

I smiled and tilted my head back so he could see my face. "You have good parents. A lot of people don't believe in therapy—they're usually the ones who need it the most. I'm glad your parents supported helping you deal with a traumatic circumstance, and wanted the best for you. Was Ivy in therapy too?"

"Yeah," he said. "She handled the whole thing far better than I did, and she was the one who was hurt. The fact that she so readily accepted her fate and moved on made me feel even worse."

"That makes sense. You felt responsible. Guilt is like a disease. It's often easier to forgive others than it is to forgive ourselves."

He moved his arms, holding me tighter. "It took me a long time to do that. Sometimes I still don't think I have."

I wrapped my hands around his arms and squeezed him back. "That's okay. It's a process. Mental mind-fucks can screw you over worse than physical ones sometimes."

"I believe that."

We cuddled in silence for a while. I watched out the window as the snow continued to fall. The flakes were huge, and I had no doubt the car would be covered in several inches by morning. As I watched, I started thinking about Cade and his family. He'd said he'd never brought a girl home before. We weren't even in a real relationship…at least, not a defined one…yet. The fact I'd added that "yet" caveat gave me pause. Was I really ready for a relationship? After all of this time? I pressed my lips together, thinking that the reaction was something I was going to have to analyze.

Cade was certainly ready…that was no secret. He'd just had me meet his sister and mom. Family meetings were usually reserved for when two people became serious. His relationship with his last girlfriend had sounded pretty damn serious, and even though his ex had idiotic opinions about Ivy, it was still strange he'd never introduced her to them when he'd brought me over after less than six months. It made me feel special, but also curious.

"Why did you want me to meet your sister?" I asked.

He didn't answer for several minutes. I was questioning whether he actually would answer it when he said, "My sister is one of the most inspiring people I know. She's outgoing, and smart, and takes life by the horns. She doesn't let anything—even a disability—affect her self-esteem. She is who she is, and you take her or leave her. You remind me a lot of Ivy. You're both smart, strong, independent, incredible women. But, like you, my sister had to overcome something. Your struggles were different, but they were still physical, emotional, and damn difficult. Yet, you both faced those fears and ghosts with absolute courage, and you did it exceptionally. I wanted you to meet Ivy. To recognize yourself in her, and see that what you look like *really* doesn't matter, B. That even when you were mistreated, you were strong and intelligent, with a huge heart, and still are—regardless of what a scale or number on a tag says." He threaded his hands between mine. "I would have fallen for you in high school as much as I've fallen for you now—because I understand that the physical representation of a person isn't who they are. I want you to understand that, too. You're beautiful, every part of you, but the parts I love the most aren't the ones on the outside."

My heart constricted abruptly, and then felt as hot as the sun, and ready to burst. Everything I'd ever wanted a man to say to me, everything I'd ever wanted a man to make me feel, was summed up in those sentences Cade had spoken. For years I'd lived in fear of relationships and being hurt again. I thought every man only wanted a woman for what they looked like, and I'd be cheated on or dumped again if I didn't fit the physical mold. Even though I'd had no interest in relationships, I was subconsciously aware of what I thought men wanted, and kept attempting to meet their standards. I didn't let men affect me like that, or anyone treat me that way in any other aspect of my life. I gave zero fucks what people thought of me in every instance, but when it came to what I looked like, I couldn't *stop* caring. Why had I allowed others to have that kind of power over me? It was a disservice to myself, and I was done doing it.

I turned over in his arms so I could see his face and look into his eyes. "Thank you."

"For what?"

"For teaching me to push past my fear."

His eyes darkened and his hand came up to the side of my face, cupping my cheek. "Does that mean you're ready for more than just dating?"

I held his gaze. "I can't imagine being your girlfriend would ever be boring."

He sawed out a breath and placed his forehead against mine. "Thank fuck."

I grinned, reaching my own hands up to his cheeks.

He mirrored my expression. "You know, it's only a matter of time before we have to get naked to maximize body heat conservation."

"Mmmm," I said, dragging my bottom lip back with my teeth. "I was thinking about that earlier."

He leaned down, his mouth a hairsbreadth away from mine. "Then why are you still wearing clothes?"

He pressed his lips to mine, the kiss hard and wanting. I

returned it with just as much need.

He pulled back, his eyes searching. "Are you sure? Because I can't do this only once, and I won't share you. I want you, Brynn. Only you. If you want something different, I need to know now. In about five seconds, I won't be able to stop."

I held his gaze, every part of me, from my nipples to my core, burning with desire. "I don't want anyone but you, Cade. Only you."

His hands went over my coat, unbuttoning it, then made quick work of my sweater underneath. I pushed his coat off as well, then pulled his shirt over his head, throwing it to the side of the SUV. My bra was red, lacy, and kept nothing a secret. He ran a finger over the cups, my breasts pushed up and enlarged with need. He took my nipple in his mouth through my bra, and I moaned as I leaned my head back. He sucked and bit, the texture of the lace rubbing in a delicious way, then repeated the tongue tease on my other nipple. "As much as I like this," he said, reaching a hand behind my back and with the skill of an expert, undoing the clasps of my bra with one hand, on the first try, "I like what's underneath even more."

"Did you practice that one-handed clasp move?" I asked.

His lips slid up. "I'm a bra magician."

"You're not kidding. I can't even get it off that fast."

He pulled my bra off, throwing it to the side. Then sat back, looking at my breasts. I was a modest C-cup. Not too big, not too small. Enough to give me a decent amount of cleavage, and an enormous amount with a push-up bra.

"Your nipples look like the prettiest pink roses I've ever seen."

I blushed, thinking it was the first time I'd *ever* been compared to a delicate flower.

He leaned down and took my nipples in his mouth again, one at a time. It was a completely different sensation than I'd felt with the lace of the bra. His tongue was rough against the sensitive skin, and when I thought I couldn't take the sensation anymore, he started alternating between sucking and biting. I was already wet, if he kept this up, I was going to orgasm before he even got inside me. I pushed him back. His eyes were dark and he didn't look happy about the interruption. "I want to see you," I said.

He pushed off of me, holding my eyes as he undid his belt. Then so slowly it was painful, unzipped his pants, and started to slide them down. His stomach was flat and hard, and I wanted to trace the muscles with my tongue. I could see the bulge pushing against the side of his jeans, but it was still covered. "I see I'm not the only one who goes commando."

He gave me a wolf-smile and slowly moved his head back and forth, still not taking his eyes from me. "I sleep naked, too."

I met his gaze. "So do I."

He pulled his pants off the rest of the way. "We're not going to get much sleeping done when we have sleepovers then."

My gaze trailed down to the thick length jutting out

from his body. It was long, uncircumcised, and perfect in every way.

Holy.

Hell.

Cade was naked.

*Master Z* was naked.

Completely, totally, beautifully naked.

"No," I breathed out the word, unable to shift my gaze away from his muscled frame and hard cock, "we won't." He pulled a condom from the wallet in his jeans and rolled it on. Even the act of watching him touch himself to put on a condom was erotic.

"I'm doing that next time," I said, jealous he'd been touching what I yearned for. I pushed him down so he was horizontal, then got between his legs. I trailed my lips down his stomach, my hands splayed out firmly on his chest, holding him in place. As I got close to him, his cock jumped, pulsing with need. My mouth was half an inch away and with a smile, I passed by him, my breath the only contact with his length, and kept kissing down his thigh. He groaned, and I grinned between kisses. I licked my way back up, and repeated the same thing on the other side, my tongue leaving a trail of craving. I wanted him as much as he wanted me. On my way back up his thigh, I stopped above him, pulled my hair back so he'd have a clear view, and took one of his balls in my mouth, sucking. His hips popped up and when I took the other ball in my mouth as well, he let out a loud groan. I wrapped my fingers around the base of his cock, like a makeshift cock ring, licking and sucking his balls, then released them, moving my lips up. I took the head first—teasing it, light licks, like the tip was a lollipop. Up, down, and around, twisting my tongue. I relaxed the back of my throat so I could take him all. "Fuck, Brynn! You're going to make me come!" My lips stretched against him and I kept going. Licking and sucking, licking and sucking, changing the depth and hardness. I could feel his cock getting even harder, his balls tightening, and just when I thought he was going to blow, I stopped. He threw his head back in frustration. I gave him a wicked look, then went back—this time adding some teeth. He moaned again, his hands in my hair. I went down harder, taking him completely. "If you keep doing that, I'm going to come," he growled.

"That's the idea," I said, the next time I came up for air.

He shook his head. "No. The first time I come, I'm going to be inside you." He picked me up, depositing me to the side, then he reached over to my waist, unhooking the button on my pants.

The zipper came down and he pulled. In one swift movement, I was naked.

He looked at me, completely bare and open to him and inhaled a ragged breath. "You're everything, B. Not just beautiful, but everything."

He leaned down, his body over mine, his length pressed into my thigh as he kissed me deeply.

I pushed him off, my breath coming out in pants. He looked at me like I was insane. "What is it?" he asked, struggling to maintain control. "Please don't tell me you changed your mind."

I looked at him like he was insane. "Are you fucking

kidding? Of course not. I've been waiting for this for months! I just forgot to take my socks off."

He froze, his face more shocked than I'd ever seen a person look. "Seriously?" His tone was full of incredulity and his eyes looked like they were going to pop out of his head.

I shrugged, unapologetic. "I can't have sex with socks on."

He arched a brow. "I've read Mistress A and she seems to do it just fine in heels?"

"That's different."

"Why?"

I wasn't exactly sure. It just was. "I don't know. But I can't do it in socks."

He pressed his lips together and took a deep breath. "If I wasn't so turned on right now, I'd want to analyze that," Cade said, "but at this point, I don't give a fuck. Get your damn socks off. Here," he said, reaching down, "I'll help."

We made quick work of the socks, and Cade was on top of me immediately, his mouth on mine. He reached down, centering himself at my entrance, then pressed into me. I gasped as he sighed. "You're so wet." His thickness filled me in every way. I'd never been with someone who I had true feelings for, and who returned them. This wasn't lust, or infatuation. This was so much more. And for some reason, that made it better than I ever expected it could be. Or maybe Cade was just that good.

He pushed in and out, holding himself above me. I watched his muscles contract with the movement, his shoulders rolling forward and back.

"Looks like holding plank at the gym is working out for you."

"And hang cleans," he ground out.

He started to move faster, and I could tell it wouldn't last much longer. I shook my head. "What now?" he asked.

"It's my turn."

His expression turned sinful as he rolled me, switching positions so I was on top…a movement not easy to maneuver in an enclosed space, but we managed. He felt even bigger this way, and I clenched my muscles around him as I went up and down. I came almost immediately. He squeezed his eyes shut, almost pained trying to hold back his own release. After a couple of seconds he opened them, and I kept going. Up and down, circling my hips. He put his hands on my ass, controlling the movement. "You don't like it when someone else is in charge," I said, more statement than question.

"Neither do you."

I pressed my lips to his, kissing him hard. "We're going to have to work on that, Counselor."

He was getting close to release when I leaned down and said, "Next time, I'm riding you backwards."

He exploded and I followed, my walls closing around him like a vice. When we were done, I fell on top of him and eventually moved to the side, nestled into the nook of his arm where I closed my eyes and fell asleep.

I woke up after about twenty minutes. Cade had apparently checked his watch before I dozed off.

My head was on his chest and I was appreciating the work of art that was his body. His tattoo was visible, and while I hadn't had time to closely examine it earlier, or the previous times I'd seen his naked chest, I had ample time now. "Your tattoo," I said, tracing it lightly with my fingertips. It was a python, coiled and ready to strike, its teeth within biting distance of his scar. It was black and green, the coils standing out with various shades of fading. The eyes of the snake were bright purple. "Ivy drew this for you?"

He was lightly trailing his fingers up and down my back and it was one of the most relaxing things I'd ever felt. "Yeah."

"She did an incredible job."

"She's going to an art college and wants to do something art-related. Maybe even become a tattoo artist. It would be a good option for her."

"She'd be great at it." I traced the coils again with my nails. "Why the snake?"

He tilted his head to look down at my fingers on his skin and the scar, a visual representation of something that had almost taken his life. "I don't have a lot of fears, but one of them is snakes. It's a reminder not to ever let the fear overtake me. That I should use the fear as a motivator to move past and overcome something instead of letting it hold me frozen."

That made sense, and I liked that the tattoo had such a deeply personal meaning to him. It was something he'd really thought about, not something he got on a whim. "And the reason it's poised over the scar?"

He paused before answering. "Because for a long time, the accident did make me fear things. It took me time to get over that. To embrace my scar as a part of myself—as a learning experience. If I'd let my injuries go and not treated them, they would have killed me. But the injuries were taken care of, and I healed. Scarred, changed, but still here. Fear is the same way. You can let it rule your life. You can let all the potential negative possibilities be the driver for your decisions, or you can take charge of your choices and not let your demons lead you. My accident taught me that we all have to deal with pain and shitty situations. The only emotion that eclipses fear is love, and they both have a similar result. Fear has the power to build you, or break you. I'll look that snake in the eye every time, and choose to fight."

My heart surged with pride for this man and what he'd been through, and how much he'd worked to become the version of himself he wanted to be. "I love that about you," I said, and was immediately surprised by how much I meant it. I loved that Cade had such a strong sense of self. He knew exactly who he was, what he wanted, and didn't let anything sway him. I felt like we complimented each other perfectly. Aside from that, I realized that for the first time in years, I truly cared for a man. And this time, it was for a man who actually deserved me.

"Your plan worked," I said.

"Mmm," he answered. "What plan was that?"

"To make me fall for you by withholding sex."

He flashed a broad grin. "Oh, I know."

I lightly punched his arm. "You're cocky as fuck."

"I am."

I eyed him. "You sound like you enjoyed the process."

"Proving that I wanted you for far more than sex?" he asked. "Oh yeah. I enjoyed that a lot. But holding out as long as I did took Herculean effort. You have no idea how many times I've had to jack off since I met you."

I shook my head, not feeling the least bit bad for him. "All of those wasted orgasms."

"I was thinking about you for every one of them."

"You could have been inside of me for every one of them."

A rumble came from low in his chest. "Now I will be." He lifted my chin so he could look in my eyes. "There are too many things I love about you to even try to start naming them."

"Well," I said, "we do have all night, so you could if you wanted to."

"Hmmm," Cade said as he started to kiss down my neck. "How about if I do that *while* I do you."

I arched a brow. Most guys needed more of a turn-around time. "Are you ready for that, Counselor?"

He gave me a dark, promising look. "With you, I'll never not be ready."

I grinned, and orgasmed three more times before a knock on the window brought us back to reality. A police officer had seen our tracks and SUV. He was there waiting to help us get out of the ditch and back on the road.

Cade wasn't the least bit embarrassed by the steamed up

windows, and neither was I.

The officer looked to be in his forties, and tried to suppress a grin as he said, "I'd ask if you need a blanket, but it doesn't look like you had a problem staying warm."

"Nope," Cade said, a mischievous smile on his face, "sure didn't, Officer."

"I'll be out here when you're ready."

An hour, and one missing bra later, we were back on the road and on our way home.

## *Tips and Tits: The Word from Mistress A*

### Swim Wear

*There's a strange epidemic going around. It's been popular in various places, in various stages since the beginning of time, but it's currently impacting swim wear. It's called: "How little can you get away with wearing." Someone sent me a link to the newest beach must-have. A piece of cloth that somehow hugs man-bits. I've studied it repeatedly, and the only explanation I can come up with for how it's staying put is magic and demons. Maybe they're using double-sided tape, but considering most dudes don't shave that region, and whine like they've been mortally wounded when they have to pluck a hair from anywhere on their body, I'm going to guess double-sided tape is not an option. These suits are vacuum sealed to a dude's man bits, leaving NO question what you've got going on under there.*

*Here's the thing: I'm not one to judge. Love what you wear, wear what you love. If that's what makes you happy, do it! But if you choose to wear one of the wrap-around swimsuits that barely cover your kiwis and banana, be prepared for stares. You might as well be wearing nothing but a dick mitten.*

It had been almost two weeks since mine and Cade's slide in the snow, and our relationship declaration. When I'd told Syd that Cade and I were exclusive, she hadn't stopped shrieking for at least five minutes. She still occasionally squeaked when she saw us together. I was happy. Really happy. I felt a sense of fulfillment I hadn't realized I'd been missing.

My phone buzzed. A text from Syd.

*Did you see Master Z's post?*

I hadn't, but I'd go look at it now.

## Alpha Answers

*Summer is coming up, and if you need a good way to cool down, I have a sweet suggestion for you. While ice cream is great in a bowl, it's even better on a person. I'm not talking about a little can of whipped cream; you can have an entire human sundae if you and your partner are both up for making a delicious mess. There are hotels that cater to this particular act. You order your dessert tray from room-service, and get a variety of yummy treats, as well as a plastic bed sheet. If you decide to take advantage of the hotel sundae, be sure to leave a massive tip, because cleaning up after this activity can't be easy. If you're interested in trying it at home, get a plastic paint drop cloth, secure it to your mattress, and drizzle, lick, and come. It's a messy ordeal, but you won't regret the sweet treat, and you can burn off the calories as fast as you eat them.*

I smiled, and texted Syd back.

*Yes. And that sundae was just as amazing as we thought it would be.*

Cade and I had discussed it and had decided to tell Syd about Master Z. She knew I'd been communicating with them both, and that I'd had feelings for them both. She would have suspected something if I'd suddenly dropped Master Z and only cared about Cade. She'd been surprised at the news, but totally accepting, and promised never to tell another soul.

Another text came through, but this time, it wasn't from Syd.

*Are you naked?*

I grinned and texted back.

*I can be.*

*You WILL be.*

I couldn't stop smiling. I had no idea I could be this happy and wished I'd given in to Cade and his relationship rules so much faster. A knock sounded on the door and I opened it for him. Cade's eyes went over me, darkening like they did every time he saw me. I'd never felt so desired or wanted, and couldn't wait to get him naked.

"Get in here and get your clothes off," I said, shutting the door behind him and locking it to make sure no one came in while we were stripping.

"Oh, they're coming off," he said. "But not quite yet."

My eyes narrowed in suspicion. "Why not?"

He took my hand and pulled me toward the couch. "It's been two weeks."

"And I've had more orgasms than I even thought possible." I grinned, pulling on his shirt. "Let's keep going and see if we can break some kind of record."

"You're relentless."

"You love me."

His eyes held mine and a surge of emotion passed between us. "Yes, I do." He reached in his pocket and pulled out a square, grey box. "That's why I got you this."

I looked at the box, then him. "You got me a gift?"

He nodded. "Open it."

I'd told him I didn't care about gifts; that experiences mattered more to me, but I didn't want to make him feel bad. I opened it and saw a delicate silver necklace with a glittery star hanging sideways, trails of something sparkly behind it.

I gasped as I held the stunning piece of jewelry up. "A shooting star! Just like we saw on our first date!"

He nodded, looking at me expectantly. "Do you like it?"

I gave him a look. "Are you crazy? I love it! This is one of my new favorite things!"

I took it from the box and lifted my hair while he helped me put it on. "I know you said you don't like gifts, that you'd rather have experiences. But this is a gift that I hope will remind you of a good memory."

I met his eyes as my fingers gently traced the star at my neck. My lips lifted as my heart burst with love for this man—a love I hadn't realized I wanted, or needed, but now wasn't sure I could live without. "It does. It's beautiful, Cade. Thank you! I'll never take it off."

He blew out a breath, leaning back against the couch. "Good thing it's not socks then. I don't think I could stand waiting for you to take off your jewelry too."

I stuck my tongue out at him as I jumped on top of his lap, straddling him. "I'm going to make you pay for that, Counselor."

He grinned. "I'm looking forward to it."

"I can't believe you're taking a vacation together!" Syd said, her voice sing-songy between the yells of people in the crowd. We were at an MLS game. Syd had won tickets, and invited me and Courtney to go with her and have a girls' night at the game. Jax was home watching Paige, and hanging out with Cade.

"Why not?" I asked. "School's almost out for the summer. I can work from anywhere. There's no reason not to do it somewhere warm and sandy." And by "do it," I wasn't just talking about working.

Cade and I had taken some of our Mistress A and Master Z earnings and rented a secluded villa in Costa Rica for a month. We planned to spend the time hiking, and being as naked as possible.

"Because up until recently, you didn't even believe in relationships, let alone shared living space."

"I share a house with you."

She rolled her eyes. "Totally different, and you know it."

Courtney's gaze scanned the area; she'd been doing it all night—almost like she was anxious. I wondered what was up. "Are you okay, Court?"

Her eyes snapped to me. "Yeah," she said, a little too quickly. "Fine."

The game finished with our team winning 1-0. Syd's prize came with a "meet the team" experience after the game. We all started down the stairs. Courtney's face fell and she looked almost sick.

"I'm going to find a bathroom really fast. I'll meet you down there."

"I hope she's okay," I said to Syd.

Syd looked a little worried as well. "Me too."

I hated being sick, and hated it even more when I was sick in public instead of home, cuddled under a blanket watching Netflix. Maybe that's what the problem had been the whole time.

We met some of the players and had a few quick photos taken. Syd was talking to one of the staff members about CARE…probably trying to get the team involved somehow. Syd was good about making connections. I excused myself to go use the restroom, and check on Courtney. As I made my way through the stands and back up the stairs, I heard voices coming from one of the alcoves. I moved toward the sounds in case someone needed help. As I came around a corner, I saw Courtney. She seemed to be having a discussion with a guy. There was a large group of people standing about twenty-five feet behind them. He was wearing a number seven MLS jersey and at first, I thought it was a fan. Then I noticed his shorts, socks over shin guards, and neon green shoes. All of which matched the exact clothes of the players I'd just met.

Courtney knew one of the players on the team.

That was obvious. What wasn't clear was why she looked like she was barely holding herself together. I stayed back, not wanting to butt in if she didn't need help. She'd been acting nervous all night. Clearly, she'd gone to the bathroom to avoid a meeting with this guy and the other team members on the field. I was certain she didn't want anyone else to know about it. She started to walk away. The guy shook his head and I heard him say, "Not good enough, Court. You're great at running, always were. I've regretted you leaving since the day you walked out the door."

She pushed her shoulders back and blew out a long breath. "That's a speech you should have given me five years ago. Before you broke my heart." Then she turned and walked away.

He started off after her but stopped, like he was trying to decide his next move. The fans that had been standing back were now surrounding him, making the choice for him. I wasn't sure what I'd just witnessed, but I knew Courtney didn't want to talk about it. Her body language alone had communicated that she needed space. I decided to wait to talk to her.

We finished the meet and greet and found Courtney on the way out. We went back to the car, our stomachs rumbling for dinner. I'd borrowed Cade's SUV because it was roomy and comfortable. Syd hopped in the passenger seat, Court in the back. "Are you feeling okay, Court?" Syd asked.

Courtney still looked shaken up, but she hid it well. "Yeah, I'm fine."

"I went to check on you," I said.

I saw her eyes get larger in my rearview mirror.

"Are you sure you're okay?" I asked.

She exhaled meeting my gaze in the mirror. "I'm fine. Just a little indigestion."

"Indigestion" was what number seven's nickname was going to be from here on out.

"Are you sure you want to go to dinner?"

She nodded. "I haven't eaten all day, plus it's one of my fav—" she stopped mid-sentence, then pulled something out from between the seats and held it up. "I'm guessing this belongs to you, B."

Syd started to laugh. "It *is* her color."

I glanced back to see what she was holding. "My bra!" I yelled. "I've been looking for this for weeks!"

We all laughed and Court said, "Good thing you won't be needing that, or any other clothes in Costa Rica."

Syd narrowed her eyes. "If Jax and I visit, the no-pants zone will have to be revoked while we're there. I love you both, but I don't need to see you naked."

"You've seen me naked plenty of times," I pointed out.

"That's different," Syd said, her nose scrunched up. "We're friends."

"You're friends with Cade," I said.

She shuddered. "Not like that."

We all laughed and I agreed that we'd have emergency

pants for times when we were hosting visitors. I smiled, thinking about how content I was with my friends, my life, and my boyfriend. I'd opened myself up to something I thought I didn't want, and I'd never been happier. I couldn't wait for the summer, and the rest of our lives.

# Epilogue

## One Month Later

We were sitting on our deck, steps away from the beach and pristine aqua water, a warm and salty breeze blowing through the air. I'd just finished my blog post for the day, and was stretched out in our hammock, ocean waves rolling onto the sand twenty feet away.

Cade came over and handed me a glass of something icy and sweet. In the past I would have eschewed it for something with fewer carbs, or replaced it with water completely. Not now. I had a man who loved me for everything I was, and I was learning to let go of the ridiculous expectations I thought society had for me, and that I'd placed on myself. It felt good to make progress, and it was even better to do it with someone who cared so much by my side. I took a sip out of the festive straw and it was fantastic. "Mmm, what's this?" I asked.

He grinned. "Collin sent me the recipe for a panty dropper."

I laughed out loud. "Well, he was right, it's fantastic…but it's not like you have a problem getting me to drop my panties."

"You rarely wear them. And I like it that way."

He settled in next to me, now an expert at couple-hammock navigation since we'd been there for two weeks. "So," Cade said, taking a sip of his own panty dropper. "What do you think will happen to Mistress A in the future?"

I shrugged, settling into his nook—one of my favorite places. "I'm sure she'll continue giving great advice."

"Even if she's not spending most of her time looking for the biggest penis on the planet?"

I gave him a broad grin. "She's extremely happy with the one she already found." I took another sip of my drink. Cade was an excellent cabana boy. "What will happen to Master Z?"

He started running his fingers over my neck, down my chest, and back again, his strokes feather light. It drove me crazy and he knew it. "He'll be using his new experiences to write about love and relationships, and how much better sex is with them."

I put the drink on the ground and placed my hand on his chest, my fingers wet from the sweating glass I'd been holding. "From the perspective of our readers, sex is sex.

It's good if you have a good partner."

He bit his bottom lip, dragging it back with his teeth. "But it's so much better if the partner is someone you love."

I blushed, still not used to the words. "You know, you never told me your original itinerary for our first date."

His lips tipped up, his eyes sparkling with mischief. "Didn't I?"

I shook my head as his fingers moved lower on my breasts, playing with the tiny scarlet strings of my bikini top. "You said you changed it at the last minute—but I know it involved a blindfold."

"Mmmm," he agreed, "and handcuffs. I'd been thinking of using both of those on you since the day I saw you in the sex toy store."

I cocked a brow. "I assume a bed was involved?"

He lifted a shoulder. "For some of the time."

I gave him a playful slap on the arm. "Would you tell me already?!"

He pressed his lips to mine in a heady kiss. I felt my top coming untied, and then felt it drop to the side of the hammock in the sand as he lifted me on top of him. My legs pressed into his sides as he pushed his fingers into my hair, pulling my head down like I was his only source of oxygen. I could feel his length growing even harder under me. He slowly untied the strings on each side of my hips, the bottoms of my bikini falling away. He looked at me, fully naked on top of him, the azure water lapping the sand in the background, and inhaled a rattled breath. "I have a better idea," he said. "Why don't I show you?"

I smiled slowly against his lips. "I can't think of a better plan."

*The End*

# Acknowledgments

This was the hardest book I've ever written, and the past twenty-three months were the hardest of my life. Losing not only a best friend, but someone I relied on so completely to help me do my job was devastating. There were days I didn't think I could go on personally, and many days I didn't believe I could keep writing without Ashley. There were several people who convinced me I could, and that Ashley would figure out a way to come back and kick my ass if I didn't. I owe them a thousand hugs and my sanity: Jennifer Miller, Sophie Jordan, Cindy Koelbl, and Kelley Crandall.

I need to give a huge thanks to my amazing production team. Dan, who did my formatting this time around because he wanted to add another title to his husband superhero resume. Robin Harper, at Wicked by Design, for my gorgeous cover, and Leland and Brittany, my beautiful cover models. Amber Garcia at Lady Amber's Reviews and PR, who helped with my release when I was feeling completely overwhelmed, and saved me from hiding under my desk and mainlining chocolate and wine. Jean Booknerd has been by my side for almost every release I've done, and I can't thank her enough for her kindness and friendship. I will never be able to replace Ashley, but it's important for me to continue producing work she would have been proud of. I knew I'd have to find new partners to help me do that. I will be forever grateful to the editors and beta readers who helped me with this book: Kelley Crandall, Cindy Koelbl, Athena Wikstrom, and Mercadeez Latimer.

To Dan, my person…and the reason I've been able to convince myself to keep breathing. You are my home, my rock, my soul mate and the love of my life. There is little I'm certain of, but the fact that I love you with my whole soul, and you are, and always will be, my constant and the most important person in my life are things I will never doubt. I'm so incredibly lucky to have you as my partner, and my best friend. Thank you for taking care of me, giving me refuge in your arms, and trying to help me even when we were both drowning in helplessness. Thank you for supporting my dreams, standing by me during the good times, and holding me up through the bad. I would not be who I am if I hadn't met you eighteen years ago, and I would not have survived the past twenty-three months without you. I thank Thor every day that I get to spend my life with you. I love you.

To Ashley, my Samwise…
I sat down to write this page, and realized I don't know how to write acknowledgments without including you. I wouldn't be here, in this place, publishing my sixth book and working on my seventh without your years of guidance. I've written a thousand notes to you since you passed away…I'm certain I'll write a million more. I've moved forward—one day at a time, remembering all of the things you taught me, and smiling every time I hear your voice in my head exasperated about a comma splice or misplaced modifier. The expectations you had

for me are a ghost that lingers, demanding me to push myself and always be better…because that's what you required of me in life, and death made me more determined to make you proud. You changed the entire course of my life by believing in me. I miss you every damn day. I will love you forever. My words wouldn't exist without you, and in that way, I feel like I get the rare opportunity to watch you—and help you—live on. Words are eternal, and your essence flows through mine.

There were a handful of people who will always have a special place in my heart for walking beside me through the grieving process, and being there as I took first steps all over again. I want to acknowledge them for helping me get to this place. Dan (of course), Karen DeVault, Sarah Coombs, Kelly King, my parents, my brother and sister, Brandy Korzep, Britta Sorenson, Krystal Hazlett, Karen Versoi, Adrie Buchanan, Tamara Snell, Jessica Brown, Michelle Kamerath, Michael Coiner, Bobbi Rice, Athena Wikstrom, Jean Booknerd, Sophie Jordan, Heather Crandall, Ali Cross, RaShelle Workman, Lani Woodland, Crystal Perkins, Teralynn Childs, and my trainer, Erin Blevins, and her husband, Michael Blevins, who both taught me I could push through the pain and do hard things. There were a few times when I didn't think I had the strength to keep writing…and at one point, I'd decided to quit. Michael wrote several articles that inspired me to keep going. His posts focus on physical training, but I can apply almost every entry to other parts of life, too. Check him out on gritandteeth.com, and check out Erin's website for fantastic recipes: shutupeat.com.

To Ashley's parents, Gary and Sharon Argyle, and her family and extended family…I'm incredibly grateful to you all. Thank you for being so gracious, and for continuing to keep us a part of your lives.

To all the readers, friends, loved ones, and even strangers, who climbed down in the pit of sadness with me and stayed there, understanding, caring, and waiting until I was ready to get out. Thank you for being there, for sticking with me, for being patient, and for helping me fight through this. You have no idea how much your words of support, love, and encouragement helped me during the waves of grief. The private messages, emails, and social media comments were like water in a desert. Your kindness means the world to me, and I want you to know how much I appreciate you being there with me in my darkness. I hope you love *Chasing Brynn*…it's the first of many books to come.

For Ashley. Always.

# Books by Angela Corbett

<u>Tempting Series</u>
*Tempting Sydney*
*Chasing Brynn*

<u>A Dude Reads Romance Series</u>
*A Dude Reads Romance-Tempting Sydney*
*A Dude Reads Romance-Chasing Brynn*

<u>Kate Saxee Mystery Series</u>
*The Devil Drinks Coffee*
*Devilishly Short #1*
*The Devil Wears Tank Tops*

<u>Emblem of Eternity Trilogy</u>
*Eternal Starling*
*Eternal Echoes*

For special sneak peeks, giveaways, and super secret news, join Angela's newsletter!
www.angelacorbett.com
Twitter: @AngCorbett
Instagram: @ByAngCorbett
Facebook: www.Facebook.com/AuthorAngelaCorbett

If you enjoyed reading *Chasing Brynn*, please help others enjoy this book too by lending it, recommending it, or reviewing it on Amazon, Barnes and Noble, or Goodreads. If you do write a review, please send me a message through my website so I can thank you personally! www.angelacorbett.com

xoxo,
Ang

# About Angela

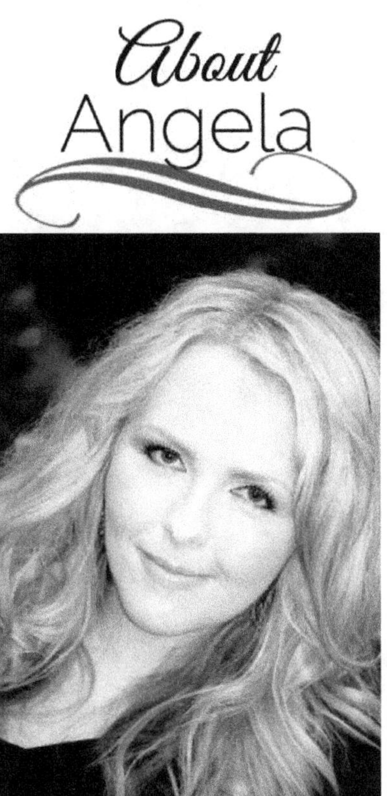

Angela Corbett graduated from Westminster College and previously worked as a journalist, freelance writer, and director of communications and marketing. She lives in Utah with her extremely supportive husband, and loves classic cars, traveling, and chasing their five-pound Pomeranian, Pippin—who is just as mischievous as his hobbit namesake. She's the author of Young Adult, New Adult, and Adult fiction—with lots of kissing. She writes under two names, Angela Corbett, and Destiny Ford.

www.ingramcontent.com/pod-product-compliance
Lightning Source LLC
Chambersburg PA
CBHW060356260626
47160CB00006B/2335
*9780989283656*